"I'M A WOMAN. NOTHING MORE. NOTHING LESS. DON'T TRY TO MAKE ME OUT TO BE SOMETHING I'M NOT.

"I'm not a hothouse flower. Nor am I a child. I'm fully grown and in possession of all my faculties and I want to spend this night—and only this night —with you."

"I'll remember," Kellen groaned, his mouth invading hers. "For tonight only," he repeated, breaking off the kiss to speak. "God, I do want you so badly."

Tessa drew back. This was not the intensity she expected of a casual liaison. It sounded too sincere, too heartfelt and genuine. Then she remembered. She was a conquest to him, nothing more.

"Don't you trust me not to hurt you, Tessa?" he asked, intrigued perhaps by her drawing back.

"Yes, I do trust you." Strangely it was true. She did trust him no matter how cynical or disillusioned he might be. It was her own wayward emotions that needed guarding against.

A CANDLELIGHT ECSTASY ROMANCE®

MATCH MADE IN HEAVEN

MALISSA CARROLL

A CANDLELIGHT ECSTASY ROMANCE®

Published by
Dell Publishing Co., Inc.
1 Dag Hammarskjold Plaza
New York, New York 10017

Dell ® TM 681510, Dell Publishing Co., Inc.

Candlelight Ecstasy Romance®, 1,203,540, is a registered
trademark of Dell Publishing Co., Inc., New York, New York.

ISBN: 0-440-15573-8

Printed in the United States of America

First printing-October 1984

For Lori Copeland—because you listen even better than you write.

To Our Readers:

We have been delighted with your enthusiastic response to Candlelight Ecstasy Romances® and we thank you for the interest you have shown in this exciting series.

In the upcoming months we will continue to present the distinctive, sensuous love stories you have come to expect only from Ecstasy. We look forward to bringing you many more books from your favorite authors and also the very finest work from new authors of contemporary romantic fiction.

As always, we are striving to present the unique, absorbing love stories that you enjoy most—books that are more than ordinary romance.

Your suggestions and comments are always welcome. Please write to us at the address below.

Sincerely,

The Editors
Candlelight Romances
1 Dag Hammarskjold Plaza
New York, New York 10017

CHAPTER ONE

Kellen Sterling came to an abrupt halt before the arched glass window of the hotel's small exclusive boutique. The leggy blonde holding on to his arm stumbled slightly and fussed in a high, querulous voice. He ignored her. She reminded him somehow of a wax flower, beautiful and compelling from a distance but which on closer inspection turns out to be a fake, curiously lifeless and disappointing. His closer inspection had lasted too long already. He shouldn't have brought her with him to this out-of-the-way California hotel; but he had been a little too drunk and lonely, and a little too much the gentleman to abandon her in the boarding tunnel when they left the Concorde in New York.

Now she ceased to exist for him completely. As he stared into the shop, his full attention was focused on the girl within. No. Not a girl, he corrected inwardly as he watched the lithe feminine movements from beyond the window's crystal barrier. A woman. Not too young, or too old, too short or too tall. She'd have to tip her gold-brown head slightly to meet his gaze and he liked the idea.

But she didn't turn his way. She was caught up in her own concerns, watching her reflection in a full-length oval-framed mirror and her assessment of her person was decidedly critical.

Then suddenly she smiled. A gesture of purely feminine satisfaction as her hands smoothed across the fullness of her hips, tugged at the waistline that was a trifle too loose, it seemed, and moved upward, hesitantly, to trace the delicate tint of apricot skin exposed by the plunging neckline of the apple-green silk dress she wore.

Kellen was entranced by that smile—captured unwillingly by an elusive charm he didn't want to acknowledge. Her smile

11

smoothed and softened her piquant features, accenting the high, curved cheekbones and firm line of her jaw, while revealing an underlying sensual warmth and brightness that brought a quick, instinctive tightening of his breath. Kellen wasn't accustomed to women taking him by surprise. Especially with a gesture as mundane as a smile.

As he watched, the smile died as quickly as it was born, replaced by an expression of calm aloofness and cool calculation that made Kellen blink, wondering if he'd imagined the intriguing gamine creature of a moment before.

Oblivious of his interested scrutiny, she whirled before the mirror, watching the shimmering apple-green pleats of her skirt alternately cling and billow around the bend of her knee. Kellen's lazy, steel-blue gaze followed the swirl of material with deceptive languor while he noted the sweep of creamy thigh and hip the lifting skirt exposed to his view. She was very definitely a woman.

"Kellen, what in heaven's name are you looking at?" the blonde complained in a whining tone that would have set his teeth on edge if he'd been paying her more than a fraction of his attention. He shrugged her clinging hand away with scarcely concealed annoyance. She meant nothing to him. He hadn't allowed any woman that hold over him for nearly fifteen years. She was a convenience, a decoration, someone to warm his bed and keep him from wakening in the night to nothing but the sound of his own breathing. He pulled her toward a jewelry display in the window with a cynical certainty born of countless liaisons. It would keep her quiet and occupied as her greed warred with her expectations. They were both aware that an expensive token of his esteem would help to avoid a scene when he sent her packing. She took the bait without a moment's hesitation, pale gray eyes darkening with an avaricious glint. Kellen was once again free to concentrate on the woman at the mirror.

Inside the boutique she smiled again, flicking a wayward strand of short gold-brown hair away from her face. This time the image that invaded his thoughts was of a medieval madonna he had glimpsed in a Rome museum. The painted figure was at once fragile and mischievous, worldly and sublime. Like the fifteenth-century madonna's veil, the woman's softly layered, shoulder-length hair framed her fine-boned, emerald-eyed features becomingly, enhancing the aura of vulnerable innocence. The style suited her, Kellen decided arbitrarily. And it was a hundred times more practical than the mane of bleached, wildly curling hair his companion wore, in imitation of the latest Hollywood sensation, he guessed. With a graceful swirl of the pleated skirt, the woman stepped away from the mirror and at that instant, as though she sensed his intense attention, she glanced across the crowded shop. She tipped her head to meet his gaze for a short blinding moment that sent a rush of heat to his loins and brought a smile of echoing sensuality to his lips. Their gazes touched and lingered before her regard moved to the female at his elbow. She blinked, breaking the private spell, and her eyes narrowed swiftly, a mask of cool detachment sliding over her face.

A quick spurt of anger replaced the desire she had aroused and Kellen's face hardened as she turned to speak to the clerk who'd been assisting her selection. She didn't glance his way again. It had all happened in a heartbeat but he had seen her disapproval of him—her disdain for a man who would play eye games with one woman while in the company of another—reflected in the emerald depths of her eyes. He wanted to stop her, ask by what right she passed judgment on his way of life. Instead he watched stiffly as she disappeared with the elderly clerk into the dressing room behind her.

"Kellen, this gold ankle cuff is adorable."

He turned his head as his forgotten companion spoke, pushing aside the uncharacteristic urge to enter the boutique, block her retreat, and tell her that this woman he was with meant less than nothing to him. Not for the first time he saw the endless parade of women in his life as she must see them: vain, silly, pleasure-loving creatures that made demands on his body and his wallet—not his heart and soul. He wasn't pleased by the censure he interpreted in that one fleeting glance. He wanted to make his displeasure known.

"Kellen, you aren't listening to a word I say," the blonde complained coyly, grazing an enameled talon along his chiseled jaw.

No hint of the angry thoughts escaped Kellen's iron control, but the narrowing of his eyes and the hardening of their metallic blue depths caused a flutter in her heart. When was the last

13

time he'd felt the need to explain his life—or his actions—to any living person? Especially a stranger glimpsed from a distance? It was a novel and uncomfortable sensation, to say the least. Who was she? He intended to find out.

Kellen Sterling very seldom failed to accomplish anything he set out to do. He was a loner, by profession and inclination. Reserved almost to the point of reticence, he could turn cynical and withdrawn in a single heartbeat. For the past five years he'd been the darling of the American wine scene, his disreputable past buried and nearly forgotten. The sins of a dozen years ago, now explained away as youthful indiscretion. But his own personal anger and pain gnawed at him still. All of the carefully guarded and sublimated frustrations in his life surged beneath the thin shell of sophisticated elegance he presented to the world, stirring below the surface, just as the sap in the vines was vibrating steadily upward after winter's long dormancy.

He was perceptive enough to equate some of his own present restlessness to the season. It would soon be spring. And in his heart of hearts he was still a vintner; a grower of grapes, a winemaker with no vines of his own to tend. Exiled from his home, estranged from his family, there seemed no point in settling down. So he contented himself with improving other men's vineyards and wines and dallying with their wives and mistresses. And because there was nothing that he could do to change the focus of his life in the immediate future, or so he believed, the bleakness of his inner pain and frustration now centered on the nearest object—the woman at his side.

"Kellen, you haven't heard a single word," she repeated, this time with no attempt at humoring him. "Isn't this a lovely piece of workmanship? Don't you think it would look well on my ankle?" She twisted her head down and studied her own expensively shod foot with interest. Then she smiled up at him in anticipation.

It was the last straw, that practiced, calculating smile. "Lovely. I'll have it sent to the suite," he growled, making his decision with his usual ruthless swiftness. He spoke more harshly than he had intended and she must have mistaken the husky intonation for desire because she smiled more broadly.

"It's the middle of the morning, darling," she giggled, linking her hand with his as she flicked her tongue over her lips like a

14

hungry lizard, "we've barely finished breakfast an hour ago." She arched her sleek body closer to his lean hardness, intending to let him see that her protests were only for show. She wanted him in her bed any hour of the day or night. "You'll wear me out if you're not careful."

"That would be unfortunate indeed. Such a waste of your talents." She missed the subtle irony in his low words completely. "Actually you misunderstand. I'm afraid something unexpected has come up. Since I can't leave California for several days, I'll have to take care of it all by phone. It's not fair to ask you to stay here and be bored to tears while I'm trying to straighten the matter out. I'll send the maid to help you pack," he directed, impaling her with chilling blue eyes.

"Pack? We just got here," she stormed, letting her voice rise sharply as a hint of the West Virginia coal dust she'd shaken from her pretty feet ten years ago snaked through her words. Kellen was a meal ticket she didn't intend to lose without a reason—even if it did mean being immured in this godforsaken —words failed her and she looked around the tiled, whitewashed lobby—this . . . monastery—she snorted, settling for the truth—in the middle of nowhere.

"It can't be helped," he sidestepped with reserve. It wasn't even possible to argue with him. He'd already withdrawn to somewhere she couldn't follow. "I'll meet you in Paris next week. I'll make the reservation while you pack," Kellen lied with no compunction whatsoever. He never intended to see her again and she sensed it also. Why he was behaving so callously he wasn't sure. Unless it was the vague restlessness that had plagued him for so long. And he was tired of her. It couldn't have anything to do with a sudden sun-streaked smile and emerald eyes.

"Oh, all right," the blonde capitulated with another appraising glance at the gold bauble. It would pay for her hotel room for several days and there was always the chance he really did mean to look her up when he returned to Paris. "If that's what you want, Kellen, darling. You're as unpredictable as an old maid." She'd handled him wrong from the beginning but there was no use in crying over spilled milk. He'd just leave her flat if she made a scene and she couldn't risk that. Not here, where her chances of finding someone to take his place were slim to say the least.

It never occurred to her that his mercurial mood change had a deeper cause. That he might be searching for something more than relief of the boredom that always shadowed her shallow, pleasure-loving world. Their relationship was purely physical. Most of her love affairs were—by necessity—and his, by cold choice. No more or no less meaningful than the current one.

What sadness could he know? she'd question if someone ever asked. His opinion was valued by authorities in the wine industry on two continents. He had money and prestige, influence, everything that mattered to her. Women were his for the taking, most, more than merely willing. Kellen Sterling combined the overpowering forces of physical beauty, virility, and sheer male arrogance into a magnetic appeal that drove women wild—and lesser men to drink. She was going to miss him, all right. But the only lasting regret that entered her hedonistic brain was the wish that she could keep him in her bed for the rest of her life.

CHAPTER TWO

"Tell me my old eyes deceive me," Magda Jurrus begged as she held the stemmed crystal goblet to the light of the bright California sun and shook her head dolefully. Tessa Mallory watched her shining coil of coal black hair as it caught the afternoon highlights. "There's a haze developing in my Pinot Noir." Magda waved off the hovering waiter who had deposited the tray and glasses on the wicker table with a careless flutter of her jeweled hand. He bowed slightly and backed away, not at all offended by his employer's autocratic ways. She was European and part of the aristocracy. What could you expect? his eyes told Tessa as he made his exit from the stone terrace where they sat.

Magda ignored him with truly haughty grandeur and poured a few ounces of the ruby liquid from an incongruous laboratory beaker into a second fragile taster's glass. With a gracious flourish she handed it to the young woman seated on her left.

"It's dreadful, I'm shattered," she exclaimed dramatically in the rich middle-European accent that hadn't diminished despite thirty years' residency in California. Mme. Jurrus was Hungarian-born and -bred, and no one was allowed to forget the fact. Few people knew, as Tessa did, that she had been a naturalized citizen of the United States for over two decades. "Tell me, Tessa dear, what do you think has caused it?" she queried, looking across the glass-topped table at the young woman studying her own goblet of the ruby liquid.

Tessa Mallory swallowed the smile that would have melted the veneer of cool aloofness she habitually showed the world and allowed the warm brightness of her personality to shine through. Her hostess was apparently serious and she wouldn't appreciate the levity. Tessa was on her best behavior, aware of

17

the honor Magda bestowed by soliciting her opinion. It was a gesture of friendship. The Pinot Noir was Magda's pride and joy, her expertise in the winemaking world was light years more advanced than Tessa's.

"Starbright," Tessa pronounced in a low musical tone. Her voice suited her understated beauty. It was restrained and refined, with an underlying cadence of earthy sensuality that took her listeners by surprise, much like her smile. "I can't detect a hint of haze. And I imagine your staff doesn't either," she added with perfect candor.

The matriarchal figure in her riotously hued, all-enveloping caftan made a second dismissive gesture toward the laboratory situated in the hillside below the centuries-old monastery. A great deal of time and money had gone into integrating the more utilitarian aspects of the hotel into the overall atmosphere. Much of the winery complex was underground, recessed into the hillside behind and below the monastery.

"Ha!" Magda snorted with Continental disdain. "What do they know? They are college boys playing at being winemakers. They use a computer to analyze my wines." She threw out the words in staccato clips, her voice dropping on the word "computer" as though it were obscene. "What does a computer know about making wine, I ask you? My Pinot Noir is like an unruly grape-child. It must be treated accordingly. It's not happy away from Burgundy where it truly belongs." She sighed theatrically and settled her well-padded bulk more comfortably into her chair. The wicker groaned in protest. "No matter how hard I try to make them happy, the vines will not thrive. A good wine begins in the soil; perhaps that is the problem? But I keep on trying; pampering, nurturing, coaxing, each step of the way. How can they do better than that with their testing and their 'computers'?"

Tessa nodded her gold-brown head understandingly, her soft shoulder-length hair swaying around her cheeks like a bell. There was nothing unusual in Magda's referring to her vines as though they were delinquent children. She was a vintner and her obsession with the small noncommercial plot they discussed was understandable. It paralleled in some degree Tessa's partner and mentor Webster Mayer's attachment to his own planting of Johannesberg Rieslings. Unfortunately for Magda, the

18

French vines were low yielding and had generally failed to respond to meticulous care and attention—from all the winery staff—as well as their owner. Magda's world-famous San Luis Winery's fortune still lay in its excellent Cabernet Sauvignon and in its up-and-coming Fumé Blanc, which Webster predicted would be the best-selling wine of the next decade. But to Tessa's journeyman's eye there was no sign of hazing—a clouding of the vintage caused by impurities or suspended particles in the red wine they were discussing—and she said as much.

"Perhaps you are right," Magda agreed, so quickly Tessa again suspected her hostess wasn't as concerned as she appeared. She was testing her guest for her own satisfaction in ascertaining how she was progressing under Web's tutelage, and for a chance to show off her wine. "I worry so," she said charmingly, rolling her r's. "Give me your opinion of the wine. It is very young," she apologized unnecessarily. "This is only a barrel sample of course. It will take time, but I would like to know what you think."

Tessa held the stem of the partially filled wineglass between her strong, sensitive fingers and swirled the wine for several seconds before inhaling its bouquet. Its robe—or color—was clear with a hint of garnet shading in the ruby liquid. The nose —or aroma—was sharp and clean, giving an impression of cranberries and spice. Tessa was impressed; it showed every indication of maturing into a complex, full-bodied wine. She tipped the goblet to her lips and let the cool wine linger in the mouth before swallowing. It was tart and biting on her tongue, proclaiming its youth.

"Cherries," Tessa said simply, "and a bit of spice. A hint of oak," she added, referring to the slight flavoring it was acquiring from its long rest in large oak casks imported from Germany. She had no use for the stilted language and snobbery that pervaded the wine industry. Tessa gave her opinion straightforwardly, as she did everything else. "It is acquiring body and character. You have a winner on your hands."

Magda nodded, pleased. "It will develop well," she agreed. "The tannin will settle, of course, leaving it soft and clean. It will be a very well-balanced wine, despite my grumblings."

"Or because of your caring and vigilance," Tessa added perceptively. If she had learned one thing in the four years she'd spent with Webster Mayer it was that every wine was a distinct example of its maker's art, mirroring his strengths and weaknesses as well as displaying its own.

"Yes. Caring and vigilance and the fullness of time." Magda repeated the words rolling them around on her tongue as she had done the wine. "All in the fullness of time."

The well-worn phrase caught at Tessa's fancy. The time this particular wine would spend aging in cask and bottle would pass all too quickly, she was sure. Sometimes lately she wanted to reach out and stop time in its passage. That had never been so when she was younger and full of hopes and dreams. To hold time still until she could take account of her life, assess her actions and her future, that's what she needed to do now before she set the world to spinning again.

"For today it is too raw and full of wild oats as you say in this country," Magda said, interrupting her thoughts. "It will be better for the waiting." She smacked her lips in anticipation of that day and changed the subject so smoothly and with such grace that no pause was necessary. "Are you enjoying your stay with us, my dear?"

The question surprised Tessa, but she replied quickly and sincerely. "It's lovely, Magda. Exactly as I've imagined Napa Valley to be. So warm and sunny. Back home it's still winter and here the vines will be leafing out soon. It's hard to believe." Tessa leaned back in the white-painted wicker lounge chair, noticing as she had before the protesting creak of its fibers as she crossed one slender silk-clad ankle over the other. She stared out over the sunken terrace at the few people splashing in the flower-and-shrubbery-ringed pool. Not a hint of their twentieth-century frivolity infringed on the serene atmosphere of the former monastery.

A quick rush of tears stung Tessa's jade-green eyes as she stared out over the valley. How odd. It wasn't like her to be so sentimental. It was probably only jet lag, bringing her emotions too near the surface. She blinked them away. Tessa wasn't about to admit to herself, or anyone else, that she might be homesick for the rolling hills and winter-gray landscape of southern Ohio after only two days in California. Nevertheless, the feeling persisted and she took a deep, determined breath, willing it away.

The small, snow-covered vineyard in her thoughts was indeed a world away from the panoramic view surrounding her. She turned her attention to the contrast. Sun-drenched, winter-dormant terraced vineyards stretched beyond the well-manicured grounds below the pool. This was California as she'd imagined it would be. Two thousand miles from the quiet rural silence and the wide expanse of the shifting ice-covered Ohio River visible from her own windows.

"I want you to feel at home during the conference. You look so pensive sitting here I thought you might be unhappy?" Magda questioned in a low voice. The words were so kindly spoken and sincere that Tessa couldn't take offense although she didn't care to discuss her feelings with a relative stranger no matter how long Magda's friendship with Webster Mayer had flourished.

"Of course not," Tessa responded not altogether truthfully. She wasn't unhappy, but neither was she pleased with the direction her life was taking. Part of her homesickness and her mood stemmed from the ambiguity of her own feelings at the moment. "I'm just tired I guess." She did smile this time and Magda returned the favor.

"I'm pleased you like my hotel."

The last statement really didn't require an answer so Tessa continued to watch the happy family group that had entered the pool as they spoke. Her green eyes were partially veiled behind spiky brown lashes and the sorrow that suddenly clouded their clear depths went undetected. The young couple and their healthy, happy toddlers were preparing to swim. The perfect California family, Tessa decided, tanned and golden, affluent, the wife and mother smugly pregnant with another beautiful baby.

"They make a happy picture, do they not?" Magda interrupted as her shrewd brown eyes followed Tessa's line of vision.

"Yes, they do," she replied warily. She knew what was coming next; still, after four years she wasn't used to speaking of her husband's death. She tensed instinctively.

"Webster has told me you are a widow, as I am. There were no children from your marriage?"

"No. I regret that very much," Tessa heard herself admit. They were skating on very thin ice. Could Magda detect the undercurrents of longing and excitement in her voice? "We were very young when my husband was taken ill," she added defensively, trying to ward off the sharp dart of remorse and anger that still sometimes found her heart when she thought of Jacky's death. Why had he given up on life so quickly? It wasn't fair. "Our whole lives were ahead of us. There seemed to be all the time in the world."

"My children were the greatest consolation in my sorrow. But you are still young, my dear. There will be time for you to love again. To make for yourself beautiful babies like that pair."

Tessa's mouth went suddenly dry and she took another swallow of the young, unfinished wine. It went down sharply and made her shiver. There had been no hint of apology in Magda's words. In her world women didn't make excuses for wanting to bear children, as many of Tessa's acquaintances seemed to feel was necessary. Magda's generation hadn't been caught up in the "baby trap" mentality and the "me" generation that had shaped the lives of so many of Tessa's contemporaries.

Tessa nodded silently, unwilling yet to speak her thoughts. Was there really all the time in the world? She didn't think so. Not anymore. The days and weeks were passing too quickly. On her next birthday she'd be thirty-two years old. Time was running out, slipping away in a decreasing number of tomorrows.

A baby. No one knew how much she yearned for a child of her own. If Jacky had lived they might have been blessed with such lovely children as the ones splashing about in their parents' strong loving arms. But Jacky was dead and life wasn't always fair. If only someone had warned her, told her when they had been young and heedless of time that Jacky wouldn't be there to share all these tomorrows with her. That she would have to explore the future—totally alone—because her love hadn't been strong enough to give him the courage to face a recurrence of the cancer that was what fate held in store for him.

"Madame Jurrus." The ubiquitous waiter had reappeared at Magda's elbow, dragging their attention back to the everyday world. "Your presence is required in the kitchens. There is some problem with the chef." He spoke formally in the presence of a paying guest and Magda rolled her eyes heavenward in exasperation.

22

"Henri is throwing another tantrum is what you mean to say," she stated bluntly. The waiter bobbed his head. "Please excuse me, Tessa, duty calls."

"Certainly. I imagine French chefs must be handled with great delicacy." Tessa smiled as the older woman rose from her seat, her caftan rippling in the breeze like colorful, exotic wings.

"One does not treat them with too much delicacy when the closest they have ever been to Paris is the East Side of Chicago," she responded darkly and made her exit.

Tessa laughed aloud, a sound like tiny silver bells, as she savored Magda's militant pronouncement. The tension was broken at that moment and the poignant mood that had taken possession of her over the last few minutes dissipated. The searing pain and heartbreak of her lost love were growing fainter with the passage of healing time, the same march of days and nights she'd been regretting just moments earlier. It was one more of life's little ironies, but she was grateful for the healing all the same.

The lobby of the venerable building was crowded with guests on this late-winter afternoon as Tessa stepped across the threshold of the terrace doors. Sunshine poured over the antique Spanish-style furnishings in abstract patterns. Her gaze wandered around the room, resting lightly on the beautifully manicured potted palms, and rough-woven wall hangings in all the colors of the warm dusty earth from which they had sprung. It was so very different from home, still wrapped in the icy solitude of a long blustery Ohio winter.

A distinct feeling of someone watching her invaded Tessa's idle survey. The sensation sent a ripple of nerves running down her spine on tiny clawed feet. She twisted her head, searching for Webster's familiar tall figure but he was nowhere to be seen. The feeling persisted, however, and she held her breath a long moment until the sensation passed. It was a foolish notion, she scolded herself, and she didn't give in to the sudden impulse to search the faces of the other guests grouped around the rough-plastered room. Instead she stepped past a recessed alcove into what was once the monks' refectory where she could admire the view beyond the plate-glass windows in the far wall.

It could have been an alien world if it were not for the high-

23

voltage power lines in the distance and the cars toiling along the valley roads far below. Acres and acres of gnarled and twisted vines stretched up the gentle slope of the hills, drawing the eye steadily higher toward the summit of lovely Mount Helena, guardian of the fertile Napa Valley. Above it all stretched a limitless sky, crisscrossed with vapor trails and so blue it hurt to look at it too long.

This was Tessa's first trip to California's wine region and she was spellbound by the countryside. To one accustomed to the low, rolling hills of the Ohio River it was a heady, fascinating view. And it seemed odder yet when you considered that a short seventy-two hours ago she'd been enduring the cold and damp of a late-season snowstorm. Now Tessa wished she hadn't added the blazer to her cream-colored, raw-silk suit because the day was definitely going to be too warm for it.

A familiar voice rose above the babble of conversation that ebbed and flowed around her as Webster's craggy tones slipped across the surface of her consciousness. Tessa turned slightly to watch her employer approach. An indulgent smile quirked her lips, a greeting she reserved for him alone. Web was the best friend she had. The best friend she had ever had. He had replaced the father she could barely remember. He was the only man she loved that fate hadn't taken from her. She cared deeply for him, admired his integrity and skill—and she was grateful to him.

They'd found each other at the lowest point in their lives—in her life at least—and she'd never regretted leaving her nursing career to accompany him into a new world. Four years ago she'd been lost, mourning, and frightened to death of going on alone. Today she had a new life, and a new career as an apprentice winemaker. Web had taken her in, giving her his gruff, undemanding companionship, while she in turn had seen to the mending of his damaged heart and indulged his passion for making fine wine. In the process he'd helped her find again the resilience and zest for living that she had lost after Jacky's death. Now she would protect their happy and secure world with her very life if need be.

"I've been looking for you all over this damned pile of stones," Web growled with a frown that many times did double duty as a smile. Seventy on his last birthday, the dynamic vint-

24

ner looked ten years younger. He shoved a hand through his short-cropped iron-gray hair and rolled back onto the balls of his feet. He was a big man, a shade under six feet tall, and almost two hundred pounds of muscle slowly turning to fat.

"The hotel is charming, you just don't want to admit it," Tessa reproved. "And hush. Magda has ears everywhere. She won't appreciate hearing you refer to this beautiful old building as a 'damned pile of stones,'" Tessa admonished. His fierce facade didn't fool many people for long. Webster Mayer was a notoriously soft touch. "It's an honor to have been asked to attend the symposium," she reminded him unnecessarily.

Web grumbled in reply. This prestigious competition was the culmination of years of hard work. He was in his element, about to prove that the delicate vinifera—the wine-giving European grapes that made California a wine power—could be grown in the less favorable climates of the Midwest. Others said it couldn't be done. But with skill, perseverance, and sheer hard work, Web had proved the experts wrong. He'd succeeded where more timid souls had feared to try. The excellent vintage they had entered in the judging was proof.

Tessa scanned his craggy countenance with a professional eye, noting his color and watching for the deepening lines around his mouth that signaled pain and fatigue. They weren't apparent and she relaxed a little, chiding herself inwardly for still treating him like a patient. His near fatal heart attack had occurred over four years ago, although he was still subject to occasional, painful attacks of angina pectoris. And he wouldn't appreciate it if he knew she worried constantly about his health. He preferred to forget her medical background altogether.

"It's too damn hot for March, Tessa," he opined, tugging at the collar of his charcoal-striped shirt. He was more tired than he admitted, Tessa deduced, even if it didn't show.

They turned by mutual agreement to the magnificent view, Tessa's jade eyes alight with the determined gleam that everyone who knew her respected and avoided whenever possible. Her mind was busy turning over various schemes to get Web to rest in the heat of the afternoon. His health was still her responsibility and she had no intention of allowing him to overdo in the unaccustomed warmth and excitement of this gathering of his peers. However, she wisely said nothing further, having learned early in their relationship that he would ignore any advice of a cautionary nature out of pure bullheadedness.

"I've been looking for a gift," Web said unexpectedly. "Something for Mrs. Basel, a little token of our trip." Mrs. Basel was Web's longtime housekeeper and Tessa's staunch ally in caring for their absentminded employer.

"Did you find something suitable?"

"No," he confessed with a sheepish, boyish grin. "I was hoping you'd have better luck." He ran his hand across his chin and scowled again. "Would you like to pick up something for her granddaughter? I miss the little tyke."

A sharp thrust of excitement mixed with anxiety streaked along Tessa's nerve fibers. It was very close to the feeling that the sensation of eyes on her back had produced earlier. But this neural alarm originated deep within herself. A gift. She wanted something for herself also, and she planned to find it on this short momentous trip across the continent.

"I'd be glad to. There are some lovely things in the boutique and gift shop. I'll bet you never even went inside," she teased, striving to regain her equilibrium as she did so.

"Right again. But I'm no good at frills and ruffles. Coming from you their gifts will be a lovely surprise." He looked pleased when she agreed to take the task. "Good, I'm glad that's settled. There's someone I want you to meet." Putting the vexing matter of souvenirs behind him, Web moved off with his usual vigor and Tessa remained staring off into the distance, a small half-smile tugging at her lips, lost in her own dream.

A lovely surprise. What would Web think if she told him she wanted a gift also? That the gift she would choose for herself was a child? A baby—all her own to love and cherish.

Perhaps if this competition hadn't come at the end of a long, hard winter when she'd had too much time to think of the future stretching out like an empty, lonely road ahead of her . . . Perhaps if Mrs. Basel's daughter hadn't contracted hepatitis and brought her tiny baby girl into their lives to awaken maternal instincts Tessa had buried under the cold layers of her mourning for Jacky . . . Perhaps if she hadn't enjoyed so completely nurturing and caring for the infant during those long, cold weeks she was in Webster's home . . . the idea wouldn't have taken such a hold on her. The acute attack of baby love would have passed when the curly-headed, powdery-smelling creature returned to her parents. But it had not. Like a virus it had hit her heart and brain simultaneously, infecting her system, overloading her defenses.

It was well and good to have decided she wanted a baby to make her life complete. She wanted the joy that watching a child grow and mature into a healthy, happy human being would provide. But was it the right decision to make from Webster's point of view? And her mother's? And should she take Jacky's parents into consideration? They still regarded her as their daughter. She didn't know, could only conjecture, and if she considered all the possible consequences too closely, she'd never go through with it.

She still wanted a child desperately, even after weeks of solitary arguments with her heart and intellect warring in her spinning brain, discussions with her inner voice both pro and con, ethical and moral, emotional and logical. She still hadn't given in. A baby would be a gift of love to herself. She meant to have it. She was strong, healthy, financially solvent thanks to Web's generosity and her own good business sense. Why deny herself the joys of motherhood? Why shouldn't she have a child to love and care for, she had asked repeatedly. And repeatedly she gave herself the familiar answer. Because you do not have the one ingredient essential to the project. A husband.

It always came back to that. The major flaw in her plan. She needed a man. But how was she going to go about finding a father for her child? There was no man in her life but Webster. No one she cared enough about to ask for such a precious gift. She didn't want a lasting relationship—that was the crux of the problem. Not now—maybe never again. She hadn't met anyone in the four years since Jacky's death that had stirred her blood or her heart. Perhaps the pain of losing him had killed her desire to love again? Perhaps she was incapable of giving her love in that way a second time? It didn't matter. What mattered was the here and now. She could love a child, be a good parent. But she needed a man.

Right now. Today. The physical timing was perfect. She knew her body and its clockwork cycles with a deep instinctive knowledge. If she could find a suitable . . . Even her thoughts boggled at the enormity of what she was planning and no acceptable word came to her rescue. Tessa took a deep breath and started again, her mind ticking off the points like a well-tuned machine. If she could find a donor . . . No, that was too clinical a word. She shook her head in disgust at her own squeamishness. If she could find a man to make love to her in the next forty-eight hours, she would leave California with a new life growing within her.

It was as simple as that, she concluded, stubbornly refusing to acknowledge any qualms she might have about deceiving this unknown male. All she required was a partner to give her a baby all her own, as Magda had so innocently phrased it. It shouldn't be such a difficult task to accomplish. After all, this was California. Sex was very casual and open here; or so they said. Tessa wasn't so sure. So far no one suitable had presented himself. Maybe she was being too picky? He didn't have to be a Greek god when all was said and done. Just healthy, and reasonably intelligent . . . not too tall, or too short. . . .

Good heavens! Tessa came back to reality with a jerk. Any more daydreaming and she'd imagine she had to be in love with this nameless, faceless male. When the time came she would do what was required. Just as she had always done what was required of her, she concluded grimly. But for now she wouldn't contemplate the physical act that was a prerequisite to conception. She would cling to her dreams of a son or daughter to bring joy and happiness to her small Victorian cottage hidden in its stand of hickory and maple. A new baby to love and cherish, with no commitment to a man that would entail any demands on her heart or, later on, her child. A man who would never even know what he had given her. That was the best way; that was the goal to cling to. If only she could find the right man. . . .

"Tessa." It was Webster's voice again, and she spun around with a guilty start to find herself staring up into the darkest blue eyes she had ever been privileged to observe.

Eyes that were definitely not Web's familiar hazel. This man's eyes were as dark as lake water at night, shaded and shuttered, yet curiously familiar. Where had she seen them before? It was a tantalizing recollection hovering just beyond her mental grasp, while even deeper in her feminine soul she knew a small spark of unbidden intuition.

It told her no casual scrutiny would be allowed to plumb those secret depths. The woman that sought to explore the cobalt pools too quickly would find herself completely beyond her reach. Drowning in liquid darkness, swallowed up . . . compelled to love or hate but never to indifference. Tessa stomped on the whimsy with a heavy rational heel as Web introduced her.

"Tessa Mallory, my assistant, and a damn good vintner in her own right," Webster intoned proudly, never one to hide her light under a bushel. Tessa gave herself a mental shake and pulled her scattered wits back into a semblance of order. "Meet Kellen Sterling, one of the esteemed panel of judges presiding over the competition tonight."

"It's my pleasure." The lean sable-haired man spoke first, extending a well-shaped brown hand in her direction. "I've heard a great deal about you from Web, Mrs. Mallory. You're one of the few female vintners I've had the pleasure of meeting."

"I'm afraid Web overstates my qualifications," Tessa replied with habitual cool courtesy, accepting the touch of his hand with some trepidation. "I'm more involved with the financial and marketing end of Vinifera Vineyards, Mr. Sterling, but I'm learning." Outwardly she remained aloof and relaxed; inwardly her hastily awakened defenses were at work building barriers, sealing her off from the aura of maleness he exuded like the expensive and subtle cologne he wore. She didn't smile or lower her eyes from his face. At some deep level of feminine awareness she recognized that it would give her unease away. With the same awareness, she knew he would instinctively take every advantage of an adversary, filing away every weakness that came to his attention and using them to his own purpose.

And she had no doubt at all that women were his natural prey.

He was a shade over six feet tall, Tessa estimated quickly, adding the two-inch heels she wore to her five-foot, six-inch height. The top of her golden-brown head was just level with his heavily lashed cobalt eyes. No man should be blessed with such long, sooty lashes, she marveled obliquely; most women would kill to possess them. His nose, above an aggressive mouth that just missed being sensual, was long and bold. Her mesmerized gaze followed the line of his stubborn chin and jaw—with what she hoped was no more than ordinary interest—lingering for an instant on the curve of his strong neck and throat before dropping to the broad sweep of his shoulders. There was a hardness in this man, Tessa conceded, hidden and muted by a patina of sophistication and good breeding, but there nonetheless, like steel sheathed in velvet. He reminded her of some great beast of prey. If that was a banal cliché, so be it. That's how such phrases came to be clichés after all, because they suited their purpose so well.

Kellen Sterling coughed slightly, low in his throat, and Tessa blinked, realizing what she'd been doing. He had remained relaxed and perfectly at ease as she studied him, seeming to find her scrutiny amusing. Now he was ready to rescind the small concession of passivity he had granted—and did so as Web continued speaking.

"Tessa's on the mark when she says she runs Vinifera, Kellen," he boasted. "She keeps our little bit of a lab functioning perfectly and she's learning the vines. Now I've only to see she develops a suitable palate before I call it quits. . . ."

His last words brought Tessa back to earth with a jolt. She hated to hear him speak of dying. As though by denying mortality she could erase it from certainty. "Web, don't talk like that," she broke in, more sharply than she intended. Tessa hated sounding like a shrewish wife and lowered her voice. "It's bad luck," she finished lamely.

Tessa was aware that most, if not all, Web's business acquaintances and even a few of his friends suspected she was his mistress. It didn't bother her and Web payed no attention whatsoever to the veiled speculations. If it didn't grow on vines and you couldn't make it into wine, it didn't interest him. Gossip had nothing to do with making wine; therefore, it was unimportant.

But Tessa avoided making any gestures, such as her last remarks, that could imply that she was indeed Web's mistress. It made her angry that she'd let Kellen Sterling's assessing regard goad her into an indiscretion. In point of fact, if she were totally honest, Tessa sometimes welcomed the deception. It saved her from the embarrassment of unwanted male attention—at least on most occasions. She frowned up into the dark blue eyes

30

watching her and recalled the earlier sensation of someone staring at her from across the lobby. Could it have been this unnerving man?

Almost as if he had intercepted her line of thought, Kellen spoke again. "I hope you chose the apple-green silk yesterday. It was most becoming." His smile showed strong white teeth, even and straight.

Good genes, or a good orthodontist? Tessa's inner voice mused irreverently.

"I did." She managed to form the words in a passable imitation of her customary tone. How did he know about the dress? Where had she seen those eyes? And that smile? It quirked the ends of his mouth but never reached the dark blue eyes to lighten and warm their reflecting surfaces. It was a totally predatory gesture that reinforced the impression of jungle sleekness; and it sent Tessa's pulses racing beneath the prim buttoned cuffs of her blouse.

"I'm glad you took it." He nodded succinctly. "It suits you. A woman with your hair and eyes should always wear summer's colors."

Tessa didn't say a word; her mind had jumped backward in a split second of clarifying remembrance. Their glances had met before—yesterday—across the crowded floor space of the hotel's small dress shop where Web had insisted she buy a new dress.

Kellen Sterling had appeared in the doorway as Tessa pirouetted in front of the full-length mirror, her usual carefully preserved aloofness evaporating as she watched the sensuous material cling seductively to her thighs and the curve of her hip. She'd lifted her gaze from the captivating swirl of silk and there he was, a tall, willowy blonde draped enticingly on his arm, her icy beauty the perfect foil to his casual elegance and dark good looks.

His eyes had touched her figure across the distance, and Tessa could still feel the tingling warmth and the breath rush from her lungs as though his hand actually brushed caressingly along her skin. No words were exchanged, but his appreciative perusal of the clinging raw-silk dinner dress had told her exactly what she wanted to know. It was a dress men noticed, regardless of the woman inside it.

31

"Tessa doesn't spend enough time on things for herself," Web said proprietarily, unconsciously strengthening the image of their involvement. "She's always far too busy seeing Vinifera runs smoothly." He sent one of his fierce, loving scowls in her direction. Web had been raised in an age where shopping and wardrobes were extremely important to most women. It was hard for him to understand her customary indifference to fashions in general and shopping in particular. She hated them. But that dress was going to serve more than one purpose.

"Mrs. Mallory must be a paragon among women," Kellen answered quietly, a hint of amusement sliding through his inky-timbred voice as he looked down, slowly releasing her hand.

Tessa felt a stain of embarrassment tint her cheeks and her green eyes darkened as she dropped her arm quickly to her side. For no good reason she could fathom she didn't want this man to think her unfeminine, but his touch had imparted a febrile heat to her squirreling thoughts. A second alarm of warning claxons went off in her brain. What was the matter with her? He was just an ordinary man. . . .

"It's been an honor to meet you officially, Mr. Sterling," she replied smoothly, hoping to change the focus of the conversation from herself before he spoke again. "But I'm afraid I must be leaving you gentlemen."

"Please, call me Kellen," he cajoled, ignoring her polite dismissal. Unfortunately the disarming effect was spoiled by his quick jungle-cat smile. It was as bright as a beacon to Tessa, and her answering smile was practiced and cool. It was time to end this uncomfortable discussion. A leer at her decolletage through a store window didn't constitute an introduction in her book. Her flashing green eyes conveyed the message eloquently.

"After yesterday I feel we're practically old friends, don't you," he added pointedly, letting his gaze roam over her at will. The predatory smile remained in place, lighting up her senses like a signal flare. He was letting her see he'd read her thoughts.

"Perhaps you're right, Kellen," she answered with ice-tinged sweetness, changing course in mid-stream. "Web's been singing your praises ever since our Riesling was accepted for the judging. I'm sure it wouldn't do to be considered unfriendly to the man who holds our fate in his hands."

"You wouldn't be trying to influence one of the judges with

that remark, would you?" he baited in return, one expressive dark brow arched over the disturbing cobalt spheres as he acknowledged her sally.

Another shiver of sensation skittered over Tessa's nerve ends. She would do well to remember this man's unsettling effect on her if she intended to indulge in any further verbal skirmishes with him. Her laboring brain insisted on dredging up the small bits and pieces of facts and innuendos that comprised her knowledge of Kellen Sterling. That he was a noted wine connoisseur and troubleshooter for some of the most prestigious names in the American wine industry was common knowledge. What did Web call him when he mentioned he would be attending the symposium? The boy wonder of U.S. enologists? How dated that sounded, but Web had been serious when he said it. Tessa also knew he was a graduate of the University of California at Davis—Web's alma mater.

Was he married? Definitely not, her interior voice answered. The blonde that Tessa had seen him with yesterday, but who was nowhere in sight today, hadn't been anybody's wife. She had sensed that immediately. Tessa decided she should probably add expert on women's clothing to her inventory. Or perhaps, more correctly, expert on women. Period. The image of the gorgeous blonde was sharp and stinging in her memory. It was also inexplicably upsetting.

"I was merely stating the obvious facts, Mr. Sterling," Tessa returned, hiding her inner assessment. "You're a world-famous enologist, there's no disputing that. You may of course take it as a compliment if you wish but I find it hard to believe so fleeting a meeting could have an influence on a blind tasting that takes place in a sealed room."

"Touché, Mrs. Mallory." This time his smile was genuine, warm and devastatingly candid, deepening the fine lines around his eyes and carving two grooves in a track between his nose and chin.

Tessa couldn't smile in return. The slight emphasis on her title caught her off step, catapulting her back to an image of Jacky, tall and straight, his red hair shining in the sun. A time before the pain of his disease and the ravages of chemotherapy had all but destroyed his youth and high spirits. Her lips thinned.

33

"Kellen, why don't you join Tessa and me after the judging tonight. They can't keep you bottled up in that room the whole evening. I know you won't be at the dinner," Web invited, his voice, comforting and familiar, helping Tessa to regain her composure.

"I'd like that. You're right, I won't be at the dinner. You can't mix business and pleasure in wine judging. I'll eat after the presentation of the medals and the validating of the scores."

"It's amazing the poor judges don't faint away from hunger, Mr. Sterling," she joked uneasily, suddenly anxious at the thought of seeing more of this man.

"I thought we had agreed on 'Kellen.' " He directed this last remark straight at Tessa while his eyes caressed her face boldly and deliberately.

"I'm afraid we won't be together long enough to get to a first name basis," Tessa answered. How silly to think he would be any different from other men. Seeing her in the provocative dress yesterday, given the rumors that always revived when she traveled with Web, what other conclusion would a sophisticated man of the world draw? He considered her Webster's property, that was certain. It had surfaced in his tone. Even if he gave her the benefit of the doubt about her relationship with the older man, he would still consider her a woman alone. She would be fair game in any case.

Of course, that was the impression she hoped to convey, but the conflicting feelings it aroused within her soul were alien to her sensitive and privacy-loving inner self. She shook off the stinging discomfort they produced. It was too hard to make any valid conjectures about this man. She knew too little about him. He hid his emotions easily and well. Much as Jacky had done. Tessa frowned, enhancing the small temper line between her brows. She had too many pressing matters on her mind to enjoy parrying Kellen's banter, or discouraging his attentions.

"If you'll excuse us, Mr. Sterling," she went on, a slight edge to her rich, melodious voice as she emphasized the formal title. "I think Web should lie down before the afternoon session."

"Quit mollycoddling me, Tessa," her employer shot back with a calculating gleam in his deep-set hazel eyes. He hadn't missed the undercurrents in their verbal exchange, it seemed. "I'm as strong as a horse and you know it. As a matter of fact

I've invited young Sterling to tour the vineyards with me. He's done some remarkable things with vinifera viruses. Too bad it's still winter, but there's a lot to be learned anyway. If we only had this climate back along the river . . ."

Kellen Sterling was young, Tessa agreed, tuning out Web's patented lament about the soil and climate of their vineyard. She glanced at the younger man's strong profile while he listened politely to Webster's harangue. He was much younger than his reputation would lead one to believe. Four years older than herself? Five? Men aged so much more gracefully than women, she admitted with an emerald pang. It wasn't fair. And it made it hard to guess their ages. On her next birthday, she'd be thirty-two years old. Time was running out.

"Web, you can play on Mr. Sterling's sympathies about your soil and climatic difficulties later. Please for the sake of my nerves, say you'll rest this afternoon. For a little while." Tessa met his hazel gaze steadily and her words were firm. She didn't make the mistake of trying to wheedle his cooperation. She'd broken into the monologue so smoothly Web didn't even know he'd been stalled in mid-tirade. "Please." She laid her hand on his sleeve in a fleeting caress.

"You worry too much, honey," Web growled with one of his rare endearments, covering her hand with his beefy paw. His feelings ran deep and strong but they seldom broke the surface. It wasn't his way. You cared, you lived that caring. It wasn't necessary to shout it out for the rest of the world to hear.

"Don't let him overdo," she directed to Kellen, switching tactics with purely feminine logic. "We're not used to this warm weather so early in the year. In Ohio it's still winter." She looked directly at him, a lioness defending her cub. Kellen studied her face with quiet intensity, nodding as if satisfied with what he saw in her composed jade eyes.

"It's the same where I come from, you know. In New York the winters linger. Even though I haven't been back for years, I can remember what it's like." His eyes hardened to metallic blue spheres and Tessa began to wonder if they were hiding pain, or anger? Perhaps both? It was difficult to decipher emotions so carefully guarded.

His life is none of your business in the first place, she reminded herself sternly. Probing into the secrets of this man's past was the last thing she intended to do. "Web," Tessa tried again.

"I'll endeavor to see he doesn't walk me off my feet," Kellen interjected, grinning suddenly as his companion harrumphed his disapproval of the subject. Again there was the fleeting warmth in his smile that changed the rugged outlines of his face. Tessa held his chilling blue gaze a long, silent moment, then gave him an almost imperceptible nod of agreement.

"What are you doing this afternoon, young lady?" Web asked, apparently missing the silent exchange. He sounded as if the thought that she would be left alone had just occurred to him.

"I'm going to find Mrs. Basel's gift, take a long, lazy bubble bath, meet Magda for a tour of the winery's lab. They have a computer," she reminded him pointedly. "And give myself a manicure, not necessarily in that order," she finished up, ticking off the points on pink-tipped fingers. "Does that sound interesting enough to give up your hike?"

"Good Lord, no," Web answered, horrified. "I've been avoiding Magda Jurrus for the last twelve hours. And you know what I think about computers," he reminded testily. "I'm going back to my room when Kellen and I are finished. I'll take your advice about the nap," he promised, forestalling any further argument.

Tessa nodded but didn't comment on Webster's remark about their hostess. She'd been a friend for many years. She turned to Kellen, the beginning of a soft, amused smile curving her mouth as she pondered Web's predicament with the enterprising lady. Avoiding Magda's well-laid snares had at least accomplished the aim she had in mind. Web would get his rest.

"I've enjoyed our conversation." Tessa turned slightly to face Kellen head on. She hoped there was just the right mixture of politeness and informality in her tone.

"It was a great pleasure meeting you officially, Tessa," he challenged in return, holding out his hand. His voice was as heady and crisp as a good deep burgundy. He continued to watch her with that combination of amusement and male interest that she found so upsetting.

"Good day." So he had read the censure in her eyes earlier. And just as easily the amusement they now mirrored. He was

36

definitely too quick to be trusted. Tessa nodded graciously, letting the use of her first name pass without comment. Meeting his blue gaze with steady green eyes veiled beneath lowered lashes, she too held out her hand.

"Until this evening." His handclasp was as warm and vital as his voice. Tessa found it more upsetting than the caress of his eyes, if that was possible. She sensed rather than felt the coiled strength in the lean fluid lines of his body beneath the gray flannel slacks and navy blue wool blazer he wore. Kellen was very definitely a man, an exciting stimulating male. Completely off limits.

He followed Web from the lobby, and Tessa remained where she was. She needed a donor, a partner—that made it easier—a partner who would ask no questions, want no answers from her. Whose face and memory would fade into nothingness in a short time, leaving her with a baby—all her own.

The man holding the plate-glass door to the terrace for Web knew far too much about her. She couldn't chance approaching a man as sought after and well known as he. It was far too risky. She needed an anonymous stranger and she was growing apprehensive that she wouldn't find him in the small hotel.

Tessa looked around the lobby, catching her lip between slightly crooked teeth. What would the few men scattered around the spacious sun-warmed room think if they could read her mind? Until this moment she had refused to consider how difficult it would be to actually accost, seduce, and take to her bed a perfect stranger.

Especially for a woman who had lived nearly as cloistered a life as the monks of old. A woman who'd known only one lover in all her thirty-one years. A woman who wanted a child. But didn't want a man.

CHAPTER THREE

Tessa pushed aside the unbleached rough-woven material covering the long, narrow window of her room and leaned her head against the cool, dark glass. It was twilight and the world outside was dissolving into an abstract painting, all smudged outlines and shadowy forms in shades of purples and grays. She lifted her head from the glass and the reflection of a calm green-eyed woman stared serenely back at her. How oddly sophisticated she looked in the classically styled raw-silk dinner dress. Its effect was just what she wished it would be.

The gown was very becoming, bringing out the rich gold lights in her hair and complementing too the velvety smoothness of her apricot-tinted skin. Tessa was much more used to seeing herself in a white lab coat or the well-worn jeans she favored for working in the vineyards. Yet, when she put on the dress, she felt the staid hardworking Tessa fade away, become as insubstantial as the face in the darkly reflecting window.

She swung around with a swish of apple-green silk to find her image reproduced more clearly in the vanity mirror on the far wall. It was almost as though a more adventurous, vivacious personality had taken her place, an enticing, sensuous changeling.

Tessa moved closer, intrigued by her musings, and leaned both long-fingered hands on the dressing table. Did she look like a woman that a man might want to take to bed on their first meeting? She didn't feel like one as yet. Still, she couldn't remember when she had owned so lovely a frock. Its softly shaped neckline dipped daringly low over the swelling curves of her breasts. It bared a good deal more of her clear skin than she was comfortable displaying, but she resisted the impulse to tug at the soft material.

First things first. Choosing a man to father her child would have to wait a few hours more. Now she needed to give her consideration to the evening at hand. After all, the dress was to serve a dual purpose. Her appearance at tonight's dinner and judging would please Webster. Meeting his friends and the very real possibility of the Riesling receiving an Honorable Mention in the blind tasting, deserved all her attention. . . . Still, later when Web had retired and she was alone . . .

Once launched on the subject of her quest, her heart refused to cooperate with her logic. The hand holding a tube of rose pink lipstick faltered before resuming its task of smoothing the tinted gloss over her lips. She wouldn't be alone—not if things worked out as she wished. . . .

The dress would make it easier, she decided. The soft material clung to the excited taut peaks of her breasts, molding to the curve of her waist, where the hotel seamstress had altered it slightly, then flaring coyly over the round firmness of her hips and thighs. When she moved, the skirt alternately pleated and furled, ending at the bend of her knee. Kellen Sterling was right. The muted green complimented her. It almost—it did— make her feel capable of pulling off the quixotic scheme that kept pushing itself to the forefront of her thoughts.

Kellen Sterling. Involuntarily her mind skipped back to their brief but intense meetings. She could still conjure his image as she balanced on one slender foot and slipped its mate into a silver evening sandal.

Tall and bronzed, innately commanding, casually dressed in a cream-colored turtleneck and camel-colored wool slacks, he had looked more like a successful athlete turned businessman than a world-famous authority on American wines. There had been nothing of the rotund gourmet, or effete, snobbish East Coast liberal that most laymen associated with experts in his field. Nothing at all.

Tessa shook her head. This daydreaming had to end. She'd found a man that would serve her purpose—this afternoon while searching through the gift shop for a remembrance for the baby girl. An ordinary man, fortyish, an optometrist from Omaha, Nebraska, a city Tessa couldn't imagine visiting in her wildest dreams. He was twice married and divorced, three children, hence his visit to the gift shop. Obviously on the lookout for a little fun and games—a meaningless fling.

Because of her training as a nurse, Tessa had been able to keep careful track of the changing rhythms of her woman's body. She had planned so carefully for this moment, longed so totally for its ultimate consequence. The odds were in her favor. If fate was kind she could conceive her child tonight. She refused to look farther into the future than that. Deep down in her soul she suspected that her courage would desert her if she failed in her quest tonight. There would be no second attempt. Larry Gelbert would provide the necessary biological partner. Nothing more.

And no one else. Tessa dropped the thin silver link chain she was fastening around the long, slim column of her throat. Larry Gelbert would do very well. It was time to put Kellen Sterling forever out of her mind. But it was easier said than done.

Tessa knew she wasn't the only woman who'd been pulled in by his lodestone appeal. That's why the agitated beating of her heart when he was near couldn't be anything but physical. It was indicative of no deeper feelings whatsoever. Remember the others, Tessa, she abjured firmly. There had been the decorative blonde . . . and the some-distance-past-middle-age seamstress in the boutique . . . and how many others? But he still wouldn't do. She believed in heredity, she told her mirrored double sternly. That's why she wanted to choose the baby's father, not take her chances on a vial of fluid from a sperm bank. She knew a donor so chosen would be healthy, of course, and the right age and height and coloring. But what about his inner being?

Tessa truly believed that people were either born with a positive outlook, serene and confident; or conversely, were born ill-tempered, cranky, dull, and out-of-sorts. Those traits were passed on as surely as a tendency toward cancer or heart disease. She wanted to know her baby's father. No matter for how short a time. It would give her a basis for the future, a framework to gauge that half of her baby's developing personality. And so far Larry Gelbert met her criteria.

Kellen Sterling on the other hand was ruthless, cynical, and —for Tessa, the most damning fault of all—he lacked integrity. Even now she could feel her color rise as she recalled her own reaction to the seamstress's opening gambit while she'd fitted her dress earlier in the afternoon.

"I hope this dress is meant to catch the eye of the gentleman who looked in at you so appreciatively the other day," she said, smiling coyly as Tessa stepped out of the altered dress. It fit perfectly.

"I'm afraid I don't know what you're talking about," Tessa prevaricated as she fastened the buttons of her cream silk blouse and pulled the gathered skirt over her hips. She was ashamed now to look back and admit how intrigued she'd been by what the woman obviously had to say.

"Why, Mr. Sterling, of course," she replied innocently, as she gestured for Tessa to precede her out of the dressing room. "He came in right after you left to buy the lady he was with a lovely piece of jewelry." She bobbed behind the counter, her left hand with its badge of her profession—a wristband of multicolored pins—fluttered toward the jewelry case. She began to fold the apple-green dress into a tissue-lined box. "They must have been having a little tiff. She was complaining about having to repack and catch a plane after just arriving. Anyway," she rambled on, taking Tessa's absently offered credit card and filling out the required form, "I saw him watching you from across the room and I wondered to myself if that had anything to do with her leaving. . . ." She trailed off. "Well, you know how his kind are. Such a handsome man. But such a scoundrel." She threw the last phrase out in a voice barely loud enough to carry over the glass counter as she handed back the plastic rectangle. Her toothy smile was conspiratorial.

For a few moments Tessa had remained silent. Her inborn, highly developed love of privacy warred with her purely feminine curiosity. Every woman loved a rake. Hadn't she read that somewhere? They most certainly were interested in them if Kellen Sterling was any indication of the breed. And Tessa was no different. She replaced her credit card in her handbag and took the bait.

"I'm afraid I've only met the gentleman once, and then very briefly." It was as close as her pride would let her come to asking for information about the man. But it was all the encouragement the garrulous grandmotherly soul needed.

The boutique was nearly empty and the seamstress looked

bored. She flashed a glance at the only other clerk and customer in the shop and leaned closer to Tessa with another waft of her heady, musky perfume. She could have been somebody's grandmother. If your grandmother had worn designer eyeglasses with tiny rhinestone initials embedded in the lenses, and platform heels that tilted her matronly figure forward at an alarming angle. Tessa smiled to herself, but no hint of her inner cataloging glimmered through the calm veneer she presented to the world. She ran leaf-green eyes over a selection of costume jewelry on the counter and fingered one particularly heavy chain, as she waited for the woman's next remarks.

"It was in all the newspapers when it happened," Elsa—at least that was the name emblazoned on her ID pin—threw out experimentally, rearranging the pile of softly colored, hand-screened silk scarves from which Tessa had just picked one in gold and browns for Web's housekeeper.

Tessa looked up quickly, swallowing the lure: hook, line, and sinker. "Well, maybe not all the papers. He was in the same classes at Davis as my nephew. So of course, the articles at the check-out stands caught my eye. It must have been ten, no twelve, years ago."

"I see," Tessa answered lamely. She'd forgotten how small the winemaking world could be. How prone to gossip and petty backbiting. What could he have done ten or twelve years ago, when he was a college student, that could still be considered a scandal in these days? Tessa was beginning to regret encouraging the woman. She picked up the dress box and the smaller one containing Mrs. Basel's scarf, the first traces of a dismissing smile on her lips, when the woman's next words stopped her dead in her tracks.

"Paternity suits are always so embarrassing for everybody concerned. Don't you agree?" she queried, snipping off a trailing thread from a scarf in shades of mauve and yellow with the bright orange-handled scissors that hung from a ribbon around her neck. The combination of colors clashed horribly. Tessa watched the flashing blade as if mesmerized. "And then to have your sister-in-law filing the complaint. . . ."

"Paternity suit?" Tessa could have bitten off her tongue but the words were already out, hanging in the still, filtered air between them.

"Yes." The clerk looked surprised at the vehemence in her tone. Her sandy eyebrows crawled up toward the halo of fuzzy ginger and gray curls that crowned her head. "The poor, innocent young thing. I'm sure she was at her wits' end and didn't know what else to do." She looked at Tessa as though she were rather dense. "His sister-in-law accused him of fathering her child. It was quite a scandal," she explained as though relishing the sordid details she was drawing from her memory. "The family's old, you know. Since way before the Revolutionary War. His father disinherited him," she added confidentially. "Or as close as you can get. Isn't that unbelievable in this day and age?" She paused expectantly, but Tessa only nodded for her to go on, hating herself for prying even so obliquely into his past, hating even more what the woman was saying.

"It nearly killed his brother, they say. He's much older than that one." She inclined her head toward the spot at the window where Tessa had first laid eyes on Kellen Sterling. "Oh, it was a juicy tidbit there for a while. My nephew always figured his brother must have caught them together—in a compromising situation, if you know what I mean—and his brother ordered her out of the house. Well, that one"—she gestured again as if unable to speak his name—"didn't do right by the girl. It's always the woman who suffers in these affairs." She kept on nodding her gray head sagely. "So she filed suit to get them to recognize her claim." Apparently taking Tessa's continued silence as disapproval, she stopped her reminiscences and settled back down to business. "Will there be anything else, miss?"

But Tessa wasn't about to let her go so easily. She swallowed the last of her scruples like a bitter pill and asked in a voice that cracked slightly around the edges, "What happened after that?" She had to know what had become of the woman who accused Kellen of being the father of her child. She didn't understand precisely why it was so important to know, but it was. Had she suffered all these years while he traveled from one continent to the next, living like a bachelor prince? "Did he claim the child?"

"I don't think so," Elsa answered, frowning with the effort to remember the exact details of the scandal. "He got drafted right after graduation and my nephew sort of lost track. He has a vineyard up in Washington State now and I don't see him as often anymore," she threw in proudly. Clearly the woman was losing interest. Or perhaps she realized she'd spoken too freely about an important guest of the hotel? Anyway she seemed in a hurry for Tessa to go.

"Surely you aren't going to leave me dangling." Tessa managed a travesty of her usual rare smile. "I'd love to know what happened. It's just like a soap opera." She didn't know whom she despised the most at that moment, Kellen Sterling, or herself for sinking so low that she'd encourage this old woman's gossip.

"Well, in this case the wages of sin . . ." The trendy grandmother trailed off, clicking her tongue against her teeth. "His brother took the girl back, he was ill or in an accident, something like that. The whole affair just died down, what with all the other things going on in the world then. It's been a long time. His father and brother and his wife run the family vineyards. The old man—Jason Sterling—is pretty feudal, they say. Surely you've heard of Sterling Hills? You're from back East yourself, aren't you?"

"Yes." Tessa didn't bother to tell the woman her home was two states' distance from the fertile, sheltered shoreline of the Hudson River where Sterling Hills lay. Webster had spoken occasionally of the fine sparkling wines they made but she never paid much attention, or connected it to Kellen Sterling. Why should she?

"Then you probably know more about him than I do," Elsa added with a hint of suspicion. "My nephew says they make some of the best champagne in this country."

"Yes. Excellent sparkling wines. Now if you'll excuse me, I'll let you get back to your other customers."

As there was only one other browser in the shop, Tessa knew her excuse sounded as thin as it was. Her conscience was getting the best of her curiosity and she slid the dressbox under her arm, hurrying out of the boutique into the identical glass-fronted gift shop beside it. For a woman who valued her privacy above everything else, she'd been shamelessly pumping a total stranger about Kellen Sterling's past. She didn't want to know anything more about him! She'd certainly not liked what she had heard. He was despicable—seducing his brother's wife. It offended her own standards of conduct—which she had every

44

intention of breaking herself this very night. It was not a comfortable conclusion. Then with her mind still swirling, she'd reached out to pick up a small stuffed giraffe and met Larry Gelbert.

That had been several hours ago; she hadn't seen either man since then but here she was, still comparing Kellen Sterling to the other candidate her unconvinced intellect proposed. It would never do. He was not the man she was searching for. Using him as a standard only made it worse, because he was as unsuited to her as the rest. It was a "no win" situation and she didn't intend to let it deteriorate any further.

She was allowing Kellen Sterling's remote, lake-blue eyes and golden-toned body entirely too large a share of her waking thoughts. With characteristic coolness she changed the focus of her musings, but the effort was tremendous. Tessa attended to the last-minute details of her makeup and located her bag and shawl as though walking in a dream. First things first: the words kept repeating in her brain with monotonous regularity. And finally they succeeded in pushing other matters to the back of her mind. A few moments later she was ready to greet Webster with a faint copy of her usually special smile when his knock sounded on the iron-studded wooden door of her room.

Tessa glanced at the slender silver face of her wristwatch. Ten o'clock. Webster would be retiring soon, his body was still firmly attuned to a schedule based on eastern standard time and that made it very late for him indeed. She lifted the lead crystal goblet to her lips and savored the fragrant, memorable taste of Magda's premier Chardonnay. Someday their vines would yield a wine of equal character. Perhaps not as polished and sophisticated as this one, she admitted, because adversity builds different characteristics in wines as well as in human beings. Their vinifera varietal wines would never be so polished, so unobtrusive on the palate . . . but they would be all the better for the struggle.

There was an eddy of movement in the group of people standing around the linen-covered table in the center of the low-ceilinged room, and Tessa saw Web reach out to pick up a small velvet-covered box from the base of a bottle of their Riesling displayed attractively with several other vintages. She'd never

45

seen him look more handsome in the wide-lapeled, slightly old-fashioned dinner jacket she'd insisted he bring along. Coupled with a less formal white turtleneck sweater and charcoal wool pants, it gave him an air of casual distinction and savoir faire that Tessa found downright sexy herself.

Magda must have thought so too. She'd cornered him in his circle of old friends and acquaintances, looking mysterious and exotic in a flowing black robe of some gauzy material with a high ebony comb and antique lace mantilla towering in the piled coils of her night-black hair. She was congratulating him yet again as she smiled down at the award he held cradled in its velvet box. A bronze medallion. Tessa smiled involuntarily in response, unaware her actions were observed by the man she hoped to avoid for a few blessed minutes of privacy.

She was still unbelieving of their good fortune. Web's Riesling had been picked from among fifteen other fine white wines to win a coveted third place prize. The only vintage outside the state of California to be so honored. It was what Web had been shooting for ever since they had made their pact to put aside separate past sorrows and make Vinifera Vineyards into a commercial and personal success.

It was Web's night and she should be joining him. He liked to have her meet his old friends from the days after the Second World War when he had made wines for some of the most famous wineries in the state. But she was edgy, disinclined to make small talk, and hoped this glass of wine would help her loosen up. She wanted to ignore the twinges of conscience that flickered out and snagged her mind when her thoughts strayed from the scene at hand. She didn't like keeping Webster in the dark, but this decision was too personal, too all-encompassing to be shared. Tessa drained her glass, deciding she'd feel less out of place if she were slightly drunk. Just enough to make it easier —just enough to make her more at ease about the step she was taking. Not enough to harm the baby she hoped to conceive.

She'd tried to prepare herself emotionally for this moment, but it was still alien territory she was entering. Having a child was not a decision she'd made lightly but with quiet deliberation, and it would have consequences stretching out to involve the rest of her life. She had a right to be nervous.

Larry Gelbert finally succeeded in catching her eye, advancing on her position like a smiling satyr. Why hadn't she noticed that gleaming, feverish excitement in his china blue eyes before? The sensation made her shiver and wish for another glass of wine as she broke the optical contact and stared down at the empty goblet in her hand.

It was too late to get away, run to the shelter of Magda's warm, smothering charm, or Web's quiet, solid bulk. She could feel the heat of his body as he halted beside her although she didn't look up. It was too late to back out now. She'd come too far, made too many promises to herself. She'd burned her bridges, crossed the Rubicon, as her high school literature teacher always used to say.

Tessa had paid determined attention to the Nebraska native all evening, learned as much of his background as she wanted to know. She couldn't back out now because she felt squeamish and uncertain. There was no reason to turn tail and run to earth because she thought he was eyeing her like a prize morsel on the buffet table. And because he had sweaty palms. Neither of those traits was hereditary as far as she knew.

But it was unsettling all the same, hence the need to keep her spirits up. Added to that was the tension of knowing that shortly she would have to ask him to her room. Tessa couldn't take the risk of his not asking her; although by the way he kept inventing excuses to touch her and brush himself against her, it didn't seem a likely possibility that he would refuse. She glanced upward through lowered lashes and glimpsed again the strange glitter. The vibrations were there between them—at least the ones she received from him were decidedly sexual. Hers, she had no doubt, were merely nervous energy. It was almost as though he couldn't wait to get her into his bed. She was his unexpected bonus on his vacation, the casual California sex he'd fantasized about. It didn't matter what she felt at all.

"Let's dance, Tessa," he urged, sliding a quick glance around the room. He grinned, showing lots of strong white teeth. "Who would believe I stumbled into this just because I missed my tour bus?" he questioned rhetorically. That he would only be at the hotel one night had tipped the balance of the scales in his favor. He'd be chagrined to learn it wasn't his blond, blue-eyed good looks that kept Tessa from turning a cold shoulder to his flirtation in the gift shop this afternoon; but the fact that he'd only be in her life twenty-four hours at the most.

"I'd like that," she lied as he plucked the fragile glass from her fingers with soft square-nailed hands and placed it on a small, round table at her side. His snub nose was peeling from too much exposure to the California sun and the red in his cheeks and neck was intensified unbecomingly by the stark contrast of his white dinner jacket and shirt. A little overweight, Tessa catalogued with scientific detachment, but he seemed kind and good-natured, if somewhat insipid; certainly he seemed primed for a fling. Once more she was reassured that she had made the right choice by the laugh lines radiating from the corners of his blue eyes. She wouldn't last past tomorrow in his thoughts, she rationalized with her inner self. And she hoped his sojourn in her memory would be almost as short.

Magda had gone out of her way to create the ambience of Old Mexico this evening, Tessa observed as they made their way toward the dance floor. Dim globe lights glowed in the beamed ceiling—brighter over the buffet table and the bar—but the rest of the illumination was provided by hand-thrown ceramic lamps with hurricane shades. A three-piece combo in Mexican costumes covered with hammered-silver ornamentation in fanciful animal shapes and intricate medallions were grouped in the corner nearest the glass doors that led to the pool and patios beyond. Their faces were shadowed by the large wide-brimmed hats they wore, and the music was soft and slow, in keeping with the restrained atmosphere, and was easy to dance to.

Tessa let herself be drawn into Larry's arms, her mind working at light speed as their bodies swayed languidly to the music and his hand roved caressingly over the fabric of her dress. Tessa held her breath, but she felt nothing beyond a slight distaste at his display. Excited by her touch, Larry pulled her nearer and Tessa didn't allow herself to object, although her hand clenched involuntarily on his shoulder as she felt him tremble with excitement and lust. She fought down the urge to reach behind her and remove his hand as his fingers splayed across her back and edged down to the sensitive base of her spine, pushing their lower bodies together so that she could feel

48

the desire in him as her thigh was wedged intimately between his legs.

This is the way it has to be, old girl, Tessa reminded herself grimly. It's no worse than you feared. In a few more hours it will all be behind you, and if everything goes as planned he will have given you a baby in exchange for the use of your body. Not a bad deal if you put it in that context.

Tessa rallied her forces and smiled up at him invitingly, using every ounce of her considerable willpower to keep her full pink-glossed lips from trembling childishly. Filled with confidence and the thrill of the hunt, Larry swept her around the dance floor until she was dizzy and disoriented. When the music slowed and dwindled to a melancholy halt, she found herself facing the entrance and looking over Larry's padded shoulder to see Kellen Sterling silhouetted in the doorway like a fallen archangel, all black and golden, storm and fury etched in the harsh lines of his face. She could almost smell the faint odor of fire and brimstone in her nostrils.

He seemed to stand in a small pool of solitude—alone even in this crowded room. His disapproving eyes raked over her flushed and breathless figure, lingering for a small, charged second on the swell of her breasts so flimsily confined by the apple-green dress, then moving slowly upward, snagging her gaze to deliberately impale her with his frosty ice-blue glare.

How dare he, Tessa fumed, forgetting instantly her unease in Larry's arms and attributing her sudden need to catch her breath to the recent exertion of the dance. How dare the man look at her as though she were a common . . .

Tessa brought herself up short. She laughed aloud, breaking Kellen's spell and surprising herself almost as much as Larry. What Kellen Sterling thought of her moral character didn't matter at all. The only thing that was important was how she felt about herself. "I'd like a glass of champagne," she told her escort, imperiously sliding a pink-nailed finger across the moist-ness of his full lips. She pulled him off the small parquet dance floor with a toss of her head that sent her gold-brown hair swinging like a bell. I need it to wash away the last of my Bible Belt, Sunday school scruples, she thought. She didn't glance toward the doorway again, letting Larry pull her into the crook of his arm as his hand rested just beneath the swell of her

49

breast. From the corner of her eye she saw Kellen advance into the room, and she gave a guilty start. Was he coming after her? It was a silly notion, gone as quickly as it had come. He wasn't really an avenging angel, after all. He moved to the table, greeting Webster and Magda, and the men shook hands. He was probably congratulating Web on the bronze medal, Tessa thought obliquely, slightly disappointed. She'd have liked to give him a piece of her mind.

"Let's get a bottle of champagne and take it to my room," Larry suggested slyly, giving her hand a squeeze that made her wince. She hadn't realized he was so strong. His lips brushed her hair somewhere above her left ear. Apparently he was satisfied that his seduction was working.

Things were moving too quickly for Tessa. She felt trapped. She hadn't wanted to be seen leaving with Larry while Web was still in the room. Her brain searched frantically for something to detour his intentions. "In a few minutes," she croaked. "Let's not waste this marvelous party. We have all night ahead of us." Larry was too pleased with her pronouncement to catch the faint ragged edge of hysteria hidden in her dazzling smile.

"Anything you want, honey," he said expansively. As it could be, Tessa thought spitefully, this evening wasn't costing him a red cent.

She glanced over her shoulder surreptitiously to see Kellen's dark head, his hair gleaming like rich satin under the ceiling lights as he bent attentively to catch something Magda was saying. Again she could feel the disapproval in his eyes as his gaze flickered in her direction. Who was he to pass judgment on her? A man who fathered a child on his sister-in-law and then refused to face the consequences.

Kellen's displeasure at her performance, and hers at his reaction, suddenly brought the power of the dress into effect. Like a sorcerer's spell, Tessa recalled the vivacious temptress that could be beckoned from within herself. She was in charge now, the real Tessa slipping away into a limbo of noninvolvement. It was the alluring woman in the mirror who accepted a brimming goblet of champagne and smiled beguilingly up into Larry's flushed face and gloating eyes.

Tessa hoped the changeling would remain in power until dawn.

CHAPTER FOUR

Her alter ego's reign was short-lived.

A hand, hard and strong, touched her shoulder and the color drained from her rose-dusted cheeks. Tessa turned to see Kellen Sterling standing beside her, his face a demon-mask of darkly lighted planes and angles. His low, growling voice invaded her senses far more quickly, and devastatingly, than the wine in her glass.

"I believe this is my dance, Mrs. Mallory." His polite words sent a chill coursing through Tessa. She rubbed her hand over the gooseflesh on her arms and opened her mouth to refuse the imperious summons.

She never had a chance.

Before she could respond, Kellen thrust her tall fluted champagne glass into Larry's spongy grasp with a mumbled, "Thanks, old man," and led her toward the dance floor. His fingers were like an iron clamp on her elbow.

"You're hurting me," Tessa grated through clenched teeth and her green eyes blazed in fury. She had the most ridiculous urge to dig in her heels and fight their forward motion. It was time she put this infuriating, overbearing man in his place. She didn't want to be held in his arms no matter how briefly or indifferently. She intended to let him know, in no uncertain terms, that his attentions were unwelcome.

"Sorry," he answered, untruthfully it seemed, as the predatory smile quirked the corners of his lips attractively. "I didn't realize you were so fragile." He guided her onto the floor and into the rhythm of the dance without missing a step. Tessa found herself following his lead with effortless ease. It made her angrier still.

"I'm not fragile," Tessa blazed, her green eyes glinting in the subdued light. She sensed her only defense was a good offense, and rushed on. "But I'm most certainly not used to being man-handled in this manner." She hoped she sounded half as hostile as she felt.

The insult rolled off his impeccably tailored back like water off a duck. "I'd never have guessed that from the display you two just put on." Kellen's words were challenging and uncompromisingly harsh, demanding an answer. Worst of all they were true. Tessa bit back a sharp retort, forced to admire his total control of the situation even as she deplored it. And the subservient position it placed her in.

"I find Larry charming," she said baldly. It was the only reply she could think of so quickly. They might have been discussing the table centerpieces, not a flesh-and-blood man. Not the potential father of her child.

"A car salesman from Des Moines?" he shot back, one dark-winged brow lifted in well-feigned surprise.

"He's an optometrist from Omaha," Tessa answered primly, but she met his gaze defiantly with eyes green as river ice. She couldn't suppress the tiny smile that curved the corners of her mouth. "And a very successful one, or so he tells me." In endless detail, she added silently.

"A pillar of the community, no doubt," Kellen stated dryly. "President of the Rotarians. A Little League coach." Was he teasing her? Could she see a faint lightening of those disturbing cobalt spheres? Or was it merely her imagination playing tricks?

"I'm not aware of his athletic prowess," Tessa admitted demurely, her emerald eyes dancing with private excitement. Fencing with Kellen gave her the same kind of giddy exhilarating feeling she always experienced looking down from a sheer drop. The utter, unshakable conviction that if she only possessed that single extra ounce of courage to push off into the void . . . surely . . . surely she could fly.

"I stand corrected," he conceded, inclining his dark head so that a wayward lock of nearly black hair fell forward. Tessa longed to reach out and push it back into place. It intensified a certain quality of rakish appeal that was hard to resist. "They don't make wine in Omaha that I'm aware of. Is he a frustrated vintner, kibitzing this illustrious gathering of your peers?"

"Not that I'm aware of," Tessa answered lightly, parroting his words. Let him speculate about Larry Gelbert all he wished. She was enjoying her own small power play. Her feeling of being able to soar, of wanting to step off into the void returned with increased fervor. But of course she wouldn't do it. She had her feet too firmly on the ground for that nonsense. It was a ridiculous notion, suicidal.

"Then what is he doing here among the elite of the 'boutique' wine crowd?" By 'boutique' Tessa knew he referred to the small wineries that catered to a limited clientele, seldom marketing their wines commercially—usually because the production was too small to be disposed of profitably that way. They depended on private subscription, their own tasting rooms, and sometimes restaurant wine lists to make a handsome profit. This valley was dotted with prime examples. Vinifera Vineyards could now be listed in their ranks—more exclusive still, as they were something of a rara avis in the wine world. Ohio was a long way from Napa Valley.

"Dr. Gelbert is touring the wine country with a select group of his colleagues," she expanded airily. The champagne had hit her with a burst of tiny brilliants that were bounding around inside her head at the speed of light. For the first time she could meet his penetrating agate eyes with a semblance of worldly sophistication. Yet as she did so she stumbled, missing a step. Kellen righted her with no hint of strain, although she knew she was no featherweight. The earth had moved beneath her feet, but no one else seemed to notice. If it were an earthquake surely someone would mention it? Kellen held her bemused regard. Now, oddly the entire room seemed to be spiraling down to the small circle of his arms. Tessa felt as if she were floating several inches above the floor as she was pulled into the solitary space that surrounded him. The eye of the storm?

Tessa would have liked to lay her head on Kellen's shoulder and stay in his embrace until the sun crept over the hills and laid rosy fingers on her cheeks. But that was impossible. She brought herself up short, breaking the almost hypnotic power of his eyes. He wasn't even holding her that closely. She might have been his maiden aunt. Several inches of warm, body-heated air remained between them. His hand never strayed from the curve of her back just above her waist, although the pressure of his fingers burned relentlessly through the thin fabric, branding their imprint on her skin. Tessa sighed, narrowing her green eyes as she shook the lingering fantasy of effortless gliding flight.

She continued speaking, unaware of her dreamy expression or a lapse of several seconds in her narrative. "Larry missed the bus with his tour group and had to spend the night. He'll catch up with them tomorrow when they come back down the valley." That was another reason he was so suitable for her needs. Their paths would never cross again.

"Good for him. Back with his own kind. Stodgy optometrists from points east."

"That's my kind, too, Mr. Sterling," Tessa reminded him rather forcefully. Determined to be civil but firm. "Good solid middle-class midwestern stock. That's where my roots are."

"And always will be with any luck. But you're a vintner now. A breed apart from the Larry Gelberts of this world." Tessa didn't have an answer for that observation. She digested it in silence. Was she a vintner? An apprentice at best, but it did seem to be taking a great hold on her life. She seldom if ever thought about a return to her career in nursing. And she hadn't for many months, she realized in astonishment. Recklessly she met his gaze head-on and saw the truth in his words. Tessa smiled and she couldn't see that Kellen felt the shock waves at the very center of his being, but his hand tightened convulsively on hers.

"Tomorrow I'm off to New York. Then to London for Christie's auctions of rare red wines. It will be a day of partings for you, Mrs. Mallory." His low voice grated on the words and his jaw hardened into fixed undecipherable lines.

The announcement gave her a curious little pang around her heart. But she explained it away as relief at his going. His moods were too quicksilver for her to fathom; it was too disturbing to watch as he changed from warm and teasing to cynical and cold in the blink of an eye.

"Are you attending as your own agent?" She couldn't resist asking the question, and it helped to get her mind off its disturbing tendency to dwell on every nuance of his strongly carved features. A great deal of money and the most rare and sought-after vintages in the world changed hands at the famous London auction house. It was part of a world she could only

54

dream about. And he belonged there, by birthright and by breeding.

"Yes and no. It's a little out of my league. But you can often pick up a good bargain from some of the lesser-known châteaux. And I have enough commissions to make it worth my while to attend."

Tessa wondered who it might be? A New York millionaire, too busy with his wheeling and dealing in the stock market to see to it himself; but a man who wanted the prestige of several priceless bottles of 1806 Château Lafite-Rothschild in his cellar? Or he might be bringing back a 1961 Mouton-Rothschild for an exclusive restaurant in San Francisco or Dallas. "You lead a very exciting life, sir," she quipped, her voice taking on the husky intonation it acquired when her interests or emotions were stirred.

"A very solitary life," he answered quietly, disturbing her with his apparent sincerity. His tone was matter-of-fact but he failed to meet her liquid gaze and she tried not to be swayed by any feelings of empathy for the man. Tessa cast about in her mind for a mental image of his unhappy sister-in-law, but failed to bring it into focus. Instead the recollection of his chic blond companion popped up as clear and sharp as a photograph and danced behind her eyelids with no invitation whatsoever.

"You're alone a great deal of the time?" The episode made her voice sharp.

"More often from choice than necessity." He must have sensed her warring between compassion and chagrin and wanted to let her know her sympathy was unwelcome. And unnecessary.

Tessa stiffened, trying to back farther out of the charmed circle of his arms. His hold tightened imperceptibly but she was as solidly trapped as if they were bound together by chains of chromium steel. "It's the nature of the business." He shrugged and Tessa could feel the ripple of sinewy muscles under her fingers. There was none of the fleshy laxity that she'd encountered in Larry's arms. "Sleeping in hotel rooms in foreign cities. Dealing with taxi drivers when you don't speak the language. My French is okay, but my German and Italian are nearly nonexistent," he disclosed, giving her another small insight into his complex personality. "Being the guest of harried vintners who don't have the time to entertain you but feel they must," he elaborated and she found herself relaxing a little in the quiet space that surrounded them. Tessa liked to hear him talk. "Endless evenings discussing another man's wines. Making conversation with his equally bored wife or mistress." Tessa stiffened, a frown shadowing her high, smooth brow. "Spending long hours in damp château wine-cellars in Europe. In big warehouselike ones in this country." He smiled sadly, but blue flecks of amusement danced in his eyes. She was being had!

"Are you trying to tell me you are to be pitied for your choice of career?" Tessa sniped because she had pictured all too vividly the solitary life he described. She didn't like knowing her emotions were so easily read. Kellen didn't want or need her sympathy, and she had shown him another vulnerable point, another chink in her own armor, to add to his arsenal.

"I think I'm a great deal more to be pitied than censured," he drawled, and this time the amusement that tinged his words was more pronounced.

"I don't believe that any man who could boast such a companion"—Tessa wanted to say "lover" but restrained herself just in time—"as the woman I saw you with outside the boutique yesterday is to be pitied in the least. Most men would envy you, I'm sure." It was a petty shot but the words tumbled past her lips before she could stop them. She was probing for a weakness that probably didn't exist.

"That's because you know very little about the world beyond your small sheltered corner of it, I suspect." He smiled with the words. Not the jungle-cat smile that immediately set her hackles to rise, but the warm, inviting smile he'd used yesterday in the lobby. It spiked her guns effectively. But not before she fired her last salvo.

"And where is she tonight?" The pause that followed her words lengthened as a murmur of voices, glassware, and Latin music floated around them.

Kellen twisted his head to look down at an elegant gold wristwatch. "I imagine she'll be breakfasting sometime soon in a coffee shop near the Hôtel Georges Cinq that she usually frequents when in Paris. At a fashionably late hour, of course." His tone dismissed the woman as easily as his next words. "It doesn't really concern us. I don't intend to ever see her again."

56

Tessa didn't speak after that. It was a warning to keep her distance. She wasn't a match for him in her present slightly befuddled state and she knew it. Still she shrank inwardly from the cold implacable voice he'd used to dismiss his former mistress. Because that woman could have been nothing less. Tessa was positive of that. Was that how cavalierly he treated all of his discarded women? If so, he would be an extremely dangerous man to love.

Kellen pulled her closer as the band drifted into another slow romantic lament without pause. Tessa let herself sink against his hard, lean strength, grateful for the respite, despite the urgent warnings of her intellect not to relax her guard. She was so drained emotionally by the sparring that the dance had seemed to go on forever. Their bodies barely touched. A casual observer would only have seen a handsome man and his beautiful partner dancing serenely to the music's sensuous beat. But Tessa was more intensely receptive to tactile stimuli than she had ever been in her life. For her the night was being drawn out on coppery lines charged with sparking bolts of static energy.

Her breasts brushed lightly against the pleated front of his shirt and she could feel the dusky peaks harden in anticipation. His granite thigh pushed against the softness of her leg. The material of his superbly tailored jacket was rough beneath her fingers and her hand curled into the curve of his neck. She would have liked nothing more than to reach up and touch the short hair at the back of his head but she did no such thing. Never in her memory could Tessa recall being this sexually aware of a man. The depth of her arousal frightened and confused her.

The music ended. Kellen stepped away. Tessa blinked in confusion, for suddenly the small dance floor was crowded with people. She looked around her with heightened awareness brought about by the combination of nerves and champagne—and Kellen—that was bombarding her with sensual feedback.

"Tessa, honey," Web boomed, smiling at her across the abyss. "Magda's invited me to her private rooms for a snifter of brandy and some more talk about the good old days with a few friends. You're welcome to join us?" He sounded unsure of the last sentence. Tessa knew he was happy seeing her with two eligible men. He often urged her to get out and start living again. Well, she was—and with a vengeance.

Tessa tried to smile her refusal as Larry sauntered up with another brimming goblet of champagne and she introduced him to Webster and the older woman.

"Nice of your staff to find me a room, Madame Jurrus." He saluted Magda with grating familiarity. "I appreciate it." His voice and smile seemed to be expanding with the amount of alcohol he consumed.

"You are very lucky we had a cancellation, Dr. Gelbert. We are usually booked full on occasions such as this. Are you interested in wines?" Magda spoke with perfect politeness but Tessa realized she didn't like the man at all.

"No, I'm not. But I do know what I like, at any rate, and this champagne is very good." He took a long swallow and coughed a little deep in his throat. Tessa wondered with a flash of intuition if his wine tasting tour had been a last-minute inspiration, something one did automatically when visiting California?

"Please have all you wish," Magda said with a slight regal inclination of her head. "And enjoy your stay at San Luis."

"Tessa?" Web inquired again. Tessa stifled a sigh. Web wasn't sure of Larry either. Perhaps she was making a mistake. Or just giving into an attack of maidenly nerves?

"No, Web. Tessa will be much happier here with these gentlemen," Magda directed, taking the decision out of Tessa's hands. She gave Kellen a smile that communicated something that Tessa couldn't decode. Apparently satisfied, the older woman tapped his black-clad arm with her lace fan and nodded her head. "Good, that's settled. Tessa needs to be dancing and enjoying herself, not listening to talk of vineyards and vines that were planted even before she was born. Come, Web, the others are waiting."

Web offered Magda his arm obediently and gave Tessa a large sheepish grin. She wished she were going with them. As her friend studied her strained, pale face, he became suddenly serious. "Will you breakfast with me as usual?"

"Of course," she answered vehemently. "I'll be ready at seven," Tessa added more calmly, summoning his smile from deep within. This trying night would be behind her long before sunrise and they could return to a happy, ordered routine. Web

58

was her solid rock in a world that was suddenly quicksand beneath her faltering feet.

"My God, what an unearthly hour to rise," Magda proclaimed into the awkward silence that followed, allowing herself a delicate shudder. Tessa took a tiny sip of the bubbly golden wine to keep it from spilling over her gown and reached up on tiptoe to give Web a peck on the cheek. "Have a good evening."

"You too, honey," he replied with gruff embarrassment and turned on his heel.

A chorus of good-nights followed the seniors out of the room. Tessa was alone with the man of her choice as Kellen indicated his intention to leave them with a curt nod in her general direction. She watched his tall athletic figure stride away with decidedly mixed emotions.

Kellen was the last barrier between her and Larry's obvious impatience to have her to himself. Tessa took another, longer sip of wine and squared her shoulders. This was it, the time to put her resolve to the test.

"Would you like to take a walk in the . . ." Larry motioned out the door, a frown creasing his forehead below his carefully styled blond hair.

"I think the word you're looking for is cloister," Tessa supplied nervously, recalling the dark sheltered walkway surrounding the hotel's main courtyard. She nodded and took his hand. The palm was damp.

A few minutes later Tessa found herself backed against a stone balustrade, the empty champagne goblet slack in her hand. Larry's swift embrace stunned her. His invading tongue dueled with her tightly clenched teeth as he bent her back over the low wall and his hands began to seek access to her soft breasts within the plunging neckline of the apple-green dress. Tessa stiffened, instantly appalled at his crudeness and her own violent reaction to it. If she couldn't endure his kisses or his caresses, how was she ever going to be able to give herself to him completely?

The thought caused her nerveless fingers to open and she dropped the champagne glass with a shattering cry of crystal on stone. Tessa listened to its echo in her heart as her naïve illu-

59

sions began to shatter in their turn. This was wrong. It was insane. She couldn't go through with it.

There had to be love involved with sex. The love she'd shared all too briefly with Jacky. The emotions her parents had felt when they chose to create their children. The passion Web and his beloved wife had known for almost thirty-five years until her death. And if you couldn't have love you must at least share the desire to give yourself in the physical act. It was what she'd been taught to believe. Indeed, it was what she did believe with all her heart. But this travesty had no element of any of those emotions. Tessa felt her stomach muscles clamp in disgust. She couldn't go through with it.

She lifted her hands and pushed Larry's feverish face and body away from hers. Tessa stared at him with eyes dark and fearful in the pale silver moonlight. Somewhere not far away a bird twittered, disturbed no doubt by the sound of breaking glass and tussling bodies. She could hear the strains of music quite clearly with some small uninvolved part of her that was feeding bits and pieces of data to her whirling brain.

With the lessening of Larry's nearness, a little of her sanity and courage returned. He'd just taken her by surprise, that was all, she lectured sternly. You were married for almost four years, Tessa. You're not a frightened teenager, or a trembling virgin. You know the touch of a man's hands, the feel of his body in yours. Tessa swallowed hard and made her decision, trying to bring the situation under control.

"Larry, please." She heard the voice coming out of her mouth and was chagrined by the way it quavered and cracked on the two simple words. She wanted with every fiber of her being the baby he could give her—even more than she wanted to run and hide. It didn't matter that her shocked intellect was screaming rape in the clamoring inner chambers of her mind. It couldn't be. She was perfectly willing to go to bed with this man.

"Sorry, baby. But I've waited all day for this. And tonight when I walked into the banquet room and saw you in that dress." His avid gaze didn't even bother with the dress. It stripped her to the skin and she stomped on a silly adolescent urge to shield her breasts with her hands to protect them from his prying eyes. His puffy finger traced the outline of her heaving breasts and Tessa shuddered, rushing into speech.

"You just surprised me, that's all. . . . Let's try it again. A little slower this time," she croaked, amazed at her own temerity. Their coming together would be an act of love. Tessa tried to hold on to the thought like a fragile talisman. The child she hoped would be created by their union would be loved by her every minute of the rest of her life. And she'd never see Larry Gelbert again.

His fleshy, moist lips descended over hers a second time and her hands clenched on his shoulders before Tessa forced herself to quiescence with an act of will. She opened her mouth to his probing tongue, but tears of self-loathing welled up under her lids. If she could only relax, enjoy his kisses, it would be so much better for herself and the child she wanted to conceive. Tessa's mind jumped unbidden to the pleasant memory of Jacky's kisses and caresses. He'd been a kind, undemanding lover. Would it be so wrong of her to recall his body and his touch to help her through this ordeal? Would she be disrespectful to his memory and the love they'd shared if he helped her through the night?

A small, choking sound began in the back of her throat and might have been a sob by the time it reached her lips if Larry's heavy unwanted weight bending her back hadn't been lifted from her with startling rapidity.

"You're drunk, Gelbert. I suggest you make your apologies to the lady and call it a night." Kellen's voice came out of the darkness with all the quiet fury of a panther on the prowl.

"What the hell?" her startled aggressor rasped, turning to face his tormentor as Tessa's hands flew to rearrange her disordered clothing.

"I said get your hands off her. Is that plain enough for you?"

Tessa couldn't make a coherent sound to save her soul. And that's exactly what she felt she'd been surrendering—the very essence of her being and the strength of her will. Now that she was released from Larry's unwanted embrace, her courage came flooding back. And perversely her anger transferred itself to the instrument of her rescue, to the tall, dark figure of Kellen Sterling silhouetted aggressively by the dim light of the banquet room doors.

"How dare you, Kellen Sterling?" Tessa hissed with something of a lack of originality. "You have no right to interfere with our . . . private . . . conversation . . ." she finished lamely, her face flaming despite the cool evening air.

"I wouldn't think of it," he grinned, and Tessa caught the white flash of his teeth in the moonlight. The menacing purr of his low voice was completely gone. "I'm here as a messenger, nothing more." Yet as Tessa risked a glance into his stormy blue eyes, she knew he was as angry as she, though his tone and relaxed stance belied the emotion very effectively. If her own senses hadn't been operating at such intensity he might have got away with the performance.

Larry, however, took the remark at face value and dropped his belligerent pose. "Who's looking for her?" he inquired acidly, but he swayed unsteadily on his feet, robbing the words of their sting.

"Her employer, as a matter of fact." Kellen looked through Larry Gelbert as if he didn't exist, as though he were too unimportant even to bother cataloging his weak points for future reference. It was Tessa's own guilty conscience that put the worst possible connotation on his words.

"My God," she cried, pushing herself away from the rough stone support, "has something happened to Web?"

"Listen, Tessa," Larry mumbled, and she turned her head impatiently toward him, seeing for the first time how drunk he really was. She looked away in disgust, barely registering his speech as she searched Kellen's face for some sign of reassurance. There was none to see. "You go see what the old guy wants and I'll meet you later . . . for a nightcap," he clarified, holding out a placating hand as Kellen shifted his weight threateningly. Larry Gelbert wasn't too drunk to know he was outclassed. But he had hopes for coming out of this confrontation with some of the spoils. "Okay, sweetheart?"

He bent forward and pulled Tessa toward him for a long possessive kiss that made her want to drag her hand across her bruised lips. As he held her stiff, unresponsive body against him, he contrived to slip his room key into her hand. Tessa's fingers closed over it automatically. She knew for a certainty she'd never bring herself to use it now but she didn't see how to refuse it without creating a scene. "See you later, baby," Larry growled and walked back toward the lighted windows of the banquet room with drunken bravado.

Kellen watched him go, muttering something low and pungent under his breath that Tessa was glad she couldn't catch. She stood like Lot's wife, seeing the ruins of her carefully laid plans settle into dust at her feet.

"Give me that key, Tessa," her nemesis ordered, holding out his hand imperiously. She responded to the tone of command without conscious thought as she looked down at the telltale key with a guilty start. Kellen took the piece of metal and plastic and tossed it over the railing into the shrubbery that lined the walkway. Brushing past the leaves, it landed with a discordant chink.

Tessa's face flamed crimson again and she stuttered in her haste and anger. "I had no intention of accepting his crude invitation," she said in her best imitation of Magda at her most aristocratic.

"The hell you didn't," Kellen snarled, grabbing her by the shoulders and shaking her like a rat terrier. "You've been acting like a bitch in heat all evening. Panting over that clod like he was the last man on earth."

It was almost enough to bring the bubble of hysterical laughter lurking in her throat to the surface. A bitch in heat. "That's a lie!" Her teeth chattered as she spoke and in the privacy of her thoughts Tessa acknowledged the truth of the statement. Had Magda and Web seen it also? Web. She'd almost forgotten why Kellen had searched her out. "Stop shaking me! I can't think," she stormed, growing brave in defense of her friend and mentor.

"Sorry." Kellen sounded disgusted with his lack of control. "You bring out the worst in a man, do you know that?" he grated, running his hand over his aggressive chin where a faint shadow of dark beard made him look more than ever like a terrorist or a bandit chieftain from an earlier age. Tessa stored up the remark as one more tiny dart of pain. It was also the truth. "I don't like to see my friends made fools of."

"I don't know what you're talking about," Tessa countered distractedly. "Where's Web, I have to go to him. Is he ill?" The urgency in her tense body and dark eyes made Kellen stop and pause, as if rethinking his position.

"He's fine. I didn't mean to frighten you. I forgot about his heart trouble." It was another piece of private knowledge that sailed right over Tessa's head.

"He's not ill?" Her voice was glitter bright and the words were as hard as diamond chips. He'd been lying to her all along.

"I'm afraid he didn't send for you, precisely. If that's what you're getting at. I'm afraid that was the inspiration of the moment, you might say." His satisfied smile looked fiendish in the moonlight.

"Of all the nerve . . ." Tessa hissed, regaining her spirit as her worry over Web subsided.

"I was fully prepared to send you back to him if necessary," Kellen returned, tugging on his left earlobe. "I still am." A distinct threat in the emphasis he put on the words brought her up short, silencing her scathing rejoinder before it was uttered. "As I said before. I don't like to see my friends made fools of."

"I . . . I still don't know what you're talking about. It was only a kiss, after all. You had no right to interfere. I can take care of myself." Her laugh was shaky and not very convincing to her own ears. She'd been outmaneuvered by an expert. Kellen knew he wouldn't have to resort to violence with a man like Larry when chicanery would do the trick. Damn him! Yet somehow Tessa couldn't bear the thought of this infuriating male believing she could betray the best friend she had in the world. Especially with a nothing like Larry Gelbert.

"Some kiss," he snorted derisively. "Gelbert's hands were all over you. Did he hurt you?" Kellen asked unexpectedly.

"No, he did not." It wasn't precisely true, her lips ached from the force of his kisses and her self-esteem was definitely bruised.

"That's good. At least you won't have to explain any marks to Web."

"I beg your pardon," Tessa replied, shocked.

"It's none of my business if you want to make a spectacle of yourself with a swine like that one. But not in front of Magda and Web. Haven't you got any pride?" His hand shot out and clamped around her wrists as her fingers curled with ancient feminine instinct into taloned weapons of lethal intent. Kellen moved with the sure swiftness of a powerful man, dragging her close to him and his angry face filled her vision. "If you're going to be the mistress of a man old enough to be your father," he said, a cynical smile twisting his mouth awry, "you have to practice a certain amount of discretion. Or haven't you learned that lesson as yet?"

Speechless, infuriated, Tessa stared into his face. The cold, proud lines dropped into place across his features but the imprint of his ridicule seemed destined to remain etched on Tessa's brain for eternity. He thought that little of her. He grouped her in the same bracket as the expensive blond mistress he had used and discarded with such ease. She burned with the shame of his accusations. And perversely she was hurt by the fact that Kellen not only believed she was Web's mistress—an impression she knew she had done nothing to deny, and had obliquely encouraged—but worst of all, he thought she would betray the older man so blantantly and so cruelly. His opinion of women was very low indeed.

It was the pain of that last deduction that made her spin on her heel to hide the tears of remorse and fury that stung her eyes. But Tessa had forgotten that Kellen still held her in a painless but unshakable grip.

"Oh, no you don't," he hissed, further misinterpreting her actions. "You're staying here with me until Gelbert is safely passed out in his room. It shouldn't take more than fifteen minutes at the most. The man can't hold his liquor worth a damn or I'm no judge." He laughed mirthlessly at his own pun. "Gelbert wouldn't have been worth the trouble you were taking to seduce him." His tone was scathing and Tessa flinched away from its arctic chill.

It was the final straw. A red haze suffused her vision and sent her temper rocketing out of control. "You ass," she whispered sharply, finding courage deep within herself. "I don't have to explain any of my actions to you. Do you understand?" Tessa was glad for something to strike out at; anything was better than this biting shame she felt. Everything was going wrong. Her dreams were turning to sand and slipping through her fingers so quickly that she didn't seem to be able to save them, no matter how hard she squeezed her hand. The tears she'd choked back threatened to overflow once again. "I'm going to my room so please take your hands off me. I don't intend to stand here and be insulted another moment."

"You'll stay until I tell you to go," Kellen returned, every bit as angry as Tessa.

She took a deep breath and held on to the last shreds of her splintering temper. "I won't take orders from you or from anyone. But since you seem bound to act as my conscience I'll tell you just once, in words of one syllable so you will understand. I wouldn't hurt Webster Mayer for the world. He's my dearest friend. I love him like a father. But I am not, nor have I ever been, his mistress."

"Good."

"Good?" It was the last thing she expected him to say and she stood stock-still, unable to decide what to do next. Kellen made the decision for her. Taking her head between his lean, strong hands he traced the path of one crystal tear that had escaped her precarious control. "My God, Tessa. Don't cry. I believe you. Don't cry. I hate it when women cry." He bent his head and Tessa held her breath in anticipation.

Was he going to kiss her? She hoped he would and her hungry body arched closer to his magnetic appeal.

And she hoped he wouldn't. Somehow she knew with the exquisite sensitivity that had been with her all evening that it would be a kiss like never before. That it would remain etched on her memory for all time like the imprint of his features. Tessa couldn't take the risk of testing her resolve. Already her unruly heart was awakened to his male command. She could almost taste his mouth and she longed for the fruition of that wish.

"You're making my head spin," she complained, feeling the siren in her brought to aching life once again by his proximity.

"It's a mutual affliction," Kellen murmured, threading his blunt, square-nailed fingers through her fine gold-brown hair. "You're an enigma, Tessa Mallory. I can't figure you out. But I want you. I've wanted you ever since I saw you in that dress yesterday." He tilted her head back to search her face and she met his gaze head-on. "Are you really the wanton you tried to convince that hapless fool, Gelbert, you were? Or are you the shy child-woman that's staring at me now from those fascinating green eyes? Or are you something else entirely? Something in between?"

Tessa wanted to tell him his words were nonsense, but his lips moved to cover her mouth just as she began the first syllable. It was total annihilation, pure and simple. Kellen didn't demand response. It wasn't in the least necessary. He merely orchestrated her surrender with consummate skill. Feather-light caresses touched the upturned corners of her lips, coaxing, enticing, entreating her cooperation.

Tessa brought her manacled wrists up between them, some small pocket of resistance holding back her complete capitulation. He retreated strategically as he felt her stiffen. But only for a second. Then so smoothly she almost didn't know when he moved, Kellen shifted his position, his thumbs replacing his lips as he urged her lips to open for the entrance of his searching tongue. With gentle persuasive pressure, he invaded the sweet moist hollow of her mouth.

Tessa's arms came up around his neck as naturally as if they'd always belonged there. Her fingers stole into the sable pelt of hair where it curled softly at the nape. She inhaled deeply, catching the faint scent of his soap—sandalwood, she guessed—and the clean, slightly musky fragrance of his skin. No cologne diminished the essence of maleness that enveloped Tessa. Its aroma would have interfered with the wine, with his sense of taste and smell. Kellen was trained to discern anomalies in parts per billion her whirling intellect dredged up out of the void. Billions, like the number of shooting stars behind her eyelids.

Tessa couldn't remember such a kiss as this. Was certain she'd never experienced such a kiss before. My God, it would be so easy to allow him to take complete control, let loose of that last bit of sanity that begged her to send him away. Honesty held her in thrall. This was the man she'd wanted since the first sight of him in the boutique window had collided with the deep, seeking need in her to conceive a child. He was the perfect male, the perfect father for her child.

He would take from her all he wanted and give her a baby in return. It would be so easy.

Tessa's unconvinced intellect gave up the uneven struggle to gain supremacy as the ageless, purely feminine urge to perpetuate the species rose up to meet and join forces with the sensuous being the dress had unleashed within her. She wanted a child and now she wanted this man—Kellen Sterling—even more.

The die was cast. And then quickly, with the speed of spoken thought, reality and fantasy collided. Kellen lifted his head, breathing heavily, and smoothed the hair from her brow. "I think I'd better get you back to your room before this gets any further out of control."

"I don't want to go back to my room," Tessa murmured a fraction of a second later. She wasn't thinking any longer. The desiring woman in the mirror would have her way. "I want to stay with you."

She held her breath as Kellen tensed. She could feel the strengthening, the contraction of muscles along the entire length of his body where it pressed against her more pliant feminine form.

"I won't be a substitute for Gelbert," he grated harshly, holding her at arm's length when all she wanted was to cling to him like a limpet.

Tessa shook her head in wordless denial. "You won't be." Kellen Sterling would never take second place to any man, she was sure of that. In that sense she spoke only the truth. But on another plane, in a different dimension or reality, she lied. He was taking Gelbert's place. He was now the means to an end. She hated the deception but it was imperative, unavoidable.

"And I'm offering nothing. Do you understand that, Tessa? Can you be satisfied with a one-night stand? Nothing more. There's no room in my life for long-term relationships. No commitments. I want you—but that's all."

For the second time that night his words were a challenge and the tone was harsh. Tessa flinched but stood her ground, her fingers tangling in the silver chain at her throat for an anguished second. Her voice might have betrayed her, made him change his mind. She didn't want him to see the child-woman he'd described staring out of her jade-green eyes. She lowered shadowed lids and pressed close once again, answering with her body. Her voice when she spoke was barely audible above the thudding of two heartbeats.

"I don't want anything from you beyond tonight." It was a pact she made with herself as well as with him. "Nothing at all."

In a dizzying rush of movement Kellen swept her up into his

arms while the moon and stars reeled in the heavens. Tessa let herself nestle into the curve of his shoulder. She laughed suddenly, a silvery note that tinkled like sleigh bells.

"What's so funny?" he growled softly, his breath tickling her ear.

"Liberated women don't allow themselves to be carried off by their lovers these days. Didn't you know that? I think I should lodge a formal protest." There. She'd actually said the word out loud. And proved she could be as nonchalant and worldly as he wanted her to be. Tessa bit her lips in the near darkness, wondering how he would react.

His arm, where it curved along her back, stiffened momentarily, then relaxed. "It's lucky for you that I'm not a liberated male or you'd have to walk." His tone was light and velvet-rough. "I guess I'm just a throwback to caveman days. A barbarian dressed in borrowed plumage."

"I'll keep that in mind," Tessa quipped, but she was far from thinking him a barbarian. His precision and grace of movement belied the charge. It spoke of leashed strength, arrogance, self-command, and even now in the formal black evening clothes, a certain virile elegance.

They reached the door of his suite and Kellen set her down, causing her to slide the full length of his body, molding her to his strength with hands that followed the curve of her bottom and allowed her to become aware of the extent of his arousal. Tessa hadn't been touched so intimately in years. She felt a fever of desire and longing rise up in her like a cloud of stinging insects. It threatened to choke off the air she breathed, arousing a passion that matched his own. Kellen released her long enough to slide the key in the lock with hands that weren't quite steady and swing open the door. He motioned her through, and she went on legs that were suddenly no more support than columns of Jell-O. The door thudded shut with the finality of a prison lock. Tessa couldn't stop herself from swinging around to stare at it.

"Would you like something to drink?" Kellen asked in a husky whisper. If he noticed her hands clasped so tightly the knuckles showed white and the blue veins were a delicate tracery under her pale skin, he said nothing.

"No, thank you. I've had enough this evening." Instinct was

again at work. Alcohol would be bad for the child. Her child. Tessa, wondering again if she would conceive, recalled that some psychologist, somewhere, had proved that conception was often psychologically primed. Women that wanted to get pregnant, he stated, even if the urge was deeply buried in their subconscious, often did conceive after only a single encounter. Perhaps she would.

Kellen touched a light switch and a small lamp on the dressing table sprang to life. It was a much larger room than her own. Three, perhaps four, of the monks' airless cells had been thrown together to create the suite. Dark beams across the ceiling at regular intervals testified to the dimensions of those old rooms. There was a bar in the far corner, its glassware gleaming dully in the fitful light. But Tessa's eyes were drawn involuntarily to the king-size bed that dominated the floor space.

Sand-colored sheets were turned back in readiness for the night and the dull orange bedspread was folded neatly at the foot. This room like all the others in the old mission was decorated in shades that were predominantly earth-toned. Golds and browns, reds, ocher, orange, and sepia warmed the expanse of whitewashed walls and covered the wood floors with splashes of bright rugs.

And Tessa longed for home. The rolling, blue-brown river beyond her windows. The often delayed spring that finally erupted overnight in the greens and yellows, pinks, lilacs, blues, and occasional sharp dash of red that called to her summer soul.

"Have you changed your mind?" Kellen asked quietly, pulling the gold cuff-links from his sleeves. He'd already draped the black jacket of his tuxedo over an ornately carved, uncomfortable-looking armchair.

Tessa stared at him owlishly. The white shirt was too stark, too absent of warmth, for the golden undertones of his skin. He needed ivory or cream to make him look his best. "No. I won't change my mind. Not ever." It was a pledge of her intention to this man she scarcely knew, as well as a vow to herself.

"I'm glad," he said quietly. "I don't think I would let you go any longer even if you wanted to." Tessa stood quietly, passively as he kissed her eyelids, her cheeks, the tip of her nose. His lips played across hers, touching quickly and moving on to nibble at the diamond stud in the shell-like curve of her ear. "There have been so many women in my life," Kellen murmured, so quietly he might have been talking to himself, as perhaps he was. "But you are different. You've been in my mind from the first moment I saw you." His breath was hot and sweet against her neck. "I don't know what a woman like you was doing with Gelbert to begin with. The man is obviously a boor. And a louse."

Tessa shivered with a mixture of desire and relief at her escape. "I didn't know . . . he seemed very nice at first . . ." she responded candidly. She stumbled to a halt as his fingers worked expertly at the tiny fastenings of her dress. The zipper glided on silent runners and the apple-green silk dropped to the floor with a sigh of relief, baring her to the waist.

"Being so trusting will lead to your downfall, Tessa. I'm surprised Web leaves you out alone," Kellen teased as he bent her slightly back to admire the bounty he'd uncovered.

"Web would never try to run my life," Tessa stated with emphasis that supported her through the trying moment. "I'm my own woman." Kellen's eyes grazed over her feminine curves and her skin tingled pleasurably where they touched and lingered. Tessa caught her breath on a tiny moan of enjoyment. She didn't mind his perusal nearly as much as she had feared.

"I don't know what you're up to," Kellen admitted, bending to place a quick hot kiss on each rosy upthrust peak. "What game you're playing. But neither of us wants to be alone tonight. And sometimes that's enough."

"I'm not playing games," Tessa pleaded, more for the continuation of his entrancing caress than his understanding. "I want to be with you very much." She couldn't explain that she wasn't playing any game. She was acting in deadly earnest.

Kellen's thumbs continued to trace erotic patterns across the delicate blue-veined skin of her breasts and Tessa's heartbeat rose in answer to the fondling. He touched her parted lips with an inquisitive forefinger, testing the barrier of her closed teeth. They opened to the stimulation and the tip of his finger slipped inside. "Are you a rose in the California desert?" he chuckled intimately, his mouth now against the racing pulse in her throat. "Is that what you are, Tessa Mallory?"

"No. I'm a woman. Nothing more. Nothing less. Don't try to

make me out to be something I'm not. I'm not a hothouse flower. Nor am I a child. I'm fully grown, in possession of all my faculties, and I want to spend this night—and only this night—with you."

She stood with a strange artificial calm as his mouth invaded hers. "I'll remember," Kellen groaned. "For tonight only," he repeated, breaking off the kiss to speak. "God, Tessa, I do want you so badly." A small moan grew in the back of her throat as his thumbs kneaded her dusky, budding nipples. "Is that what you want?"

"Yes." Tessa's hands roamed over the soft, shimmering fabric of his shirt but she didn't shrink away from his kiss or his hands as they rested below the ripe curves of her breasts.

"Then it's settled. Love me, Tessa."

Tessa drew back, frightened despite her resolve by the sternly leashed passion in his voice. This was not intensity she expected of a casual liaison. It wasn't right. It sounded too sincere. Too heartfelt and genuine. Then she remembered he must have perfected his technique in countless such meaningless encounters. The hunger she sensed in his stance and tasted in his kisses was only that of the hunter closing in on his quarry. She was a conquest, nothing else. And he was the means to an end. "Don't you trust me not to hurt you, Tessa?" he asked, intrigued, perhaps, by her drawing back.

"Yes. I do trust you." Strangely it was true. She did trust him, no matter how cynical, bitter, or disillusioned he might be. It was her own wayward emotions that needed guarding against. "But it's been so very long. So very long . . ." she mumbled against his throat, relishing the strong, even beating of his pulse against her lips. She pressed close, unwilling to have him gaze on her nakedness so fiercely. The onyx studs in his shirt bit into her soft flesh. "I'm nervous, I guess," she admitted with a shaky laugh.

"Making love is like riding a bicycle. You never forget," he lectured with humorous sternness. "And I won't allow you just to stand there and accept my advances like a dreaming maiden. I want you to love me in return. Touch me, Tessa," he urged in a low, rough-edged whisper. "Undress me. Now." Again that arrogant, instinctive tone of command she could not ignore.

For a moment Tessa was stunned, remaining lifeless and stiff, like a helpless plastic doll. Kellen waited, tense, expectant, as she sorted through the myriad whirling intricacies of her thoughts. Tessa had never undressed a man before. Not even Jacky. He'd always taken the initiative in their lovemaking. It was the way he preferred it. And Tessa was content with that arrangement, happy when he was happy. But that wasn't the root source of her unease.

She had had no intention of letting herself get so involved. In her vague fantasies of this night, this act, she'd looked on herself as a detached and passive vessel to be filled. Standing here now, partially unclothed, was part of what she expected to occur. But not to participate as a lover—and equal partner—in the coupling. She wasn't sure she wanted to.

Then her hands reached up, almost of their own volition, and tugged at the stubborn knot of his tie as she worried her lower lip with her teeth. Nothing was going as she'd planned for it. She would have to adjust to the changes or give up her quest. And to her amazement she was discovering something else. Her entire being, body and soul, was attuned to one man and one man only. Kellen.

It hadn't been Jacky's face—although in her distress she'd called on his ghost—that rose up to shield her from the reality of Larry's fumbling, lustful caresses. It had been Kellen's chiseled features she saw. The simple recollection of that single fact struck her with seismic force. She hesitated, the onyx studs that fastened his pleated shirt shining like dark crystals in the palm of her hand as she digested the evidence of her musings.

Not Jacky's face, she thought distractedly, while Kellen silently watched the emotions flit across her fine-boned face. He plucked the shining studs from her nerveless fingers and dropped them in an ashtray on the dressing table. Not Jacky's face. And it was all right. The admission didn't hurt, although she searched her heart for the familiar sting of grief and guilty pain. It wasn't there. The hurt was gone.

It was all right. Tessa smiled—the first time for Kellen alone. She didn't know it then, wouldn't understand completely for months to come, but she'd said good-bye to her mourning in that single heartbeat. She would soon be at peace with herself. Her memories of the man-boy who'd died too soon taking her first, rather desperate love to the grave with him had found their proper place, tucked away in a shining corner of her mind, leaving her free to enter the future.

Tessa stepped into Kellen's embrace as he shrugged out of his shirt with sharp, quick movements of his muscled arms. Their mouths touched as he held her head between his hands, and her breasts brushed coyly against the lightly furred hardness of his chest. When she felt his immediate, and pronounced, response against her lower body Tessa repeated the action, reveling in her own newly discovered ability to please. She raised on tiptoe, her tongue touched his, withdrew, touched again, before she let it dart between his lips with hummingbird quickness. She liked the sensation of warm, moist darkness. Kellen tasted of good wine, smooth and rich—and of passion. This time she allowed her tongue to linger and explore.

His hands moved across her shoulders, following the curve of her back, resting at the sensitive tip of her spine as he pulled her close. Tessa gasped at the heat his touch ignited. It was as though a flare had exploded deep in her middle and now burned with a fierce bright flame. She groaned, scarcely audible even to Kellen as he captured and swallowed the small sound before it left her lips. The kiss was endless and over far too quickly.

Kellen released her reluctantly and motioned to her feet. Tessa looked down, stepped away, kicking off the flimsy silver evening sandals, feeling smaller and more lost in uncharted space than before. It was as though she had developed tunnel vision, her universe was narrowing down, coalescing into this quiet lamplit room. She could see no familiar landmarks, couldn't see beyond the man who was quickly and efficiently divesting himself of shoes and socks. Kellen reached for her again, tugging the lacy cream-colored slip and clinging pantyhose down over her rounded hips. His fingers traced the outline of her bikini briefs, and then they too were gone. Tessa stepped from the last of her clothes with unconscious dignity as Kellen studied her beauty with shining lake-blue eyes.

"You are as lovely as an English garden," he breathed against her hair, his hands luxuriating in the opulent curves and valleys of her body. "Your freshness. Your perfume and dew-covered silkiness." Tessa could scarcely make sense of his husky, whimsical words. Her hands too were bent on exploration and her blood pounded through her veins in a rushing torrent of sound and fury.

"I've always wanted to visit England," she whispered as the name of the small green island snagged and held on a jagged shard of her splintering reason. Tessa tried to retain a remnant of the worldly facade she had erected but it was increasingly difficult to form coherent speech.

"I'd like to be with you there." No warning bells sounded. Tessa was too far gone to fathom a deeper meaning in his voice.

Her hands tugged at the waistband of his slacks, anxious now to have the last of the obstacles between them removed. She eased them over lean muscular hips as greedily as he had done for her.

The spell of the green dress was holding. She felt no reservation; all she desired was to be with him, touch him, caress the granite angles of his well-honed physique, feel him within her.

No more clothing hindered them as Kellen pushed her down into the bed's softness and the beckoning comfort of the cool sheets. Tessa had forgotten how marvelous it felt to have another human being at your side. She liked it very much.

Hesitantly at first, then with a passion she could neither fully explain nor hope to contain completely, Tessa touched her lover. With sensitive blind fingers she perused the curves and hollows of his strongly carved face, then more boldly and deliberately she followed the sculpted lines of his torso, discovering the intriguing contours and textures of his skin. Her fingers reveled in the fine crisp hair covering his chest as she registered the fact that it was not so dark a brown as his brows and lashes.

Her liquid green eyes closed against the dim light of the lamp on the table as she let her hands stray lower still, following the tapering V of his ribs and waist, spreading light butterfly caresses over his tightly muscled buttocks and steely thighs, until with great daring her questing fingers closed over the heated source of his manhood.

"Tessa, my God," Kellen breathed, pulling her hard against him, rescinding the privilege of dominance he allowed her in exploring his body.

"I wanted to make this last until dawn. But I can't. I won't. You're like a fire in my blood. I want you now." His teeth surrounded a dusky rose peak and the sharp caress coupled with the sensuous kneading pressure of his hand along her thigh was almost more than Tessa could endure.

"Kellen, please. Don't make me wait any longer." His hand had inched higher, spiraling toward the very center of her being. Probing gently, preparing the way for complete surrender with persistent, exciting strokes, he made her ready. Tessa clutched at his shoulders as her hips moved in ancient erotic invitation that communicated itself to the man at her side in urgent waves of need. "Please, Kellen. I want you with me. Now."

His weight moved over her, but he withheld what she wanted most. "Tessa." His voice was raspy with suppressed desire. "Are you protected?"

"What?" The words cascaded over her like cold water. "I don't understand." She looked perplexed. Tessa was so aroused she could scarcely answer coherently. Her hands savaged the rippling muscles of his back as she tried to pull him closer still.

"Tessa, you're a nurse. Web told me." He sounded amused, but a raging fire kindled deep in his eyes. The sparks jumped between them like current between points. His face looked starkly defined and devilish in the soft, diffused lamplight. Like a woodcarving in solid black oak. He'd captured her wrists in one strong hand and now he pulled them over her head as she struggled to bring her mind and body back under her control. Little meaningless things intruded on her awareness, the feel of her hair tickling the insides of her elbows, the ticking of a small travel alarm on the bedside table, the rustle of the pillow as Kellen shifted his weight. What if he had had a vasectomy, she wondered. That would be horrible. Why hadn't she considered that possibility before? Then, as if in answer to her musings he spoke. "Are you protected?" he questioned bluntly. "This thoroughly delightful activity is designed with an ulterior purpose, you know."

"Yes . . . I know," she stammered.

"Do I take it that means you prefer I take the precautions?" he asked solicitously. He reached across her to open the drawer of the bedside stand. "It will only take a moment."

"No!" Tessa wondered if she'd actually repeated the single negative syllable more than once, or if it were really only reverberating endlessly in her head. "No, that isn't necessary," she croaked. "There's no need . . . for any further . . . precautions." She was well aware she still blushed like a schoolgirl, but if only she could keep him from guessing at her real reason for objecting so adamantly. "I . . . I mean we don't need to . . . worry about it." She stumbled to a halt. Somehow she couldn't bring herself to tell any more lies.

"Good." Kellen shifted his weight again, nudging her thighs apart with his knee, his mouth moving over her ear, nibbling, tasting, making it hard to breathe or to think at all. He released her hands and wrapped them around his neck. "That's all I wanted to know. It's something better not left to chance." His face was bitter and Tessa couldn't help but remember the story of his past. No, he wouldn't want to be caught like that again. How close her plans had come to disaster, all because she'd blocked such a complication from her mind. She had been sure of Larry. She recalled all her carefully casual questions about his children. Kellen also had a child. A child he didn't want. Wouldn't even acknowledge. He was a man who'd been caught at love's game once before. He wouldn't make the same mistake a second time.

His solicitude had nothing at all to do with concern for her welfare. She wasn't deluded enough to believe that. But it was yet another reason that he must never ascertain her real motive for seeking him out. He wasn't an adversary to be taken lightly. He would remember her words. And if he ever came to know how she had used him, he would have his revenge.

"You're like a crisp glass of your own Riesling, Tessa. You go to a man's head so quickly and so subtly he doesn't know he's drunk until he can't think of anything else." Kellen again reached a long arm across the bed and Tessa stiffened, afraid for a split second that he had changed his mind, didn't trust her assurances that there was no need for precautions. "I like to make love in the dark," he explained, flicking off the light switch before gathering her closer to place a string of incendiary caresses along her collarbone, following the path of her silver chain until it dipped coyly into the scented valley of her breasts.

"I don't mind," Tessa responded, completely breathless as his hands claimed her once more in the soft, linen-scented darkness.

"Making love in the dark is the ultimate tactile experience." And Tessa was learning she preferred it also.

Kellen didn't speak again, but concentrated his energies on giving her pleasure. Impatient now, he shifted his weight, parting her legs further, lowering his head to capture her mouth in a kiss so daring, so erotically charged, that Tessa's soul lurched on its already shaky foundation. Gently he entered her, considerate of her more tender feminine configuration. To Tessa it was merely an even more satisfying continuation of the seeking kiss. He lifted her hips, positioning her more comfortably, never pausing in his sensuous plunder of her honeyed mouth until he rested deep within her.

Tessa moved instinctively in answer to his primitive urgency, responding to him with every aroused fiber of her being. She existed at flashpoint, needing only some new unknown sensation to catapult her into ecstasy. But Kellen had discerned her outer limits with ageless male power. His movements were maddeningly controlled, holding her at the ragged limits of sanity—withholding the ultimate and final spark that would set off an internal explosion capable of hurling her into the void. His lips wandered lower, tasting the dewy rose of her nipples, tugging at the glittering invisible connection between her heart and her womb.

And Tessa too was rediscovering the glorious treasure of his male body. Tasting, kneading, tracing out the lines and angles, exploring the curves of his physique, with an awakening feminine hunger that she'd never known she was capable of feeling. He was familiar and strange, rough and tender, man and god, all bound together in the ancient dance of passion they engaged in.

So she moved with him, undulating like a sultry temptress, calling on arts learned from Mother Earth, giving and taking in her turn, carrying him with her on her journey to the stars. Tessa climbed ever higher, joined to her lover in increasing fervor. Together they touched the sun as he offered her his gift of life. She held its gilded fire for a timeless second in her hands, felt its heat sear through them both as they cried out in mutual release. Then, together still, they plunged over the edge of the chasm—and floated, joined, down into the valley of the night.

CHAPTER FIVE

Moonbeams sparked like cold fire on the rippling surface of the courtyard fountain. The figurehead, a bronze Gabriel, lifted his trumpet to the heavens while water cascaded over his robed feet and stirred dark reflections all around. Tessa trailed a hand among the lily pads, scattering the tiny goldfish inhabiting the stone bowl, and marveled yet again at the sensuous beauty of the small private retreat. Palms and ferns nodded and sighed in the corners while flowering plants nestled at their feet, soaking up the lingering heat of the sun-warmed red tile floor.

Separated from the hotel proper by a high adobe wall, the snug haven housed Magda's collection of tropical birds. Above her head fine, almost invisible wire mesh protected the avian guests; and if you listened closely enough you could hear them ruffling their wings and muttering in their sleep like old ladies dozing on a park bench. Somewhere in the branches there was an English nightingale—Magda had assured her—and if she sat very quietly he might sing. Tessa had never heard a nightingale's song and this seemed as pleasant a way to pass the time as any—until she felt safe enough to go to her room.

Tessa was hiding. She needed this time alone to sort out the increasingly confused jumble of conflicting sensations that bombarded her from all directions. She knew Kellen was looking for her. Had seen her part from Web after his speech at the closing banquet. It would only be a matter of time before he tracked her down.

She was losing control of the situation. When Kellen had appeared at their table this morning, Tessa had nearly scalded herself on her second cup of coffee. He should have been gone long before her deliberately delayed breakfast. She was aware his flight had been scheduled to leave at an early hour, that knowledge was part of her master plan. What had made him stay?

Kellen's glib explanation of a restless night and oversleeping may have fooled Web, but Tessa knew better. His glittering blue-black eyes were fixed on her flushed face and she sensed his determination to have her alone. Kellen wasn't ready to end their tryst—or to have her make the break? Tessa wasn't sure which was the case. But she was instantly on her guard.

He'd produced a wicker picnic hamper packed with delicacies straight from the hands of Hénri, Magda's ersatz French chef. And Web, all unknowing, had seconded the idea of a trip into the hills. Tessa couldn't decline without sounding churlish and arousing his suspicion so in the end she went, much too weak to deny herself the pleasure of Kellen's company, although she was breaking yet another of the cardinal rules with which she'd provided herself in this dangerous game of deception.

Hours later, even though silver moonlight now bathed her face and a cool breeze danced across the courtyard, she could close her eyes and return to the warmth of the place Kellen had chosen for them. The negative image of sunlight glistening among the oak leaves answered her mental summons with the speed of thought. The rushing uninhibited gurgle of the stream at their feet replaced the fountain's civilized murmur. The rest of the world might never have existed. They were two alone. It had been so peaceful, so tranquil Tessa had been lulled into believing the man stretched out on the blanket at her side was only a harmless tabby cat. Not a sleeping tiger.

She could handle the situation, Tessa decided, watching a very brave, or foolhardy, ant crawl across the lemon yellow cotton of her wraparound skirt. There was no need to worry that they would become more involved. This day was a miracle. A dream of a day that she had no right to enjoy. At least not in the company of the man her reawakened body still ached for. Tessa caught and caged the wayward thought in the blink of an eye. That kind of dreaming was what she must guard against. She had to keep things light and carefree if she was to emerge heart-whole and fancy-free. And that was easy enough to believe. Until he kissed her.

Like the seed of many disasters it started innocently enough,

Tessa recalled. She had finished the remains of a flaky apple tart and set her glass of lemonade down on a flat rock beside the blanket as Kellen crossed his corduroy-covered legs at the ankles and propped himself on his elbows. Tessa had flicked away the invading ant and her hand was still poised in mid-air when Kellen reached out with deceptive languor and pulled her down beside him. "And what are you up to now, Mrs. Mallory? Destroying the ecosystem? I bet you pulled the wings off flys when you were a little girl."

"I did no such thing," Tessa sniffed in mock offense, remembering some of the antics she had indulged in, in her tomboy days. "I was a perfect little lady. I have two older brothers who saw to that. And I wish you wouldn't refer to me as Mrs. Mallory in that odious tone of voice," she went on before she could harness her tongue. "My name is Tessa. Or more precisely: Theresa Anne Catherine Litton Mallory," she recited playfully as his fingers traced the curve of her jawline, igniting tiny charges of electricity in her belly. She could feel every sinewy inch of his body along the softer more curvacious length of her own. Tessa's breath grew short and jerky with escalating passion as they settled more comfortably on the blanket-covered grass.

"A name as Irish as the Blarney Stone, Mrs. Mallory," he whispered in a thick brogue against her ear. Tessa shivered pleasurably and laughed. She was still in control.

"I'm three-quarters Pennsylvania Dutch. And just as stubborn as a good hausfrau should be. Mrs. Mallory is my mother-in-law," she retorted, coming back to the main point.

"In that case you should be Ms. Mallory, or better yet, Ms. Litton. Or do you keep the title as a protective disguise. Like you use your relationship with Web as a shield against getting involved again?" His lips had found their way to her mouth and Tessa was quickly yielding to the persistent mastery of his hands and tongue. The question jolted her rudely back to reality.

"Why do you say that?" she demanded, pulling her head away from the magnetic appeal of his lips on her hairline.

"Women like you don't engage in one-night stands, Tessa. I should know." Several buttons of her pale yellow cotton shirt had already given way to his marauding fingers and it took several seconds to halt their progress with her own trembling hands. The statement finally managed to register on her passion-dulled intellect.

"I want to know why you came to me. What were your motives for last night?" he continued slowly and deliberately, his hand reaching behind her head to tame her wind-blown hair and force her to meet his eyes. "Because I don't intend to play second fiddle to a ghost any more than I would to Webster or that drunken fool, Gelbert."

Tessa broke the gentle bondage and flew out of his encircling arms like a fury. Anger came to her rescue in a boiling, steaming cloud of rage. Being Mrs. Mallory had been part of her shield against returning to the world of the living, it was true. But she'd only just discovered that self-knowledge. Kellen was circling too close to questions that she had only begun to find answers for herself. And more dangerous still—how long would it take him to uncover her real reason for seeking him out?

Again Tessa was reminded of a panther stalking its prey, searching out the hidden weaknesses of an enemy. She couldn't chance that happening to her secret. "You aren't playing second fiddle to anyone, Kellen. What I felt for my husband has no bearing on this situation. I loved him very much. But he's dead. He was twenty-seven years old and one minute he was alive—and the next dead in a head-on collision with a semitrailer rig." It was the carefully rehearsed version of the accident she told everybody. "He has been gone for over four years. This relationship"—she made the word sound as scathing as her shaking voice would allow—"was to be purely physical. Or don't you recall your own words to that effect?"

Her head came up and she faced his angry blue gaze boldly. "This is nearly the twenty-first century. Women have been granted the privilege of indulging their desires." She spoke with deliberate intent. "You were mine."

For an endless stretching moment Tessa feared she'd gone too far, pushed him past the limits of his self-control, but Kellen conquered the spurt of rage that convulsed his chiseled features and his voice when he spoke was low and steady. "Tessa, stop it. Let me explain. . . ."

"No!" She couldn't have him exchanging confidences. She already knew too much about him. That he liked Ravel and

Rachmaninoff. That he was equally at home with the music of Willie Nelson and Scott Joplin. He was a football fan, although he'd played tennis and soccer in college. His favorite authors were Tom Wolfe, Ray Bradbury, and Zane Grey. An eclectic selection, even he admitted. He was ticklish, as she was. And he was a demanding lover, gentle and yet primitively aroused, insistent that she take an equal share in their coming together. She'd liked that—liked it all very much. . . .

"No." Tessa repeated the word to convince herself as much as to forestall him. Kellen reached out a strong brown hand to cover hers where they twisted on her lap. She shrugged him off. "A one-night stand, I believe you called it. No promises of tomorrow. Didn't it occur to you that I meant what I said then? I don't want any entanglement. I knew real love once. I don't want to cheapen that." Tessa wondered if she sounded as hard-edged as her words. "Don't spoil it, Kellen," she pleaded more softly. "I shouldn't have come with you today. You broke the rules by asking; I broke them by accepting. I don't think I should see you again. Please take me back to the hotel."

"If that's the way you want it." Something in her proud set face must have convinced him. He ground out the words every bit as angrily as she. He didn't speak again and Tessa knew he would never forgive her for being the one to end it. She piled things helter-skelter back into the hamper and marched resolutely toward the rented car he'd arranged for. The short ride down to the hotel was a nightmare of icy silence. Tessa never wanted to go through another like it in her life.

What she had naïvely hoped would be a few more hours in the golden California sun—a chance to know her baby's father—had turned sour. That she was pregnant she had no doubt. Call it wish fulfillment, call it instinct, the fact remained. She knew. And she was glad.

Tessa stood up with an abrupt jerky movement and a dozen goldfish turned as one and disappeared under the concealing lily pads. She touched the mandarin collar of her linen sheath, a slender gown slit from ankle to hip, as she continued her agitated musings. The pain of the afternoon had receded and now that she understood what had made her react to Kellen's questions so violently, she could be more objective. She had been comparing Kellen and Jacky. It was as simple and as devastating as that.

It wasn't fair to her husband and she knew it. (But all the same, she hadn't been able to control her fantasizing.) That's why Kellen's words had struck so deeply into her heart. She had compared the only two lovers she had ever known. And Jacky came out the lesser of the two. Huge enervating waves of guilt swept over Tessa and she whirled away from the fountain in turmoil. Quite simply, Jacky had never been able to bring her to the heights of ecstasy that Kellen had achieved in just one night.

This stranger had driven her mad with passion, far beyond her imaginings. He was relentless in his pursuit of pleasure and she'd lost all inhibitions in his arms because he'd insisted on taking her with him each step of the way. She would have allowed him to make love to her again this afternoon under the trees and the canopy of the western sky. She would welcome his touch at this moment. She still wanted him very much.

But Jacky had never been able to perfect his technique in such countless meaningless liaisons as Kellen indulged in, she reminded herself with brutal honesty. Jacky had been young and impatient, that was all, untutored in the art of pleasing a woman so masterfully. He'd never ridiculed her, or caused her pain, but she'd never felt so completely alive under the caresses of his hands and his lips as she had with Kellen.

Her fingers closed over the fragile leafy petals of an azalea planted in a wall niche and she bent her head to sniff the bloom. It had no particular scent and Tessa backed away disappointed. It was somehow evocative of their coming together—Kellen and her. There was no deeper basis for the beauty of their passion. She mustn't succumb to that self-deception. Desire without love was only shared lust.

Still she could never forget last night. Tessa looked down at the crushed petals in her hands and let the soft breeze blow them away. She smoothed the long, straight skirt of her berry-pink gown as she let her thoughts turn ever farther inward. Somewhere in the dark early hours before dawn this morning, she'd awakened yet again to the touch of Kellen's hands on her breasts and the slightly scratchy feel of his beard when his lips brushed her face and drifted dreamily lower to feast on the bounty of her soft, warm nipples. She'd lost track, hours before, of the times they had made love. But that time, in the pearly predawn light, had been the last. The full moon that earlier highlighted her upturned face in a silvery wash had set long before. And when it was over, when they had shared yet another wordless communion, Kellen had fallen asleep with his head on her breasts.

Looking back, it was hard to tell how much longer she'd allowed herself to savor the warmth of his body, tangled so intimately with hers. But the minutes passed all too quickly. Sleepy birds attuned to the rhythms of a new day piped tentative scales in this courtyard and somewhere a door had opened along a corridor before Tessa slipped out of the big bed like a rosy wraith.

Kellen had stirred, reached for her, frowned in his sleep, and rolled onto his stomach, restless but too deeply relaxed to waken completely. She didn't want to leave him then. She didn't want to leave him now.

The nightingale began to sing. A liquid, melodious sound that shattered the quiet of the night with crystal droplets of sound. Tessa held her breath, poised in the darkness, willing the birdsong to continue. She didn't hear the faint scraping of the big old-fashioned iron key in the lock. Nor Kellen's almost silent footsteps on the tile. But the nightingale did. His song died away. . . .

"Tessa."

She spun around at the sound of his velvet voice. Her anger, fear, confusion, melted away as quickly as he covered the remaining few feet between them and reached out to take her hand in his. The last clamoring remnants of her warning senses were torn away in the hurricane of sensation his voice and his touch evoked within her. He could be so disarmingly tender when the occasion demanded. If Kellen had made a single move that she interpreted as threatening, Tessa could have commanded her resisting brain to move her away—out of harm's reach. He didn't move. "I thought I might find you here. Magda often gives a key to her favored guests."

"I was just leaving." Tessa had no intention of staying here in this garden that came perilously close to encompassing all of the romance of Old California.

"You've done a good job of avoiding me." His tone was matter-of-fact, as though they were discussing the weather. He cocked his head, the pelt of coal-black hair catching a stray wink of moonlight and absorbing it into the raven depths.

"I thought it best. I told you that this afternoon," she sidestepped.

"Is that why you came here? Did you think I wouldn't have access to this courtyard?" The arrogance in his voice was unmistakable.

"This is the way I want to remember California," Tessa replied, ignoring the taunt in his last words. "Not the smoke and heat and noise of the ballroom . . ." she said, trailing off.

It was easy to tell herself so righteously that this ache in her heart was only an emotional reaction to their night of shared passion. Nothing more than her reawakened physical needs—and his lust. It was brutally clear. She had only to see it with those eyes.

"In that case you can't leave without a good-bye kiss. Every lovely señorita deserves that much of a memory of San Luis," Kellen growled. Tessa was enfolded in his arms too quickly to protest effectively and she felt enervated by the barely leashed excitement he radiated like a dark sun. "Just one kiss. No strings attached, the way you like it." He waited for her affirmation and she didn't disappoint him. Kellen's mouth took her and his tongue coaxed her lips to part as he explored the hollows of her cheeks, deftly with intimate familiarity. Tessa stiffened slightly, heeding a short-circuiting neural alarm, then relaxed, her overwhelming need for him shutting out the still, small voice of protesting intellect.

Kellen's hand, strong and hard, slipped inside the slit of her skirt, pulling her close, letting her know the extent of his ardor, his palm settling just below the curve of her bottom. Tessa shivered with mingled desire and humiliation at her own weakness. It was as if the events of the afternoon had never happened. As though the opiate taste of his kisses possessed the power to wipe her mind clean of thought and reason.

"Tessa, it's been a hell of a long day," Kellen admitted, resting his forehead against her hair. "I've been waiting for you to change your mind and come to me. When you didn't I started looking for you. I can't let you walk out of my life without a backward glance, bargain or no bargain."

Tessa heard the words with a pang that shot through her heart and soul. Kellen, don't, she pleaded in silence. Don't hurt me like this. I barely know you. Don't let me find now, that you might come to care.

"I don't usually come after my women like this." The simple statement acted like a flint sparking on the steel of her temper.

Women. One of many. A small flame of anger grew from the spark in Tessa's brain. She was a desirable object to him, that was all. In the cold light of reason Tessa could see that she'd deluded herself into thinking there could be something between them, when it was nothing but a tangled web of circumstance and physical chemistry that combined to dull her judgment and color his every word in rainbow hues. She was a stupid fool.

"I want you to come away with me, Tessa," Kellen rasped, as though he had trouble forming the speech. "I'll take you to England, Italy, to France."

To Paris? Where he'd sent the blonde.

"Any place on earth you want to go."

"Kellen, don't say anything more. I gave you my answer this afternoon. I'll stay with you tonight." Her voice broke on the words, she knew she was too weak to deny herself that poisoned pleasure. His kiss stopped her again. The hunger and searching were still there. Tessa was almost swayed by his intensity as his probing tongue gloried in her surrender. But could he have loved her so wonderfully and so well last night if he hadn't developed his skill in countless such encounters? She didn't want to admit that, but she did. "I'll stay with you just one more night." She was close to hating her weak, desiring self at that moment. The first time her principles, her high ideals of single parenthood and independence were put to the test, she was within a single heartbeat of abandoning all of them for the sake of a man's touch.

"Not only for tonight . . . I want you tonight and every night. . . ."

Tessa reached up to place her fingertip against his lips. "What are you trying to say, Kellen?"

"I thought I did say it." He smiled down into her confused face. The heart-twisting smile she would carry in her memory for eternity. "It's very simple. Come away with me. I'm asking you to be . . ." He paused for a second and watched her strained face, his own emotions unreadable behind a mask. "I'm asking you to be my mistress."

The pain was even worse than she had feared. His mistress. The blow nearly doubled her over. He was treating her exactly as he treated the blond woman. Exactly as she told him she wanted to be treated. It was far more humiliating than when he'd only believed her to be Web's mistress.

Don't delude yourself any longer, you fool, her mind shouted into the multicolored pricks of brightness that studded the whirling darkness behind her eyelids. You were on the verge of believing there could be something between you. And nothing more substantial than your own intrinsic refusal to admit you could have a sexual relationship without any bindings of the heart or mind. All this will get you, Tessa, is a broken heart and no way to protect the baby you're carrying.

The baby. The child that might very well be growing within her already. She'd pushed it from her mind these last few minutes. It must be her first consideration now—from this moment on and for all the future. She had to break this painful encounter off quickly—and forever. "I have to go to Web. He'll be expecting me to say good night. We'll talk later." Cowardly but it would work. She'd run out of the courtyard and never see him again.

"We'll talk *now*. Web's a big boy. He can get into his jammies all by himself. You haven't accepted my invitation," Kellen answered almost playfully. He didn't really think she would turn him down, she realized. Most women probably didn't—and God help her, she wanted to be one of them. The only one. Her hesitation seemed natural to him, she thought in panic. The scheming and posturing of a designing woman. She'd played her part too well.

"I can't leave Web," Tessa elaborated. "I couldn't go with you. Even if I wanted to."

"Web won't hold you back if he knows it's what you want."

Now the small flame of anger inside her flared brighter and expanded to fill her whole being. "You don't care a bit that I have commitments to Web and Vinifera, do you," she asked hoarsely, swallowing the tears in her throat.

Kellen turned abruptly, surprise showing plainly on his face. She'd moved away from him instinctively, and when he reached out to bring her back into his arms, the fountain effectively shadowed his features. His voice when he spoke was even and cold, completely alien to her ears.

"Forgive me. I lost my head for a moment. Of course, you couldn't go like this without telling him. I've been living root-less for too many years." He raked a hand through his hair, showing more agitation in the gesture than Tessa had seen be-fore. "I'll come back for you in two or three weeks. Can you be ready for me by then?" Kellen looked past her as he spoke, his eyes focused on a future that could never be. How much of that future would she have shared with him? A few weeks? A month or two? A year at the most?

"No." The single word tightened his hands on her shoulders with a grip that brought tears to her eyes.

"What do you mean no? I'm asking you to spend the—"

Tessa broke in abruptly. She never wanted to know how he had intended to finish the sentence. "I can't leave Web." How could she say it without giving everything away. Already the lies and pieces were beginning to escalate alarmingly. "I have too much at stake. I can't risk what I have with him." Were those words selfish and conniving enough to carry her point?

He'd asked her to be his mistress as easily as he must have become involved with the blonde he abandoned so abruptly. That was no basis for building a relationship. It had to be bro-ken off quickly. Tessa had responsibilities of the heart and con-science. Commitments—a good solid old-fashioned word. And commitments must be honored. After last night she could no longer order her life to suit herself.

"Web won't hold you if you don't want to stay with him," Kellen insisted roughly. "I want you, now. We'll give him time to find a suitable assistant. But that's my only concession."

"Do you think that's all I am?" Tessa jumped on the words, forced her quaking voice to answer. "His assistant? You told me I was a vintner. I am. I've invested too much . . ." Tessa was going to say she had invested too much love and caring in Web's life and the vineyards, but she stopped herself. She had to be as hard as he if she was to come out of this confrontation with a whole heart and her secret hopes protected. She wasn't wearing the green dress, but she called on its spell to sustain her. "I've invested too much of my life and my energy in Vinifera to go traipsing off to Europe like a common whore."

"Whore, Tessa? That's a word that can backfire easily." His voice was dangerous, low and dark.

"Yes, whore." My God, couldn't she say the word without blushing. Perhaps not. But pride and strength of character came to her rescue, bolstering her sagging courage. She had to end this quickly and get away before she began to believe she saw pain and hurt beneath the icy fire of anger in his dark eyes. She'd used this man as callously as he wanted to use her. She'd taken the life force that was his alone to give and absorbed it for her own selfish purposes. He'd never forgive her for that.

"At least you'd be honest then. There are more ways to whore than by selling your body."

Tessa's hand flashed out of its own volition and collided with his cheek in a stinging slap that sent splinters of pain racing up her arm. Kellen never moved, never flinched, although Tessa knew he could have stopped her if he wished. "I never want to see you again as long as I live." She swept out through the wrought-iron gate on a flaming column of rage that lasted all the way to the door of Web's room. There pride alone held back her tears long enough for her to lift a hand and tap on the panel to say good night.

CHAPTER SIX

"I don't think I need to explain what caused you to faint in the vineyard this afternoon, do I?" Dr. Laura Hunt questioned in her pleasant Kentucky accent.

"No. I'm perfectly aware of my condition," Tessa responded, a bit defensively as she adjusted the tie belt of her paisley handkerchief-style tunic top. She didn't want to dwell on the dizzy light-headed feeling that had pitched her forward into Web's arms. "It's not such an unusual occurrence in pregnant women."

"Pregnant is right. About sixteen weeks along, I'd say," Laura responded sharply.

"Seventeen and a half," Tessa corrected, turning with her rare smile to face her frowning friend. Two pairs of eyes, gray and green, met across the small office and locked for a long second before Laura smiled also. "All the more reason why you should have been in here months ago. Is this why you've been avoiding Stan and me lately?"

So that was the underlying cause of her doctor's coolness, not disapproval of Tessa's pregnancy as she had feared. She would have to guard against this tendency to be so defensive. "Partially," Tessa admitted with a rueful shrug. "Your eyes are too sharp, Laura. As a physician you're as discreet as a fencepost. As a friend . . . well, you're as nosy as . . ."

"Spare me the comparisons, please," Laura laughed, accepting the unspoken apology with a careless wave of her hand as she propped one ample hip on the side of her battered oak desktop. Her sandaled foot swung free above the green and white linoleum-covered floor. "I can't find a thing wrong with you, other than the obvious. And that's not very obvious," she said cattily. Keeping her own figure from expanding more rapidly than it already was occupied a great deal of Laura's attention. "No wonder you had me fooled." She looked calculatingly at Tessa's almost flat belly. "You're carrying well. Wide pelvis," she opined sagely. "What exactly happened today to make Web bring you in here in such a tizzy?"

"I scared him half to death," Tessa confessed with a rueful grimace. "It was a combination of the heat, humidity, and sleepless nights, I suppose. I didn't really faint, you know," Tessa went on, settling into a Windsor chair opposite her friend. On the wall behind the desk Laura's diplomas shared equal billing with crayoned drawings provided by her children and photographs of her happy young family. "It was just a dizzy spell," Tessa explained more fully. "Web panicked, that's all."

"I take it you haven't informed him of your condition?" Laura asked, treading warily, sounding out her patient's sensitivities before making any comments or suggestions. Tessa could read her like a book, and relaxed against the back of the uncomfortable chair.

"I will as soon as we leave here. This morning's episode has forced my hand."

"And the baby's father?"

"Will never know," Tessa stated bluntly, pushing a fine curl of damp hair away from her temple. Even at its maximum setting the air conditioning couldn't keep up with the late afternoon July heat. She stood up abruptly and moved to the window, staring out at a string of grain barges making their way slowly down the muddy Ohio to Cincinnati and points south. "This is my child, Laura," Tessa went on softly, emphasizing the pronoun slightly. "I made the decision to go into this thing with my eyes wide open. I'll carry the baby and raise him alone. That is my choice."

"Is that why you postponed coming to me this long?"

"No. I've just felt very solitary these past few weeks. It's hard to put it into words. I wanted to adjust to the situation on my own. Do you understand what I'm trying to say?" Tessa could hear, rather than see, Laura fiddling with a plaster of paris paperweight decorated in gaudy primary colors with more enthusiasm than skill by her nursery-school-aged son.

"Of course I do. Being pregnant causes great changes in a woman's life. Emotional and physical upheaval is as good a way to explain it as any. It's perfectly normal to need time to deal with the situation and the changes in your body."

"Yes, that's it." Tessa smiled self-consciously at her whimsy. "It was my secret. A feeling of at last being a link in the great chain of life. A very precious knowledge that I didn't want to share. But now the cat's out of the bag, so to speak."

"And you've very neatly avoided any arguments against continuing the pregnancy by the simple expedient of remaining silent."

"Possibly," Tessa concurred with a faint flush that she hoped would be attributed to the heat. "Although I wouldn't consider terminating this pregnancy for any reason whatsoever."

"Does that include the possibility of producing a deformed fetus?" Tessa whirled from the window and clutched at the sill for support. She searched Laura's round, good-humored face, her green eyes suddenly dark with anxiety. "Did you find anything wrong?"

"No." Laura responded with patient emphasis. "And I don't expect to find anything in the blood tests we took either. They were all routine procedures. Don't get excited," the red-haired doctor defended, raising a hand to ward off Tessa's piercing green stare. "I'd be derelict in my duty if I didn't bring up these points, Tessa," she reminded her friend. Tessa nodded and relaxed her clenched hands with an effort of will. "There is no denying the longer a woman delays pregnancy the greater her risk of complications. However, you're a long way from being an elderly primigravida," Laura said, smiling, having used the medical term for a woman pregnant with her first child. "But you're not twenty-two years old anymore, either. We have to take every precaution." Laura rose from the desk and crossed the room to stand by her friend.

"I want to see you back in here in two weeks. I'll make arrangements for an ultrasound scan. It will help determine the baby's size and weight more accurately, although you sound very positive of the date of conception."

"I am," Tessa replied, her eyes on the distant hills of Kentucky. She watched them waver in a green and gray shimmer of heat. Laura's eyes slid sideways to evaluate her preoccupied friend's mood, but she continued on in the same professional tone. "I should recommend an amniocentesis. . . ."

93

"No." Tessa was firm in her refusal. "There's no indication of any abnormalities. I know as well as you the incidence of Down's syndrome and other birth defects rises with the age of the mother. But it wouldn't make any difference. The father is young and healthy." That was all she intended to say about Kellen even to Laura, her closest friend. It was part of the pact she had made with herself. One of the rules of this venture into single parenthood. "I'm healthy and a nurse. I'll take care of myself, I promise. But I'll want my baby no matter what."

"You're being blunt, Tessa. So will I," Laura returned with equal candor. "I'm not one to belittle the strength of maternal instinct. We all have a biological clock ticking away inside, ready to go off without warning and force a life decision on us whether we're in line with society's dictates or not. There's no doubt in my mind that you will be a good mother. You're perfectly capable of raising a child alone. Many women are opting for single parenthood these days. I'm not questioning your motives for bringing a child into the world in this way. But giving birth to a handicapped baby is a tremendous strain both emotionally and financially. It is not too late," she hesitated for a second, her professional responsibilities warring with her deeply held personal convictions as a mother and a woman. "It is not too late to terminate this pregnancy if that is the case."

"Whatever the reason, the answer is still no. This is my baby. I've felt him move within me these last few days. I'll take the chances. I'm not being sentimental," Tessa said harshly, trying to make Laura understand the depths of her commitment to the course she'd chosen. "I have quite a sum of money set aside, and thanks to Web's generosity, I own a share of Vinifera that will enable me to raise and educate a child comfortably. I've considered all of this countless times." Considered it all those long, solitary nights since they'd returned from California and Kellen's dark-angled features had intruded on her dream-haunted sleep, stealing her rest. "I'm committed to carrying this child."

"Then I won't pry further," Laura said, taking off the stethoscope she'd draped around her neck and laying it on the desktop. "We'll keep an eye out for the usual complications. You know enough to report anything out of the ordinary: persistent headaches, any bleeding or spotting, excessive nausea or pain. Watch your salt and caffeine consumption. No pain medication or drugs that I haven't okayed. Get plenty of rest and eat right. Your weight is fine," she sighed enviously, scribbling away on a prescription pad as she talked. "So is your blood pressure. Here's a script for vitamins, follow the label directions. Any more questions?"

"No, Doctor," Tessa answered obediently, her hands crossed over the slight rise of her belly. "I'll be a good girl."

"I hope so. Now as a friend, not your doctor." Laura moved forward to envelop Tessa in a faintly antiseptic, violet-scented hug. "Congratulations. What do you want, a boy or a girl?" Tessa laughed out loud for the first time in weeks, blinking back the easy tears that plagued her so often these days. "Hormones," Laura sighed indulgently, reaching for a tissue box in the desk drawer. "You're my last patient this afternoon. Let's talk babies."

Ten minutes later Tessa and Laura walked arm and arm into the small haphazardly furnished waiting room adjoining Laura's office. No one was in evidence but Laura's elderly, intimidatingly efficient nurse. "Webster Mayer is in the backyard with the children," she informed her employer with a sniff as starchy as her white cap and uniform. "He's as bad as a child himself these days worrying over this young woman when anyone can see she's as strong as a horse. Senile old fool." She was still muttering as they glanced conspiratorially at each other and walked out into the yard.

It didn't take long to spot the tall, gray-haired man leaning over the playfence under a huge, spreading oak tree. He was engaged in serious conversation with Megan, who had just passed her second birthday and Anthony, almost five and very conscious of his dignity. The noisy, happy blond-headed children were busy excavating in a large sandbox as Web directed the engineering feat.

Laura herself had delayed starting her family until well into her thirties. That was one reason Tessa knew she hadn't questioned her motives as closely as another physician might have done. "Biological clock" had real meaning to Laura. Now at forty-one, her small rural practice flourishing, her husband comfortably established with a prestigious Cincy law firm, she had told Tessa she was considering the advisability of a third pregnancy.

Tessa was grateful for the confidante she'd acquired in the other woman. Although the mechanics of pregnancy were as familiar to her as to any nurse, she still had never experienced them firsthand. Tessa would never concede that, along with the exhilaration she felt, she was scared. As she had told Laura earlier, she'd lived in isolation these last few weeks, sealed off from the everyday world by an invisible wall. But now as the baby stirred to life within her, she wanted to come out of her shell. Face the future and start her new life enthusiastically. Get on with it. And at any rate, her secret would be hard to keep much longer.

The children spied their mother at the top of a slight rise above the sandbox and set up a clamor that echoed out over the river. Web directed his attention toward the women. His face showed such an expression of relief that Tessa's heart contracted with love and happiness. She felt the same way about him. He was the father she'd never been privileged to know, a friend for all time. She wondered how he would take her news?

"Well, Laura," he asked, ignoring Tessa as she greeted the children. "Betty told me to come out here. I was cluttering up your waiting room and you two were gossiping in your office. How is she?"

"She's fine. Too much sun is all. I'd advise her to wear a hat in the vines. And stay out of the heat of the day. That advice is for both of you by the way, so add another fifteen dollars to the bill for my second diagnosis," she joked, lifting her daughter from the sandbox and giving her a kiss on her small pug nose. The baby squealed in delight.

"You're sure it's nothing more serious," Web probed. "She looked awful keeling over on me like that." He scowled fiercely in Tessa's general direction as she knelt to scrutinize Tony's barricade against star invaders.

"Thanks for the compliment," Tessa broke in, saving her friend from any more white lies on her behalf. "We'd better be getting back before Mrs. Basel and the vineyard crew think I've been taken off to the hospital. Everyone has made entirely too much fuss over a dizzy spell."

"Go home, have a light nutritious supper, and get some rest,"

Laura recommended, a child on her hip and one clinging to her cotton skirt, muddy, sandy handprints now decorating her long white lab coat.

"Whatever you say, Laura. I'll see she follows your advice," Web promised. "It's my turn to be in charge. I've had enough of you two giving me orders this spring." He silenced Tessa's objections automatically. He did look better than he had since their return from California. "Get in the truck, young woman."

Tessa smiled and shrugged resignedly. "It's a conspiracy," she complained, looking at the stern faces of her friends.

"You bet your bottom dollar," Web agreed, opening the door of their nearly new blue Ford pickup, the Vinifera logo emblazoned proudly on the side. The children waved an enthusiastic farewell as he adjusted his sunglasses and they pulled out of the drive.

Back on the highway Tessa watched the blue-brown waters of the busy river until they turned up into the hills. Butterflies set up a silent drumbeat in her stomach, and the smaller, lighter flutter lower in her abdomen answered the nervous reaction. Tessa couldn't help smiling. The baby's movement these last few days had made it all worthwhile. She knew the first night she felt the faint quickening ripples like a fish swimming, a feather's tickle, as she lay sleepless in her antique-filled bedroom that everything had been for the best.

Her baby was alive. No longer a shapeless mass of budding, dividing cells. He would be a whole person. A complete blueprint of his future was diagrammed into each gene—a tiny heart now beating rhythmically, and strong, separate organs growing and maturing with each passing day. Hands, feet, toes, fingers, a head recognizably human. He was already an individual. Boy or girl? It didn't matter. But all hers.

It had been a happy secret to press close to her bruised heart. Perhaps she had gone about this quest all wrong. It was hard to say with any degree of objectivity. Kellen's memory was a persistent ache in her heart. At times she'd wake in the night and call his name. Nothing but silence and night sounds of an old house in restless slumber answered her. She'd roll over in her too big bed and tell herself it was only the tremendous changes in her body that made her want him so. Women were conditioned by heredity and society to have a man to be with them.

To share this great experience. This was one of the adjustments she would have to make to the situation of being a single parent.

"What did Laura find out?" Web questioned as they rattled onto the private twisting road to Vinifera.

"I'm pregnant, Web," Tessa said baldly, watching for her first glimpse of the big old antebellum house and barn. She wished he would remove the reflecting sunglasses so she could judge his reaction more easily.

"Pregnant?" Web shot back as if he had heard her wrong.

"Yes, as in going to have a baby," she joked, but her voice cracked on the words. She wanted to be as carefree as possible. She failed miserably.

"I see," he answered quietly, his eyes on the road ahead. Tessa looked down at her hands, not sure what he expected her to say. "Will you be marrying the man?" Web asked next.

"No." Tessa stopped to clear her dry throat as Web brought the truck to a halt. She kept her eyes on the cloud of dust following their progress as it caught up with them and began to settle back onto the gravel surface. "I don't even want the father to know, Web. It wouldn't have worked out between us. I knew that from the beginning." She'd stick with the truth as much as possible. Just as she always did when she told anyone of Jacky's death. It really wasn't so hard to lie, after all. Only to lie to someone you loved and trusted. She kept her eyes on Web's big strong, work-roughened hands.

"I met a man this spring, when I was dealing with the hotel chains. When you were ill," she reminded. Web's several angina attacks—the first one the night she'd left Kellen in Magda's garden—had left him depressed and irritable for several weeks. Tessa had taken over negotiating several lucrative contracts with some of Cincinnati's most prestigious hostelries. It was a feather in Vinifera's cap and she was proud of her achievement. But when her anxiety over Web subsided she could see that those trips were also a perfect cover. Web was the only person that could link the time she'd spent with Kellen to the baby's arrival. It was vital to cloud the issue. She went on with her well-rehearsed scenario. "He was only in the city temporarily. He went back to his life. I have mine. I want to keep the baby to raise myself. Can I count on your help and support?" Tears filled her green eyes, making them appear huge and luminous in the harsh afternoon light.

"Of course, my dear. But bringing a baby into the world out of wedlock . . . It will be very hard on you." The sunglasses came off and he shifted his bulk to face her directly.

"I'm aware of that. No one would have questioned why I want a lover or a husband, Web. It's the same reasoning with a baby. I want the loving relationship a child will give me. I want to know the joy of raising a child. I'm prepared for the problems," she assured him. "Anyway, people aren't that narrow-minded anymore," Tessa concluded hopefully.

"I'm not so sure of that in this part of the country. There is always someone to point fingers and make judgments," Web warned, gesturing off into the distance.

"I can handle that." But could she? When it was no longer possible to hide her condition, would she be strong enough to shrug off the stares and whispers of her neighbors and acquaintances? She'd have to for the baby's sake. It was incredible what she could do for the baby's sake.

"Tessa . . . I don't know what to say. I'll love your child as though it were my own grandson—or -daughter," he amended hastily. "I'd offer to marry you and give him my name if you'd accept the arrangement."

"Oh, Web, that's the nicest thing anyone's ever said to me. I'll cherish those words all my life." Tessa scooted across the hot vinyl seat and gave him a quick peck on one leathery brown cheek. "All I need is your support and acceptance. I can handle all the rest."

"You've got all of it, honey," he growled, replacing his sunglasses to hide the suspicious misting in his hazel eyes. "I may be old, but I'm not old-fashioned. I know times are changing. But I can't help believing you cared more for the man than you're letting on. You're not the kind of woman to engage in casual flings, Tessa. He didn't break your heart, did he?"

"No," she lied. "I'm heart-whole and fancy-free."

"I won't ask any more questions about it then until you're ready to give me the answers." He changed the subject back to the baby adroitly as he put the truck into gear and they rolled slowly toward the garage behind the main house. "If anyone can handle a twenty-four-hour-a-day job like this, it's you. And between Mrs. Basel and me, we'll have the little tyke spoiled rotten inside six months." He sounded as though he relished the idea. Already her child was giving others joy and happiness. She had made the right decision.

"Good thing I got in some practice with Mrs. Basel's little granddaughter last winter." Web broke off, his hands deft on the steering wheel as he eased the truck into the big old garage. "Is that what gave you this idea, Tessa? Having that baby in the house?"

"Partially," she admitted. "But I've always wanted children. Jacky and I were too busy with our careers when we were first married. Later, after he became ill, he refused to consider the idea, although I wanted his child very much. Then it was too late."

"Time heals us all, Tessa. Let's look to the future." For the first time in weeks Tessa believed he meant what he said. "When can we expect this blessed event?"

"Probably early in December. I'm not quite sure yet." She blushed slightly and plodded on. "After vintage at any rate."

"Efficient to the very core, aren't you," Web scowled with his dual-duty frown. "Even planned that for slack time, did you?"

Tessa blushed a deeper rose. "Well, not precisely. But it is good timing all the same." That little bit of banter broke the ice and Web talked happily of his plans to be a surrogate grandfather as he walked her through the windbreak stand of pines to the rear door of her cottage. Tessa parted from him with a happy sigh of contentment and hoped her next hurdle would be crossed as easily.

CHAPTER SEVEN

Tessa trailed her hand in the dark, warm water of the northern Indiana lake where she'd spent so many childhood summers. The same hot, brassy-gold sun that would make the Ohio Valley a steamy cauldron today beat down on her straw hat benignly as she lazed in an old inner tube. A stray breeze pushed her out of the shade of their ramshackle dock and she kicked her way farther out into the lake, combining Laura's prenatal exercises with relaxation as neatly as anyone could wish. She was glad she'd taken Web's advice and come home. Her family had listened to her carefully worded announcement with varying degrees of disbelief and eventual acceptance, parceled out the farm chores as if nothing out of the ordinary had happened, and packed up most of the crowd for a week at the lake.

Tessa went along, vaguely grateful for the reprieve in answering a barrage of questions. They would all stand behind her, she was sure. Yet her mother's attitude was the most surprising. And the most upsetting. Tessa paddled in a slow circle to watch with lazy, contented amusement the antics of her three nephews as they fished among the lily pads. Her second brother, Jerry, father of the two youngest boys, was anchored in another rowboat nearby, plugging for bass under a weeping willow and keeping a sharp eye on the orange-life-jacketed trio. Her mother, dark and tiny and a dynamo of energy, traded recipes and family gossip with her placid sister-in-law in the shade of the camper's awning. Tessa wondered idly if they were also discussing her situation. She didn't really care at the moment. She was too lazy to worry today. Still, she found it hard to put the conversation she'd shared with her mother completely out of her mind for any length of time.

"Theresa," Margaret Litton had lectured sternly the morning

101

after Tessa arrived in the rambling old two-story farmhouse where she'd been raised. "People are designed to bring up a baby in pairs. I don't recommend a woman doing it alone unless it's a necessity." She'd picked up the conversation where it had been broken off last night. It was an ability of hers that had fascinated Tessa all her life.

"I don't intend for the baby's father to ever know," Tessa explained patiently for the second time.

"You should tell the father," Margaret insisted, swishing a dishtowel over the countertop with agitated swipes. She'd washed the breakfast dishes at her usual breakneck speed, leaving Tessa far behind in the drying. "I think he has the right to know."

"I barely knew the man, Mom," Tessa elaborated, sticking to the story she'd concocted for Web's benefit. The forks she was drying rattled in her hand. Her mother was much harder to fool than Webster.

"I don't believe that, Theresa," her petite, cupcake-round mother said flatly. "Oh, I'll agree you may not have known him for long. We won't get into that. But I refuse to believe you just picked a Tom off the fence."

"Mother," Tessa giggled self-consciously, a little shocked at the analogy.

"That's right. I am your mother. I gave you a better set of values than that," Margaret sniffed, pulling the plug so the soapy dishwater gurgled down the drain in a miniature whirlpool that was a fair imitation of Tessa's whirling thoughts. "Whether you want to believe it or not you must have special feelings for the man. You wouldn't have done what you did and face the possibility of looking at his child every day for the rest of your life without feeling strongly about him."

"I did barely know him. It was a purely physical attraction," Tessa reiterated, trying to defend her action cerebrally.

"Sometimes that's the best way to start," Margaret came back with the surprising retort. Tessa had never considered her mother a sensualist. "People nowadays want everything all worked out. They discuss it all to death. It's all relationship—not love affair—more's the pity. They make contracts and business arrangements out of what should be the greatest adventure, the greatest learning experience of two lifetimes. It's a shame, that's what it is. And you took something from him, my girl. Don't forget that. You took something that was his alone to give. That's not right. You're carrying and claiming a baby that's only half yours."

"It's all mine," Tessa said angrily, slamming silverware into the drawer. She didn't like being goaded into defending herself by words that brought her own doubts to the forefront of her thoughts. "That's the whole point of having a baby alone. I don't want to love any man again. It hurt too much. Can't you remember how you felt when Daddy died?" Tessa couldn't remember her father, who was killed in a farm accident when she was scarcely two, leaving Margaret to raise three children alone.

"I think of him every day. But time helps so much, Tessa honey. And your father and I had a dozen good years, and all the memories that go with them. I had you and your brothers to help me go on."

"My position is the same."

"No, it's not," Margaret stated firmly. "You and Jacky had so little time. You should get on with your life. Love again."

"I am," Tessa laughed nervously. "Wouldn't you say having a baby qualified in both respects?"

"No, I don't." Her mother stuck to her guns. "Because you're doing this out of selfish love and that's not the same. It's not right. I just hope you realize your responsibilities to the baby's father as well as to the child. He has a right to know. You should tell him before it's too late." With that cryptic statement she hung her towel on a wooden rack, reaching up on tiptoe to give her frowning daughter a quick hug. "I'm going to feed the hens before we pack the car. Think about what I've said," she urged more gently and sailed out, letting the screen door bang shut like a final exclamation point.

"I'll think about what you've said, Mom," Tessa whispered aloud. "But I know I'm right and we've been arguing a moot point. Kellen knows nothing about the baby. And I'll never see him again for the rest of my life."

Funny how her mother had hit the tender spot in her own heart so accurately, Tessa marveled as she rested one tanned hand on her stomach. She could look at her life with Jacky more clearly now. She had let him go—sometime—these last

103

few months. And the guilt she'd carried since his death was ashes. She hadn't failed Jacky as she feared for so long. He had failed both of them. As long as there was life, Tessa believed, there was hope. But Jacky had given up hope. That cold November day when the doctor had told him his remission had ended, that another round of chemotherapy and radiation treatments would be necessary to contain the invading cancer cells she had seen it in his eyes—he gave up the struggle.

All his life Jacky hadn't tried to be different. He'd merely failed to be the same. And in the end it was too much for him. The bent toward reserve and melancholy that manifested itself as the shyness Tessa first found so attractive was intensified by the pain and distress of his disease. His basically gentle introspective nature was brutalized by circumstances beyond his control and the terrible horde of self-doubts and uncertainty that plagued him finally took over his life.

Tessa was at last bringing all the scattered bits and pieces of her thoughts into some kind of perspective. And she was unaware of her eldest brother's appearance with his two daughters in the compound. Nor did she see him stop to speak to their mother as he divested himself of workshirt and shoes. Clad only in cut-off jeans, he picked up a second inner tube and lowered himself into the refreshingly cool water.

She'd loved Jacky with all her passionate young heart. But that love hadn't been enough to make him want to fight to stay with her. It was the hardest fact of all to face, but she did.

And how much, she wondered with the clarity of hindsight, had her own sense of purpose, her clear resolve and success in her chosen field, added to his anguish? She never knew—would never know. That last night he'd taken his copy of the pathology reports, kissed her good-bye at the door of the hospital when he dropped her off at the start of the night shift, and driven their beat-up old Datsun coupe into the path of an oncoming semi. He'd died instantly.

Now she could see the fault was in Jacky, hidden deep inside, far from view. Perhaps if he hadn't become ill it wouldn't have surfaced at all? But the past couldn't be changed. She could live with what had happened. And she wasn't going to look back anymore.

She could love again. Kellen Sterling's possession of her had awakened that sleeping part of her soul. She had laid to rest her fear of never being emotionally available to another man. But neither could she allow her life to be defined forever by the few hours of white-hot passion she had shared with Kellen. That was something she could not live with. If there was no continuing, no relationship, no matter how tenuous, she wouldn't have to worry about never being free of Kellen. That was what she couldn't put into words for her mother in the kitchen that morning five days ago. It was only what she could admit to herself this very minute.

It was why, when her happy, surprised sister-in-law asked if she wanted a girl or a boy, she'd stated her preference in no uncertain terms. A girl. Because a boy that looked like his father would remind her for the rest of her life that she feared she had fallen in love with a man she knew less than forty-eight hours. A man she couldn't have. The truth was Kellen Sterling had given her the child she desired, and had stolen her heart in return.

Cold, sparkling droplets of water rained down on her straw hat, bringing Tessa out of her reverie with a rude shock. "Tessy, wake up. I've got news for you," Frank called, using a pet name she'd hoped never to hear again.

Tessa glanced around and sent a cold spray of water in her brother's direction in retaliation for the dousing. "Frank, when did you get here? I didn't hear you drive up," she questioned, a little out of breath after the chilly bath. Tessa surveyed her burgeoning stomach with a critical eye. She'd seemed to blossom alarmingly in the week since she'd left Vinifera.

"I have a message for you," he hollered above the noise of a passing power boat. He came alongside and grabbed hold of her tube with a strong hand as the floats bobbed in the choppy wake. He was burned a deep mahogany, from his fingertips to the middle of his forearm, then less darkly up to his broad shoulders. Another dark area highlighted his face and neck. A farmer's tan, they'd always joked among themselves.

"What's the news?" Tessa quizzed lightly, putting her own darker thoughts away for the long, lonely hours of night. "Are soybean futures up the limit this afternoon?"

"Don't I wish," Frank answered fervently. Tessa's quarter-share in the family's grain and dairy operation was the basis of her baby's nest egg. That and her investment in Vinifera Vineyards.

"The most important thing first. I might not get you alone anywhere else on this darned lake. Abby would be here with me if she could get out of the Four-H judging," he explained unnecessarily. "But we wanted to tell you right away. Granted, this baby thing," he went on, gesturing to her rounding belly, "gave us all a lot to consider. Whether or not we think it's the best decision you've ever made isn't important; we're behind you one hundred percent. You know that."

"Thanks, big brother," Tessa said, clasping his hand with a quick, hard squeeze.

"I know that Simon and the girls are older than Jerry's kids." He squinted against the sunlight and ran his hand through his thinning brown hair. Tessa held her breath, afraid she might burst into tears if he told her what she wanted most to hear. "But we'd like to apply for the job as guardian for the newest Litton if you'll accept our application."

"Oh, Frank. You don't know what that means to me." Newest Litton. Yes, that's who her baby would be; the newest member of the Litton clan. Someone to care for the child if she should die was one of the last most pressing worries she'd had about her venture. If Frank and Abby would agree to be the baby's legal guardians, she could rest easily from now on. Tessa looked quickly toward the horizon as tears threatened once again to make a mockery of her composed facade. "You drove all the way up here just to tell me, didn't you."

He grinned across the arm's length of hot black rubber that separated them. "It's only an hour's drive, Tessy, and the girls wanted to swim."

"I can't tell you what a relief this is. It means more than I can ever express. I'll have all the papers drawn up immediately when I get back to the city next week."

"We'll sign whatever's necessary," he promised, kicking up huge waves with his feet as one of the girls paddled close on a rubber raft. It had been agreed in the family counsel that the children wouldn't be told until closer to the baby's birth. As Jerry's wife Ellen put it so succinctly: "The boys drive me crazy to visit Aunt Tessa when there isn't anything as interesting as a baby in the works. Halloween is plenty soon enough to let this little secret out of the bag!"

"Anytime you're ready. Now for my second message. I think you'd better pack up and head back to Cincinnati when I go home this evening."

"Has Web had another attack?" Tessa questioned, as usual jumping to conclusions where the elderly man was concerned.

"No, but he didn't sound any too good," Frank admitted. Viticulture was close enough to farming to earn Frank's interest and sympathy. He and Web had great respect for each other. "There's a problem with the vines, Tessa. Must have shown up right after you left to come up here. He mentioned something about a virus . . . or something." Tessa's stomach turned over and a cold, sticky fear took up residence in her heart.

"Are you sure he said 'virus'?" A virus in the Rieslings would mean disaster for Vinifera. Especially if it spread to the more commercial French-American hybrid grapes that were the backbone of Vinifera's existence. And her own major source of income.

" 'Virus' was the term he used," her brother assured with a frown. "My hair may be going, but my hearing's still okay. He's called in some expert from New York or California. Says if anybody can nip this thing in the bud it's him. Web wants you to come home."

Kellen has done some remarkable things with vinifera viruses. The words seared through her brain like a comet's trail of fire.

"Did he mention this man's name?" Tessa managed to get the words past the constriction in her throat. The very foundation of her world was shaking beneath her and Frank didn't even seem to notice.

"Yeah, I think he did," Frank shouted, paddling away to ward off a determined attack by both his giggling daughters. "It was Kevin, or Kenneth or something. I've always been bad with names," he apologized.

"Kellen," Tessa said with false calm and only as much interest as she thought the situation indicated.

"Yeah, that sounds right. Kellen Sterling, I think he said. Want me to drive you back to the farm tonight so you can get an early start in the morning?"

The sun was low on the horizon, already lost behind the hills as Tessa turned east onto Highway 52 and headed along the last short stretch that would return her to Vinifera and her inevitable meeting with Kellen.

She'd spent yet another restless night debating the advisability of this return. Totally alone. For the first time, as she listened to her mother's gentle breathing and her nephews as they tossed and turned, asleep in the camper's dark confines, she'd fathomed the depths of her isolation from everyone she loved and cared for. Tessa couldn't confide her reluctance to return to Web to a single living soul. It was a devastating revelation. It would be so easy to stay here, with her family, ride out the storm, then try to make Web understand why she'd deserted him when he needed her. She would be failing in her duty to try to save the vines that meant so much to them both. But she would be protecting her precious secret from discovery. She'd never felt so torn in her life.

Frank hadn't understood the seriousness of what he told her yesterday. A virus rampant in a vineyard meant the total destruction of the vines. The simple word had dropped the bottom out of her secure little world. It took years for vine shoots to mature and produce grapes capable of being made into wine. More years for the wine to age and become marketable. Years of loss of income and prestige. It would mean ruin for Vinifera.

Tessa couldn't stay away; she'd known that immediately although her reason argued persuasively for her to do just that. It would mean that Kellen could discover she was pregnant. It was a gamble, but she had no choice. If only she'd told Web the truth from the beginning, things would have been easier to manage. But she hadn't and he'd called in Kellen to help. Now she could only hope to keep lying to Web and Kellen without betraying herself.

So she'd planned her arrival very carefully. Dinner would be over. Mrs. Basel would be in the large, cheery kitchen in the rear of the house. Kellen might even have retired to his room. Probably the blue one with the Eastlake-style furniture that Web usually offered his guests. She might not have to see him at all this evening. While comforting, the thought was also curiously disappointing. Once before in his company she'd felt able to leap off the edge of the world and fly. The feeling was upon her now. And it was a dangerous temptation because she knew that when he was joined with her she could soar.

No one was sitting on the brick patio that fronted the big columned white house as Tessa drove slowly along the curving gravel drive. But light glowed welcomingly behind the large fan above the double front doors, and there was also a light in the blue room directly to the left. A rental car was parked beside Web's Pontiac and the pickup. He was here.

A traitorous elation swept over her skin like icy wind. Tessa suppressed the wayward excitement with grim fortitude. No matter how many ways her mind proved to her that thinking about Kellen was a waste of time and a threat to her precious serenity; no matter how many ways her intellect found to prove that he wasn't right for her or the baby, he was still the man her unruly heart had chosen to love. "And the last time you saw him, Tessa Litton," she surprised herself by saying aloud, "you slapped his arrogant face and told him you never wanted to see him again in your life."

CHAPTER EIGHT

"We bottled fifteen hundred cases of our De Chaunac and Baco Noir reds last season." Web's voice boomed out of the semi-darkness as Tessa paused in the gloom of the seldom-used formal dining room to smooth her damp flyaway hair with fingers that trembled slightly. "The same number of cases of Seyval Blanc and our Niagara in the whites. Of course, you'll find the Niagara a trifle unsophisticated and foxy for your palate, I imagine," he concluded, with a reference to the more grapy bouquet and taste of wines made from native American vines such as the Niagara.

Tessa took a quick step forward and halted in her tracks, one hand outstretched to steady herself against a cherry ladder-back chair. Her legs suddenly threatened to buckle and drop her unceremoniously to the carpet. "Don't underestimate the strength of your market, Web." Kellen's voice carried clearly from the morning room where Tessa had known she would find them. She clung to the chair, gathering her reserves for the coming trial, her ears tuned sharply to every nuance of his speech.

"I've found it's best to judge a wine on its own merits, on a regional basis, as they do in Europe. There's quite a demand in the East and Midwest for a cheerful, fun-loving white like your Niagara."

Web grunted his approval of Kellen's opinion of the marketplace. Tessa could almost hear him mentally congratulate the younger man's grasp of his subject. Tessa moved forward on silent sandaled feet, drawn by curiosity and something far stronger and harder to analyze. A fascination as dangerous as it was irresistible. She paused in the doorway for a long moment, watching the two men. Kellen stood by the French doors to her

110

left, a snifter of brandy in one strong, brown hand. He was even more handsome than she remembered, his face clean-shaven and darkly tanned, his body lean and rangy like a runner's. He was turned in profile, watching the last of a mauve and coral sunset fade from the western sky. The angle of his jaw and cheekbones was more sharply drawn than she recalled and there were harsh lines running between his nose and the corners of his mouth—as though he'd forgotten how to smile. Tessa pulled her bemused gaze from the tall, virile figure of her baby's father and glanced toward her friend.

Web was seated in his favorite broken-down easy chair. He looked strained and worried, but his color was good and he wasn't favoring his left arm as he often did before an attack. His hair was standing up in springy salt-and-pepper tufts as though he'd been running a hand through it in agitation. So their conversation hadn't been all so sedate. Had they been arguing politics before she came in? Or discussing sports? She would have liked to know.

Tessa relaxed slightly, aware for the first time how tense she had become. She resisted an urge to massage the tightness in the small of her back. Several times lately she'd caught herself doing just that, arching her spine, thrusting her pelvis and stomach forward as though to find a more comfortable position for her growing burden. With conscious effort Tessa kept from crossing her arms over her thickened waistline. No one on earth could tell she was pregnant in the free-flowing, many-pleated sundress she wore. No one.

She moved into the room, looking like a summer sky in the turquoise linen dress. Her hair, which had a tendency to curl in the humid summer weather, was held back by antique ivory combs—a thirty-second birthday gift from Web—and her apricot-tinted skin, darkened to a lush peach by the sun, glowed with health. Web saw her first and was out of his chair with the speed of a much younger man, but Kellen never moved from his stance at the window. He might have been a pagan idol carved of stone. Beyond him a breathtaking view of the winding Ohio and the hills of northern Kentucky faded slowly into the twilight.

"Tessa, you're back. I've missed you," Web said, coming forward to lead her to a chair. "Have you eaten? There's some

111

duckling and potatoes left in the fridge. Mrs. Basel outdid herself for just the two of us."

"No, thanks. I've already eaten," Tessa refused. The thought of the richly flavored duckling that was one of the housekeeper's specialties set her queasy stomach to churn alarmingly.

"Then a glass of sherry?" She'd taken Laura's advice that a small glass of wine in the evening was the world's best soporific and would do the baby no harm. But not tonight. Tessa could feel Kellen's eyes between her shoulder blades. She knew it was unforgivably rude to turn her back on Web's guest, but she needed the few extra seconds to compose herself. She had to get this initial encounter over with quickly and escape to the comfort and safety of her own home.

"No, nothing, please," she said, vetoing the second offering. "I just wanted to let you know I was home, safe and sound. Is there any progress on the problems in the vineyard?" She turned to face Kellen at last. It was devastating. Their eyes met and held as they had in the hotel dress shop all those months ago. Tessa's heart leaped upward and began such an erratic beating against the back of her throat she was afraid it could be heard all over the room.

My Lord, she conceded silently. Her mother had been right. How could she face the reality of a boy child that would share those eyes and that arrogant sweep of broad shoulders, or a little girl with a heart-twisting smile and luxurious coal-black hair, if she didn't love the man who'd helped create that child with her?

"Good evening, Kellen," she whispered into the stretching silence, her questions about the vines blown out of her head by a strong wind of desire. Her next words were louder and steadier by a conscious directive of her will. "Thank you for coming to our rescue so promptly. When I left to visit my family last week there was no sign of trouble here at all." She was babbling and she knew it, but at least she was back on track. And anything was better than his continued silent scrutiny.

"It's good to see you again, Tessa," he answered, his voice unexpectedly warm and sensual. What little of Tessa's color remained drained out of her face.

He wasn't finished with her. She had to get out of this small sunset-washed room. Every atom of his deceptively relaxed

112

frame held danger signals for Tessa to read. He was still on the hunt, still interested in her. Because you were the one who got away. Nothing more, she told her palpitating heart bluntly. He can't guess your secret. It's only that you bested him once. He won't allow it to happen again.

"Kellen only arrived this morning himself, Tessa," Web explained, eyeing her critically. "Most of his early tests won't have any readable results before morning."

"I've made myself at home in your lab. I hope you don't mind." His words challenged her to object.

"Why should I mind?" she answered with haughty reserve. She would have to keep her distance, that was imperative. She might as well begin this very minute. "Web, if you gentlemen will excuse me, it was a long drive and the traffic on the interstate was terrible. I'd like to make an early evening of it." Tessa gave Web an apologetic, beseeching look and turned her back on Kellen's tall, sport-shirted figure for a second time. "I'm sorry to be such a wet blanket."

"Don't think a thing of it. I warned you about overdoing," Web scolded, unheeding of her sharp warning glance. "You have to think of your health."

"I'm only tired from the traveling, Web," Tessa responded with her rare chiming laugh, not wanting to pursue the subject of her health any further. "I'll see you in the morning and you can fill me in on the details. Good night, Kellen." She turned to him one last time.

"Until later, Tessa." He saluted with his brandy snifter, his cobalt-blue eyes never leaving her face. Tessa smiled, cooly and without meaning, as she sailed out of the room, head high. But once in the high-ceilinged, marble-floored foyer, she had to clutch at the oak newel of the staircase to keep from falling.

It had been harder than she imagined to meet him like that. Not to be able to reach out and touch him, to hold him close and feel the length of him against her. She did love him. Any self-serving doubts she may have harbored were swept away the moment she looked up into his secret blue gaze. How was she ever going to get through the next few days?

Tessa stepped dripping from the shower, gazing longingly at the high, old-fashioned, claw-footed bathtub across the oakwainscoted room. She would have loved to settle down in its porcelain depths and soak away the fatigue of this long, grueling day, but she'd opted for a quick, cool shower instead. The air conditioning had been off in her Victorian, gingerbread-trimmed cottage for seven whole days. It was stifling.

Toweled dry, Tessa wandered into her bedroom and lifted a long, fleecy, orchid-hued robe from the walk-in closet in the small adjoining dressing room that would soon be the nursery. As she did so, she caught sight of her reflection in the cheval glass in the corner, and dropped the robe on the white-on-white quilt that covered her big brass bed.

It was the first time in days she'd taken the opportunity to study her changing body. Her skin felt slightly dry and itchy and she automatically picked up a tube of jasmine-scented body lotion and began smoothing it over her arms and shoulders. Her breasts were heavier, the skin an iridescent pearl-white and blue-veined, the nipples darkened and enlarged, exquisitely sensitive, as they had been since the beginning of her pregnancy.

No stretch marks yet, Tessa noticed with smug satisfaction as she smoothed the cream over her stomach and thighs and the backs of her knees. She really hadn't changed much at all— until she turned in profile. As always, Tessa couldn't quite believe what she saw. She ran her palms over the damp, smooth skin of her waist and abdomen, shaping her hands to the growing roundness. A slight perceptible movement greeted her caress. The baby was stronger now, the faint rippling, fishlike motions of days ago had given way to determined thumps and recognizable kicks. Tessa smiled with a deep contentment. It would be worth every minute of shameful deception—if she could keep her precious secret from Kellen.

Her soul-searching these past weeks had brought her to many disturbing conclusions. Tessa had come to believe she loved Kellen Sterling, a man she barely knew. But was it only because she was so vulnerable? Recalling the dark days after Jacky's death, she also recalled the wonderful days of falling in love. Slowly, luxuriously, completely. There was no such thing as love at first sight. Tessa had always scoffed at the romantic notion. She'd taken a perfectly understandable infatuation and used it as a defense mechanism, that was all. It was the escape her mind had provided when she found Larry Gelbert's caresses so unacceptable. She was versed enough in psychology to recognize that. And Kellen had been the object of that delusion.

It was all so simple really. And it hurt so terribly.

Tessa grabbed the robe and belted it tightly around her. It was still too warm to contemplate sleeping in an upstairs bedroom and too early. She would go outside and check on her roses. She started down, trailing her hand along the railing of the walnut staircase she'd stripped and refinished two winters ago when she'd bought the dilapidated, two-bedroom brick overseer's cottage from Web.

She'd spent so many happy hours here, painting, papering—with authentic turn-of-the-century prints—refinishing the elaborately carved mantelpiece over the living room fireplace, overseeing the addition of a redwood deck beyond her combination kitchen/dining room at the rear of the century-old house. Another stab of worry knifed through her. How would she keep up her mortgage payments if the vineyards failed?

The sliding glass doors off the dining alcove rolled open and Tessa stepped barefoot into the honeysuckle- and rose-scented darkness. Stars twinkled in the night sky and already a hazy mist rolled up from the river. Hot, humid, heavy with the scents and sound of growing, living things, it was another typical summer evening in the Ohio Valley.

Tessa stepped down into the garden, kneeling to sniff a ruby-petaled rose. She flicked idly at a full-blown blossom and watched the petals drift into the mulch surrounding the plant.

"Do you always garden in your bathrobe?" Kellen's voice came out of the darkness, followed by his person. Pipe tobacco drifted toward Tessa as she stood with unhurried grace. She wasn't about to let him unsettle her again tonight. Once a night was enough for any woman.

"I haven't seen my roses in a week. I didn't know you smoked a pipe," she shot back, adamant that the subject of the conversation not be herself.

"I don't very often anymore. It's bad for the taste buds, you know. And they're my stock in trade. Just an old habit, I guess. Sometimes I need something to do with my hands."

Warning claxons went off inside Tessa's head. Yes, a pipe did make a good prop for a man's hands. Especially hands like Kellen's—strong and lean, made to love a woman. Now she knew where the old saying about barefoot and pregnant had come from. She felt so terribly vulnerable like this. And she was naked beneath the enveloping folds of fleece. If he should reach out with those entrancing, magical hands, she'd be lost. Tessa backed prudently away and turned to mount the steps to the deck. She felt safer, protected from his magnetism with the redwood railing, upright and substantial, between them.

"Did you drive in from the airport?" she asked, searching hurriedly through her mind for a neutral subject, although she would rather have found one a little more stimulating than his mode of transportation.

"Yes." Kellen knocked the unsmoked pipe against the iron birdbath near his hand, ground the smoking tobacco under the heel of his shoe, and stepped into the glow of the porch light.

"I was surprised to hear Web hired you."

"You didn't know anything about this problem?" One dark brow climbed quizzically toward the wayward lock of hair on his forehead.

"I've been away," Tessa explained once more. "Can you save our vines?"

"I'll try. If it's a virus, you know there's not much I can do. The vines will have to be destroyed and a new vineyard planted from unaffected stock." It wasn't very encouraging; he was dismissing her whole future with those words. Tessa postponed asking any technical questions until she knew all the facts. It was a way of hiding her head in the sand until she felt she could face it. "Did you find your family well, Tessa?"

Why did she feel as if he was baiting her? The comment was polite and perfectly within reason. From any other man she would have blessed his change of subject. But not with Kellen; his conversation was like a tennis game. First the ball was in her court and then his.

"I found them very well and happy. Worrying about the crops and the price of grain. . . ." She trailed off, embarrassed.

"I'm sorry your visit had to be cut short."

"I wanted to be here with Web." But she was sorry too, more sorry than he would ever know. "How did Web find you, Kellen? . . . I thought you were in Europe for the summer." Tessa let a small amount of her puzzlement show in her voice.

"No. I was only there for a few weeks last spring. I've been bouncing around California in the meantime—and Magda can usually run me to ground—as she did in this case." He advanced to lean both tanned forearms on the railing, his face barely inches from her own. Tessa straightened hurriedly, but he reached out and caught her trembling hands. She fixed her eyes stubbornly on the bowl of his pipe where it protruded from the pocket of his expensive navy sport-shirt.

"If you flew in all the way from California you must be tired," Tessa whispered with a quiver in her husky, melodious voice.

"Actually I wasn't that far away. I've been visiting my family also." He said it wonderingly, sadly, as though he didn't quite believe it himself. "It's the first time I've been home in over a dozen years."

"I'm sorry your visit was spoiled. . . ." Tessa whispered. A shooting pain of aching need seared through her breasts at his touch. How dear he looked outlined by the darkness of her garden and the stand of sighing pines beyond. A second, sharper pain jabbed through her. If he was visiting his family he must have seen his sister-in-law and the child he wouldn't claim. Her fingers writhed in his painless confining grip like small birds fighting to be free. Kellen looked down at them as if he didn't really see them and released her.

"It wasn't actually spoiled," he said tightly. "Things aren't all that different at Sterling Hills." He changed the subject abruptly and continued on in the same hard-edged voice. "Tessa, I want to apologize for the things I said that last night in Magda's garden." As before, Tessa was convinced that apologizing for his actions was something Kellen Sterling rarely did.

"Don't," she interrupted. "I'm the one to apologize. I slapped your face. That was inexcusable behavior." Tessa reached out, unable to deny herself the pleasure of a fleeting caress along his chiseled jawline. "I thought I could handle that kind of casual relationship. I was wrong. After all, I suppose I should be flattered you asked me to be your mistress." Tessa smiled sadly down at him. She wished she had accepted.

Kellen reached up to circle her wrist, turning his lips into the palm, kissing her with infinite tenderness, his tongue flicking out to taste the jasmine of her bath oil. "I meant it as the highest compliment I could pay you. Not as an insult."

Tessa shivered uncontrollably, torn between wanting and the need to keep her distance. "I know that now. . . ."

He had moved as though to join her on the deck. When she held up a restraining hand, he hesitated and stepped back, releasing her. "Are we starting over, Tessa? Very well, if that's the way you want it tonight." He shrugged. "I'd better allow you to retire," he said formally. "Web tells me you've been under the weather these last few weeks. I hope you've seen a doctor. Fainting spells aren't to be ignored."

"It's nothing really," she replied, grateful for the reprieve although the subject was an embarrassing, potentially dangerous one also. "I'm afraid it's Web's way of getting back at me for the weeks I bullied him into resting and cutting back on his work when he was ill this spring. Please don't think anything of it."

"Magda told me that Web had an attack before you left California."

"Yes, but that was after . . . after I left you. It had nothing to do with my refusal to go with you." Her head came up proudly.

"I'm sure it didn't. At least not directly." He sounded curiously detached. Tessa was almost disappointed in her easy victory. She had assumed he would pounce on the weakness in her story.

"I'll be in my lab by seven," she rushed on, moving into the open doorway and neutral territory. Seven o'clock was an hour before she usually went to her small domain near the winery.

"I'll meet you there. I should be ready to read my prelims by then. Don't think you'll get away from me this easily every time, Tessa." There was a slight edge to his voice. "Business before pleasure. . . ." His tone dropped several nerve-tightening levels, making the skin crawl along her spine. "But I don't intend to let what we shared fade into such platonic state-of-the-weather, state-of-your-health tête-à-têtes as this one." Tessa jumped as though she'd been shot. "Beware." Kellen smiled dangerously. He had outmaneuvered her again.

"Good night, Kellen," Tessa replied, pulling the tattered shreds of her composure tightly around her. She deliberately ignored his last provocative comments. What could she possibly say in retaliation?

118

"Pleasant dreams, Tessa." He was gone as quickly and as quietly as a breeze through the garden. Pleasant dreams? He was far off the mark there. If she closed her eyes at all, Tessa was sure it would be nightmares that galloped through her sleep.

Surprisingly she slept dreamlessly and well. It was exactly twelve minutes past seven o'clock when Tessa descended the half dozen steps into the cool brightness of her lab. The building had originally housed a dairy and was situated about ten yards from the winery itself, but when the wind was right the yeasty, sweet smell of fermenting grapes penetrated even here. Lately it had made her temperamental stomach take exception. Today the air conditioning unit in the window hummed softly and Tessa breathed a sigh of relief.

Early as she was, Kellen was there before her, seated at a high stool, his dark head bent attentively over the microscope. He did not look up; he was completely absorbed in his work. Tessa reached past him and pulled a long white lab coat from its hook, watching him covertly beneath her spiky brown lashes. She slipped the coat over the sleeveless fuchsia tent dress she wore and hoped no one would come in and comment on her sudden predilection for dresses, instead of her usual jeans or cut-off shorts. Thank goodness she hadn't announced her pregnancy to Mrs. Basel and the vineyard staff. Heaven did sometimes smile on poor foolish sinners.

"Would you like some coffee?" she asked by way of a safe greeting. Kellen looked up from his microscope, rubbed the back of his neck with one tanned brown hand, and focused on her peaches-and-cream figure at his side. The electrifying voltage of his smile made Tessa suck in her breath in a whistling rush. The charge that flowed between them hadn't diminished despite her determination to keep her distance. The chemistry was more vital and alive than ever.

"I thought liberated executive career women like yourself did not make coffee anymore," Kellen taunted. "Isn't it in the equal rights amendment or something?"

Tessa made a face and looked down her nose. "I do it because I'm very good at it. I don't care for inferior coffee. But you may pour your own if that will make you feel more enlightened," she quipped, once more experiencing the almost narcotic high he alone could provide for her.

"No," he answered equitably. "If you're willing to act as chef you can pour. I take mine—"

"Black?" Tessa smiled questioningly, dizzy with the exhilaration of balancing on the cutting edge.

"Black." The jungle-cat smile curved the corners of his mouth and Tessa felt a heated surge of wanting course through her.

Kellen watched her for a long unsettling moment before turning back to his tests. Tessa busied herself at the coffee machine, measuring water in a glass beaker, ladling coffee granules into the filter with a generous hand, all the time totally aware of his interested perusal.

This is how it could be if they started over, began a romance on the right foot, for the right reasons. A relationship that would grow and mature with every day spent together. A father for her baby. . . . Tessa nearly dropped the steaming cup as she brought herself up short. That kind of thinking would lead to nothing but heartbreak. How could they begin a normal relationship? There was nothing normal about what had passed between them. Even if he knew her secret and accepted the baby. How long would he stay before he became restless? A few weeks? A few months? What could that portend but more pain and complications in the years ahead? No. Kellen was the enemy. He had the power to destroy her serenity—and her future happiness. She couldn't give in to these hormone-induced fantasies, to use Laura's favorite phrase. She was in this thing alone. There could be no other alternative.

Tessa set the cup down beside Kellen's arm, marveling at the deceptive steadiness of her hands. Inside she was a quivering mass of conflicting desires and contradictions in logic. "Have you found anything encouraging?" she asked to keep her thoughts at bay.

"It isn't a virus." Tessa bit her lips to still the happy outcry that threatened to break forth. "Nothing else definite as yet, but take a look for yourself," Kellen offered.

He slid off the high stool and motioned her near. Tessa went, unwilling to chance being any closer but too curious to decline. She adjusted the eyepiece and looked down at the smear of unfamiliar stained cells. She could feel Kellen's breath stir her hair as he bent over her, his slim gray-chino-covered hips propped nonchalantly against the marble tabletop as he sipped his coffee.

"You can see by the shape of the organism," he directed conversationally, "that it's definitely not a virus. I haven't pinpointed the microbe strain yet; but my guess would be it's some mutant form of one of the more prevalent grape diseases. We're more or less breaking new ground here with this soil and climate as far as viniferas are concerned. It might be slow going for a few days, but we'll come up with something to combat it."

"Then you think the vines can be saved?" Tessa was almost afraid to ask the simple question. The organism on the slide resembled nothing that she was familiar with. Plant pathology was an area of viticulture Tessa hadn't yet been able to study in depth.

"It's not necessarily fatal, as a virus would be," he admitted cautiously. "But with as much scorching of the primary leaves, and the probable reduced sugar content in the grapes we do save . . . well, your harvest will be way off this year. I'm sorry."

Tessa knew high natural sugar levels were absolutely essential in the fermentation of superior wine. Low sugar content was something every vintner hoped to avoid. But at least there would be a future for the vineyard. "A curtailed vintage is a small price to pay." She looked up, her eyes soft and shining with relief as she swiveled on the stool. Kellen took advantage of her change of position to place one long tanned arm on either side of her, barring her escape. "Will it spread to the Seyval and Baco Noir?" she whispered throatily, the subtle scent of his spicy aftershave made it hard to draw a deep, sustaining breath. Both varieties of French-American hybrid grape bordered on the Riesling planting.

"With the right preventative treatment and any luck at all, I'd say no," he answered, catching her bemused gaze and refusing to relinquish it. "We just can't be sure until I isolate the causative agent. Those varieties have enough vinifera parentage to make me want to hedge my bets," Kellen admitted, a frown carving two grooves between his thick, dark brows.

"I see." Relief made Tessa reckless. Now with his qualifying statement some of her apprehension returned. "I think I should go tell Web right away. He's been so distressed."

"I think not, Tessa," Kellen purred roughly. "That's what I'm being paid for, remember. I'll tell him later." He leaned closer, teasing her knees apart with his until her skirt rode high on her satiny thighs and he stood intimately wedged between her legs. The erotic movement disrupted Tessa's thought processes very effectively, as he intended it should.

She arched back, putting both hands on his chest, afraid he might take her completely in his arms. She couldn't chance that. Not in the thin cotton dress. "Be careful," she warned in a tight, husky voice. "The shelves behind us. They're not very stable. One of the supports is broken. . . . I keep forgetting to tell Web . . . that it needs fixing." She twisted her head to stare up at the dangerous shelving. She couldn't be sure Kellen even heard her warning. With catlike grace he smoothed her hair behind one ear and leaned forward to nibble audaciously at her earlobe. Tessa saw the pale green, rough-plastered walls spin before her eyes but she kept on talking. "I suppose I should move some of these chemicals . . . they're volatile . . . even toxic . . . some of them."

"Volatile is a very good word for you, lady vintner," Kellen murmured, his lips on her hairline. "You remind me of a bottle of champagne. Perfectly composed, even a little nunlike until someone stirs your blood . . . and you explode in his hands." His tongue darted into her ear, making tiny forays into the inner recesses. Tessa shivered in delight.

"Kellen, don't," she whispered in desperation, her pulse and respirations quickening deliciously. When she turned her head to escape the evocative caress, her lips were captured in a deep, stunning kiss that left her no energy to oppose him. Kellen's tongue plundered her mouth, stealing her willpower and her need to resist. Her arms were locked between them, keeping him from pressing his body too intimately against hers. Her fingers clutched at the open collar of his shirt, her thumbs grazing the tight, springing dark curls of hair on his chest. Tessa was galvanized by the flame of desire he ignited and the fear that erupted in its wake.

She wanted Kellen so badly she could have pulled him with her to the floor and made love—then and there—ardently, and with no thought to the consequences of her actions. It was madness pure and simple.

"Tessa, I want you back," Kellen growled against her runaway pulse, as his seeking lips wandered the rosy column of her throat, drinking in the beauty of her petal-soft skin, tasting the powdery freshness of her collarbone where it emerged from the square neckline of her dress. "I'll love you so wonderfully and so well you will have to admit there's a bond between us that can't be broken."

A bond. He was too close. Too close again to guessing what she hid from him. Tessa dragged her scattered reason back from the high cliffs of desire where it had flown at his touch.

"Kellen, you must stop this. You seem to feel because I allowed you to make love to me once . . ."

"More than once. . . ." She could feel him smile as his fingers tweaked at the buttons holding her dress closed against his marauding mouth.

"More than once," she admitted weakly, tears sneaking up to flood the corners of her jade eyes. "You believe I found that experience so novel . . . so unique. . . ."

Kellen raised his head, grinning devilishly. "On the contrary. I know you found it unique. . . ."

Anger began to stir under the embers of passion in Tessa's brain. The tears retreated. How dare he act so superior, so male. He had known even that about her—that the fulfillment he gave her had been the finest, the most complete, she'd ever experienced. It was the final humiliation.

"Let me go!" Tessa pushed her hands hard against his chest, levering herself back against the table in doing so. Beakers and bottles on the shelves above her rattled ominously. Kellen's hand streaked out to steady the Bunsen burner on the stand beside her. He backed off a step and Tessa flashed away from his side.

"You gave yourself to me completely that night, Tessa," he stated with total conviction, turning to confront her quaking body. "Nothing you can say or do will make me change my mind about that. It went far beyond the usual exchange of physical gratification." His voice was the low, leonine growl that raised the short hairs at the nape of her neck. He was arrogant and uncompromisingly virile, his hands folded across his chest, his legs crossed negligently as he leaned back against the high table.

"You don't have any right to make such judgments," Tessa hissed from several feet away. "You don't know anything about me. How I think, what makes me Tessa Litton. Perhaps I'm that passionate with every man that takes me to bed."

"Tessa." His warning tone halted her mendacious, vitriolic flow of words.

"I make my own decisions about my life," she went on, drawing herself to her full height despite her pale, strained face. Her hands were dug deep into the pockets of the lab coat. They balled into small fists as she fought for composure. "I only wanted you that night. It's the same today, there is no difference." She had to keep her anger up front. It was better that way. It couldn't hurt any more. This way she could cauterize the wound as she created it. He must never know how much she cared.

"Very well. Perhaps it's too soon for honesty. If that's the way you want it—no strings, no commitments—so be it. But I intend to have you again, Tessa," he said harshly. She'd snapped his quick temper yet again. "From that night onward you've been mine. And what is mine I keep."

Stark terror careened through Tessa's mind, driving out every other consideration. She was incapable of recognizing the need that underscored his arrogant words. *What is mine I keep.* The horror came to a halt somewhere near her heart, just above where the baby slept. *What is mine I keep.* The words repeated over and over like a death knell.

"I'll be available to help with anything you feel necessary in the vineyards," she said as she whirled and nearly ran up the stone steps into the heavy morning air. "Otherwise I think it's best if we don't see each other alone again." She didn't intend to give him a chance to respond, but slammed the door on her words.

Outside the sun beat down out of a cloudless sky and promised yet another scorching day of heat and possible thundershowers. It would make the job of containing the as yet unnamed menace in the vineyards that much harder. Repeated spraying or dusting with the chemicals Web and Kellen decided would be most effective would be necessary to control the damage. If the weather didn't cooperate it could still spell disaster for the vines. And it would delay Kellen's departure several more days.

No matter what direction Tessa turned there were pitfalls. She wasn't very good at deception. She should have told Web the truth from the beginning. But how could she have foreseen these tangled circumstances when she began this quest? Now she didn't have an ally in the whole wide world. There was only herself to rely on. And it was so hard to keep all the lies and their accompanying entwining half-lies straight. Tessa was more unsure of her role in the scheme of things than she had ever been before.

Had she conceived this child with all the right motives foremost? Conflicting emotions warred within her as she trudged back to her small, welcoming house. Had Kellen been only the means to an end? Or was he the true catalyst to her half-formed dreams of conceiving a child? Her head ached with the strain of sifting through the miasma of want and need to the bedrock of objectivity.

If only she could stay away from Kellen's tempting dangerous presence, she would be able to put things back into perspective. She was in no shape to deal with such weighty issues when so much of her energy must be spent in deceiving—everybody she loved.

Tessa glanced down at her watch, feeling uncharacteristically sorry for herself. Only eight o'clock on a sunny July morning and she already ached as if she'd been on her feet for hours. Tessa stopped walking and placed a hand on the small of her back, hoping to ease the growing knot of tension. Protecting her baby would give her all the strength she needed to deal with Kellen. Tessa straightened her shoulders and made her balled fists relax. She didn't exactly know what she would do next; but it would be what she felt was best for her baby. Not Kellen's baby—hers and hers alone. That conviction helped ease a little of the heartache, but not much. It only made her feel more isolated and lonely. No matter what occurred it was going to be a long, trying week.

CHAPTER NINE

Tessa spent the next three days barricaded in her home like a beleaguered guerrilla fighter in a mountain stronghold. Hiding was childish and didn't solve her problems but her overloaded defenses knew no other way to cope with Kellen's intoxicating presence in her life.

He seemed to be everywhere. In that quiet hour after sunrise his voice carried through her open window, rousing Tessa from restless sleep. Each morning, concealed behind lace curtains, she watched him prowl among the grapes as he directed the workmen spraying the infected vines in the early dawn calm. In the adjacent vineyards Web oversaw the placement of a chemical dust provided by the state department of agriculture. It would help protect the more hardy hybrids, their heavy burden of leaves and new canes, the clusters of hard unripe fruit, held up by an extensive network of wire frames.

Seeing Kellen there below her, day after day, stripped to the waist like a black and gold demigod among the green and blue of vines and sky made Tessa yearn to reach out and touch him. Her woman's body ached for him as badly; she didn't know how well she could hide the acute need she felt for him, so she continued her self-imposed isolation.

Yet tonight the restless longing had driven her out to the vineyard, away from the infected Rieslings where the powerful chemicals made walking inadvisable for her, and into the healthy Niagaras that were far more at home in the humid river valley.

Overhead huge cumulonimbus clouds boiled up against a darkening sky like puffs of genii smoke, blotting out the sun, bringing early twilight. Night birds stirred to life and the cicadas shrilled in the trees along the riverbank. The air was heavy with the scents of the countryside, the vines, and rich earth. The storm she'd sensed for several days had finally chosen its hour to arrive. But still Tessa lingered, fighting her well-grounded midwestern fear of severe storms along with the equally explosive possibility that Kellen had seen her come out alone. If he found her—unchaperoned by Web's restraining presence at the dinner table, or by one or another of the vineyard workers following her into the lab for a glass of icewater, or a short friendly chat—Tessa was virtually defenseless.

Silhouetted against the dying light, head back, eyes turned heavenward, Tessa scanned the storm for signs of wind or hail in its gray-black depths. She flipped a strand of hair from her cheek and caught a flash of movement from the corner of her eye. Kellen had appeared at the top of a rise. She was trapped. He'd outflanked her carefully chosen position by coming up from below her, cutting off her retreat to the house. A sudden gust of wind flattened her knee-length yellow gingham painter's smock to her middle. Tessa plucked hurriedly at the material, hoping the vines hid her profile from Kellen's view.

"What are you doing all the way down here?" he ground out, catching her by the shoulder and spinning her to face him. "Don't you know the weather service has issued a tornado watch for this county?"

"I haven't been listening to the radio," Tessa admitted, fear and a strange exhilaration making her eyes huge and beguilingly emerald in the fading light.

"I'm not surprised you don't know what's going on. From what Web tells me your antique-filled little hideaway probably doesn't run to such modern contraptions as radios. Come on. I'm getting you out of here," Kellen ordered darkly, suiting action to words.

Tessa hung back obdurately, dragging her feet although she knew the storm would break any minute. "You don't have to spy on me, Kellen Sterling. I've lived in this part of the country all my life. It's going to storm all right, but not right away. And this one won't spawn any tornado. The feel's all wrong." Kellen didn't bother to take exception to her unscientific explanation but pulled her determinedly along behind him. "Kellen!" Tessa jerked her hand from his grasp with frantic strength.

He turned on her so quickly and so smoothly, Tessa nearly

ran into the rock wall of his chest. A heavy, damp silence settled around them. Tessa pulled up short, backing into the vines, feeling the rough edges of grape leaves at her back.

"You're enjoying this, aren't you?" Tessa strained forward to catch his low, gruff words above the suddenly gusting wind. "You have been calling the shots, leading me on to dance to your tune, ever since I got here. I'm through with waiting, Tessa. No more of your chaste maiden routine. We're going back to your quaint little sanctuary and you are going to tell me exactly what you are up to. Why before you were as wild and passionate and willing to be loved as you are eager to avoid me now."

"I haven't the slightest idea what you mean," Tessa managed to stutter, her eyes dilating in the sudden darkness.

"You want me as much as I want you. Still you deny us both that pleasure." Kellen spelled out his argument with devastating candor. "You tell me you aren't a woman to play games. So there must be another, more logical reason. What is it?"

A few large tentative drops splattered around them, making a lie of Tessa's prediction. She was aware they heralded the deluge. She held her tongue. Off in the distance, above the steadily rising wind, the rain came closer, dancing on the vine leaves with increasing fervor.

"Damn this storm," Kellen breathed furiously. He glanced out at the already rain-obscured river below them. "Come on." His words were the cue as the heavens chose that moment to open and soak the two mortals in a stinging spray of ice-cold rain. Tessa gasped as her hair and smock were instantly plastered to her skin. Kellen grabbed her hand and they raced off between the widely spaced rows of vines. The rain came down so hard that it beat on the leaves like an army of maniacal drummers, each playing a separate cadence, and each more frenzied than the last.

Tessa couldn't see. She couldn't hear above the noise of wind and rain. She could only stumble along in Kellen's wake, dripping and shivering as lightning crashed around them in jagged flashes and thunder roared a demonic accompaniment to the fray.

Suddenly the rampaging downpour ceased to batter her. Tessa halted, disoriented, as Kellen pulled her roughly against

128

his side. She sucked air into her straining lungs and looked around, realizing groggily that they had found shelter in the old gazebo below her house. The octagon-shaped room had been erected at some long-forgotten date for the comfort and enjoyment of wasp-waisted ladies in high-necked voile gowns and picture frame hats as they dallied in the company of their witty escorts, resplendent in derby hats, white gloves, and spats. Tessa pushed her streaming hair from her eyes. She could almost see their ghosts, flitting genteelly through the rain-strengthened shadows of the old summer house.

She wondered fuzzily what it would have been like to live in that simpler era, when the radiant heat of Kellen's body so near her brought sanity careening back. Tessa lunged away but it was too late. His arms circled her, pulling her close, molding her shoulders and bottom against the angled contours of his body. Tessa went rigid straining to move free. His arms came around her to cross at her waist and enfold her in an iron embrace she could not hope to break.

"Now I've got you exactly where I want you." His breath tickled her ear. Unbelievably his voice held the deep, teasing note she loved. "There will be no more hedging now, Tessa. No more secrets between us. I'm tired of playing tag with you."

Tessa waited, her breath stuck deep in her throat; she plucked at his restraining hands, but she knew there was no escape for her. For a moment longer Kellen held her trembling body close, then his hands moved downward, tracing the swelling curve of her belly. Tessa felt him hesitate, stiffen, knew exactly the moment he made the only logical deduction possible.

Abruptly, dizzyingly Tessa was whirled to face him. It happened so swiftly, she couldn't take it all in. But he knew. She saw the discovery in his face. Kellen Sterling was aware of her secret.

"You're pregnant." The words were as hard as the pelting rain on the roof. Inside the summer house a cold artificial calm prevailed. Somewhere behind Tessa the roof began to leak and the monotonous drip was louder than the sound of wind and rain and the thunder's cymbals.

"Yes," Tessa whispered, eyes wide with anguish. "I didn't

want you to know." Liar! Her traitorous heart had wanted him to learn her secret all along.

"This is why you've been avoiding me. Why you didn't let me come near you. Why are you hiding it? Whose baby is it?" Kellen grated, his finger digging mercilessly into her shoulders. Tessa wanted to cry out against the pain, but she didn't.

"Mine," she answered huskily as she watched his blazing blue stare with softer, pain-filled green eyes.

"Is it Web's?" Kellen looked puzzled, completely off balance for the first time in their short, volatile relationship.

"The baby is mine. . . ." How easy it would be to take that way out. Let Kellen jump to this most obvious of conclusions. Web would understand. He would forgive her when she told him the circumstances. He wouldn't betray her; and Kellen was enough of a gentleman not to confront the older man with his suspicions. What was one more lie added to the growing weight of those she already carried? Caught up in a tangle of deceit that she'd woven with her own words and actions, Tessa was thoroughly disgusted with herself. Once she'd accused Kellen of a lack of integrity. Was she any better? "The father's identity isn't important," she croaked, fighting tears. "The baby is mine."

Tessa had hesitated a fraction of a second too long. She could see Kellen form his own conjectures, draw his own conclusion. His large hands stretched out, gathering her protesting form closer as they traced again the blossoming outline of her waist and belly.

"It's my child." The sudden blaze of elation from his cobalt eyes was lost to Tessa in another dazzling flash of lightning. "It's my child," Kellen repeated in a ragged, triumphant voice. "Tell the truth for once in your life."

Tessa was stone-cold scared. She'd always believed Kellen would be a formidable opponent if the occasion warranted. Now she was sure of it. *What is mine I keep.* She felt as bedraggled as a kitten someone had tried to drown in a burlap sack. And as weak. The tapestry of her carefully orchestrated future was unraveling faster than she could stitch it back into place. For one of the few times in her life Tessa took refuge in a woman's most potent weapon. Shining crystal tears spilled down her wet cheeks unchecked.

130

"Answer me," Kellen demanded hoarsely. "You got pregnant that night we made love. This child was conceived then, wasn't it?"

Great, shaking sobs racked her slender form as Tessa lifted her hands to her face and cried as if her heart would break. She shook Kellen's slackened grip from her arms and lifted her tear-streaked face to find him staring down at her with a strange disquieting gleam in his hard blue eyes. "Biologically you are the father, but your contribution was microscopic. The baby is mine. I'm carrying it. I will give it life at the risk of my own." The words were unforgivable, she knew, but she said them anyway.

"I hardly call my contribution microscopic," he grated through clenched teeth. "At the time it was absolutely essential, don't you agree? And most welcome to the prospective mother, if I remember correctly."

The sarcastic remark struck home. Why did he have to remind her she was putty in his hands, totally unable to resist his sexual appeal. "I hate you," Tessa shouted childishly as she evaded his outstretched hands and stumbled down the steps, wanting only the sanctuary of her own softly lit bedroom.

She could hear Kellen's angry shout, the pounding of his feet, as he started after her but she ran on heedless of the driving rain. She couldn't face him again. It was too much to cope with all at once. Blinded by tears, hampered by the slippery rope-soles of her sandals, Tessa couldn't adjust quickly enough to the sudden change in footing as she sped blindly along the needle-covered path to her home. She tripped on a pine root, stumbled, and sat down hard, still crying like a lost soul.

Kellen was on her prostrate form in a second, dragging her upright to stare angrily down at her bowed head. "What did you pull a stupid stunt like that for?" he rasped. "Are you trying to purposely hurt the baby?" Tessa wouldn't look at him, did not see that the anguish in his cobalt gaze matched her own for a brief second before the dark shutters of self-control were dropped into place.

"Hurt the baby!" she blazed at his accusation, finding her voice at last. "Don't be a moron. You don't lose a baby just because you slip on the grass."

"How do you know, you little idiot," Kellen raged back. "Have you ever been pregnant before?"

"No." Tessa shook her head, special wonder shining like an inner sun from green eyes that rivaled the pines around and above them. "Never. I'm sorry I said those awful things," she whispered, lifting her hand in a gesture of peace. "I don't know what made me say them." In a single fluid movement Tessa was scooped into Kellen's strong arms and held tightly against his chest for the second time in her life. She was too tired, too spent with weeping, to protest as he carried her through the rain-drenched rose garden and into the house. Blessed quiet replaced the storm's fury.

"Where's your bedroom?"

"Put me down," Tessa pleaded in a voice that wasn't as steady as she wished. "I'm perfectly capable of getting there myself."

"Tessa." What power did he hold over her that the mere sound of her name spoken in that tone compelled her to obedience?

"It's the first door at the top of the stairs. You're dripping water all over my carpet," she wailed, looking down over his shoulder at the wet trail they left on the stairs.

"Hush."

Again she subsided, too bemused to protest effectively. "I'm sorry for what I said," she began apologizing again as tears threatened once more.

"It's all right," he murmured gently against her wet hair, lowering her feet to the floor. "We'll get everything straight as soon as you're warm and dry. Are you sure you didn't hurt yourself when you fell?"

"Positive. I'm as strong as a horse, really." Tessa swallowed a gurgle of nervous laughter. "Laura, my doctor, says once the little . . . sweethearts . . ." Tessa hesitated. She didn't like to think she was superstitious. Laura had used a much more colorful noun, but Laura had two beautiful children. She could tempt fate. Tessa could not. "Once they grab hold nothing will shake them loose until they're ready."

"To hell with your doctor's homespun philosophy. You nearly scared the wits out of me taking off like that." They stood entwined for long, quiet seconds as the fury of the storm

132

beat outside the snug haven of her bedroom. Tessa watched beneath lowered, rain-dappled lashes as Kellen looked around at the oak and maple furnishings, the wide antique brass bed, the half-open doors to the blue-tiled bath and darkened dressing room. He stood in the center of the room, his hands on his hips, his rain-soaked shirt molded to his powerful shoulders and chest. What was he thinking at this very moment? Did he want her as badly as she needed him? Tessa dared to think it was so. Yet she was hopelessly uncertain of her next move. She shivered uncontrollably, galvanizing Kellen into action.

"Get those wet clothes off," he ordered gruffly. Tessa's head snapped up and she glared defiantly into his fathomless blue eyes. She might as well give up trying to read any meaning into their reflecting depths. That time—if there had ever been one—was past. He only allowed her to know those small bits and pieces of himself he was willing to share.

"I beg your pardon." The haughty words were overruled by a wayward sneeze. "Excuse me," Tessa mumbled contritely from behind her hand.

"Strip I said, or I'll do it for you," Kellen repeated in a low growl that was no less easy to ignore than a shout. "I'll run you a hot bath."

"I'm not getting in a tub when it's storming like this," Tessa declared mutinously, pointing out the window with a modicum of her usual cool reserve etched on her pale features.

"I see your point about the bath," Kellen conceded as a bolt of brassy-gold lightning struck the soaked ground close by. "Then get into bed. I'll find you a towel to dry your hair."

"And one for yourself. You're still dripping all over my Axminster." Tessa remained standing near the window. She spoke over her shoulder, fingers tracing the meandering path of a rain-drop on its journey down the windowpane. The only light came from the bathroom where Kellen rummaged through her linen closet. She couldn't undress in front of him. Tessa felt shy and uncertain. He wasn't reacting at all as she had imagined he would. She'd fortified herself to resist an angry, cold man. Kellen was too quiet, too much in control. It only made her more apprehensive. As so often before, Tessa compared herself to a cornered mouse as a great cat toyed with its prey. She couldn't

133

allow him to have the upper hand any longer. She had to assert her independence. Tessa turned to face him.

"What are you waiting for?" Kellen stood in the bathroom door like an immovable oak in the forest.

"I'll get undressed as soon as I've seen you to the door."

"Oh, no you don't, Tessa. We've far too many important matters to discuss. You won't send me packing this easily." His voice was stern and Tessa bristled defensively. She noticed he was minus squelching shoes and socks. He evidently meant what he said about staying. But he always meant what he said.

What did her bathroom look like with his things in it? Tessa shivered again with mingled desire and distress as her clammy dress adhered uncomfortably to her chilled skin.

"Now, Tessa."

It must be his use of one-syllable words that made her feel so helpless and submissive to his will, she fumed, as her hands went obediently to the buttons of her smock. She kicked off her ruined sandals petulantly. If he spoke in sentences like a civilized human being, she could deal with the commands, reason her way out of this predicament. It was when he reverted to aggravating male aggression, cultivated over countless millennia, that Tessa found herself at a loss, betrayed by as many centuries of subservient feminine conditioning.

"Turn your back," Tessa directed as a third and fourth button opened and parted the smock to her waist. She wasn't ready for him to view her swelling body. Not yet. Possibly never.

"No, I will not. Just keep going," Kellen urged as she halted to glare into his reflecting azure stare. He shook out a pale blue towel and wrapped it turban fashion around her wet and probably straggly hair. "That's better," he commented, voicing her own consensus of her appearance. "You don't look like such a bedraggled waif." Kellen pulled her hands free of their stranglehold on the dress and slipped it down over her shoulders and wrists. It dropped to a sodden heap on the floor, taking Tessa's sustaining anger with it.

She felt betraying tears of weakness and humiliation well up and begin to spill down her cheeks. She came close to hating him as Kellen tugged at the strained elastic waistband of her half slip. It met the same fate as her dress. Tessa stood, cowed and subdued, in an almost transparent nylon bra and lacy briefs. She was absolutely defenseless.

"Don't look at me like that," Tessa cried out, unable to restrain the anguished plea. She didn't want Kellen to think her ugly or grotesque. She was too tired, too anxious of what was to come, to face that contingency. How would he react to the sight of an obviously pregnant woman? Men were conditioned to want their women svelte and shapely. She would soon be neither of them. And Kellen more than most men must be averse to the growing swell of her belly and the new heavier curve of her breasts. Tessa's churning brain reminded her of those unpalatable facts with great vigor. She made a grab for her housecoat where she'd dropped it carelessly over the back of a chintz-covered slipper chair that morning.

"Tessa, please don't hide from me." Was there the faintest note of pleading in his inky voice? Tessa hesitated. Kellen reached behind her and flicked the clasp of her bra; the thin lacy wisp fell away. He held her struggling hands so she couldn't cross them over her blossoming stomach. "God, Tessa, you're even more beautiful than I remember." Kellen's arms came around her, crushing her to the hard rock wall of his chest, driving the breath from her lungs.

Kellen's mouth came down demandingly on hers. Tessa couldn't voice her half-hearted protest at his handling of her person. She struggled against his superior strength, knowing she would surrender eventually and completely to his dominance, but knowing equally as painfully that it would solve nothing between them to make love.

Kellen tamed her instinctive rebellion quickly and with pride-demolishing efficiency. His hand came around the back of her neck, holding Tessa still as his other arm clamped her firmly to him. His mouth plundered hers and he didn't release his punishing hold until she ceased to squirm in his arms, her cold lips warming beneath the heat of his mouth, opening like the exquisite petals of a dew-kissed rose. His kiss tasted of sandalwood and rain, Tessa's of salt tears and summer gardens.

When at last Kellen allowed her to move, Tessa remained quiescent, her beating fists now stilled, twined around his neck enchantingly. Kellen altered his position slightly, teasing her rubbery legs apart, fitting her hips close to the complementing saddle of his loins. Tessa sighed deep in her throat, the husky inviting murmur of a woman lost to loving. She wanted him so badly, needed him so desperately, that nothing else mattered at all.

Heaven and earth could cease to exist around her and it would be of little consequence. Tessa had been waiting for this embrace an eternity of solitary days and nights. The loss and heartache of the past, the almost assured pain of the immediate future, were nothing compared to the pleasure of this moment of love; and the incandescent heat Kellen ignited deep in the core of her being. When he broke the contact of their hungry mouths for less than an instant, Tessa moaned, rising on tiptoe, aggressive and assured, to resume the probing caress.

She molded to him, a golden fertile goddess, jealous of any stimuli intruding on the enchanted circle of her lover's arms. "Love me, Kellen, block out the world, the storm. Don't leave me dangling like this somewhere between heaven and hell," Tessa begged, and she didn't care. It seemed so right, so ordained, that they should join this way. Kellen groaned like a soul in torment as her lips teased his. He opened to her honeyed caress like a starving man who had been given a feast, while his hands molded her rounded bottom to the force of his passion. Tessa ignored the cold scratch of wet denim along her legs, the sudden chill of his belt buckle against her naked flesh.

She was elated. For the first time she'd felt the surge of purely feminine power that originates in the trembling arms of a strong man brought low by a woman's touch. Tessa slid her hands over the sinewy tapering V of his torso, lost in her own erotic fantasy until her hands on his back made contact with the clammy, clinging material of his wet cotton shirt.

"Strip," Tessa whispered provocatively, amazed at how quickly she'd banished her worries and fears. They were there, of course, she wasn't that deluded, but the heavy leaden weight had receded to a spot below her heart and for the present she ignored its sting. Tessa gazed up into Kellen's cobalt-blue eyes, boldly, watching passion flame and spark in the impenetrable depths. "I don't want you catching your death of cold in my bedroom. It would be hard to explain to the hired help."

"You do it." So only nominal control of their lovemaking was to be granted. So be it. Kellen kept his hands on her hips,

136

tracing small circular patterns on her belly with his thumbs as she fumbled with the buttons of his shirt. His touch sent rocketing charges of desire streaking through her abdomen. Her fingers were stiff and clumsy. Tessa pulled the tail from the waistband of his jeans with a jerk, reaching up to slide it over the wide sweep of his shoulders. It joined her discarded dress in a slowly widening circle of soaked carpet. They didn't notice. Grabbing a towel from the chair where he'd dropped them, Tessa motioned Kellen to lower his head.

He watched her for a long, searching moment and then did as he was bid, dipping his head. Tessa rubbed the soft terry through the thick sable pelt, smiling in satisfaction as she did so. Perhaps she could learn to handle this great beast of the jungle. She would most certainly relish the opportunity to try. When all the warmth-stealing moisture was dried away, Tessa threw the towel into the growing heap on the floor.

"Kellen," Tessa said hesitantly, both small hands on the sides of his face, directing his gaze deep into her own. "This won't settle anything between us. I'm afraid it will only create even greater problems in the future."

"Hell, I know that," Kellen grated harshly between clenched teeth as Tessa's hands slipped along the tanned column of his throat. She frowned, almost unaware of her erotic exploration of his shoulders and the enticing curve of his collarbone. "Tessa, we have problems and complications we haven't even become aware of as yet. But I've thought about you every day for the past five months. And damn near every minute—day and night—of the last week. I want you so badly I can taste it. Don't refuse me now."

"It will complicate the situation so horribly." She tried again, searching for the right words to outline her position. It was beyond the cold-deadened capacity of her intellect. Only the desiring feminine center of her was capable of reacting.

"Can it be more so?" Kellen asked, perplexity sounding in his low voice. "I thought I'd never see you again. Then out of the blue I get Web's call. I came here to try my hand at wooing and winning you a second time. I find you carrying my child. And hiding the fact." Tessa felt goosebumps rise on her arms, her warning senses alive to the threat in his voice. A threat so subtle, so deeply hidden, he may not have been aware of it himself. *What is mine I keep.*

"I never wanted you to know." Tessa's innate honesty forced her to confess the truth. No more lies if she could avoid them.

"Why the hell not?" It was a mistake. His voice frightened her by its intensity. "Because you made an error when you thought you were protected? It's as much my fault as yours. I should have taken the precautions that night." He erroneously assumed the pregnancy was accidental. Was that why he had reacted so calmly? Tessa wasn't sure.

"I'm having trouble taking it all in. So are you. I can read the confusion and uncertainty in your eyes." Yet Tessa could read none of his deeper feelings in the shaded and shuttered blue spheres. It kept her at a disadvantage—off balance.

She took a deep breath, fighting back treacherous tears. Now she would have to make her position clear. Her dream of a baby so completely her own that the father would never know was fragmented beyond repair. But not her ideals, her commitment to single parenthood and the path she'd chosen to follow. "I want this baby for myself alone. That's why I hid my condition from you. I don't want to be involved with any man. I told you that in California. I planned this pregnancy—I meant for you never to know." She held her gaze steady waiting for his rebuttal.

His reaction when it came was characteristically quiet and controlled, although his eyes narrowed as if he'd been struck a telling blow. "We don't have those options open anymore, Tessa. Either of us." The words were sinister. What options did he consider they had? Somehow that he would want her to terminate the pregnancy never even entered her thoughts. Kellen valued life, in his own maverick fashion, as much as she.

Did he love her? Want to marry her and make a life together? That was the ultimate delusion, and Tessa thrust the temptation to dwell on the precious fantasy to the back of her mind with heroic effort.

A long rolling crash of thunder punctuated Kellen's final statement and Tessa cringed in his arms, caught up in her dark musings. She wasn't strong enough, composed enough, now to argue her point further. Tomorrow in the bright objective light of day she'd make her position clear. The baby was hers alone.

How final, how sad, those words sounded echoing through the empty chambers of her brain while Kellen held her safe in the body-heated darkness.

Her breasts were pressed against the tantalizing roughness of his chest, her breath came in short, quick gasps as he moved lightly against her, teasing the enlarged dusky peaks, catching a budding nipple and rolling it gently between his thumb and forefinger.

"Damn, don't cry, Tessa. Not tonight. A truce," Kellen murmured, kissing a salty tear from her pale cheek. With quick, precise movements he stripped her clinging panties from rounded hips and divested himself of his wet jeans.

Totally, magnificently naked, he lifted Tessa from the floor and deposited her on the firm, unyielding mattress. She watched him through tear-spangled lashes. He was breathtaking in his male beauty, his sinewy body limned by the storm's fitful light. Tessa gloried in the broad sweep of his shoulders, the narrowing line of waist and hips, the long corded length of his thighs. She ached to draw him close and lose herself in his virility. Tessa held out her hands in wordless feminine invitation.

"We are best together in the night," Kellen sighed, catching his breath on a groan as Tessa rose up to pull him down to her. She could feel the mattress reconform to his added weight but she kept her eyes shut tight, savoring the afterimage of his physique that lingered behind her eyelids. "Best together when we let our bodies speak for us," he murmured, settling to rest beside her. "From now till sunup let me hold you, love you, feel our baby move in you. That's all I ask, nothing more, nothing less."

"My baby, Kellen," Tessa whispered obstinately, as he took her in his arms, pressing her back deep into the pillows as he pulled the light sheet and blanket over them both. Kellen's hands tangled in her hair, loosening the towel, spilling the damp tresses over his fingers as he tilted her head for his seeking kiss. His body moved over hers, slowly, tantalizingly, until Tessa felt she would go mad with wanting. His lips trailed down over her throat, branding her with kisses no less electric than the lightning beyond the window. Her hands lightly savaged his back, drawing painless furrows along the ridges and valleys of his rib cage, fitting her palms to the rounded hardness of his biceps and the sloping curve of his collarbone. Tessa was lost in the joy of her tactile exaltation of his masculinity.

Kellen's lips left her sensitized, almost painful nipples and moved once more to take her mouth in a kiss so charged with sexuality, Tessa nearly exploded beneath him. She arched upward, begging their joining, entreating his entry with pleasuring caresses of his pulsing manhood. She was elemental, woman seeking what she needed to make her whole—nothing more.

Her boldness was catalytic. They were too keyed up, had repudiated each other too long, to expend any more precious darkness on love play. Kellen's knee came between hers with vital energy, proclaiming his urgent male need. Tessa answered with trilling feminine notes of desire, moving beneath him, inviting the coupling with parted lips and open thighs. Their tongues met and mingled as he entered her satin softness with a hungry moan of delight. Kellen was skilled, and tender, primitive and giving, the perfect lover. But a small, worrisome corner of Tessa's brain would not bow to his erotic mastery.

"My baby, not ours," she repeated, her frail incantation against his total takeover of her body and soul. "That's the way it must be." His lips left hers momentarily, suspending his narcotic movements to position her more comfortably below him. "Do you understand, Kellen?" He had to be made to see that incontrovertible fact.

"No more words. No more bargaining." Kellen's mouth covered hers, blocking out her voice, and his hands took control of her erratic arcing body. His hunger now controlled her will as well. Achingly, delightedly, Tessa followed his lead, arching into his velvet-sheathed steel thrusts, her world condensed in a mind-tightening spiral that whirled her toward the void. She clutched at Kellen, anxious that he should join her as she careened toward infinity. He sensed her need, quickening his rhythm until Tessa ceased to think at all. She could only feel him with her, in her, surrounding her, as they cried out in mutual release. Tessa's body was racked with glittering spasms that dissolved her into stardust before she re-formed to float slowly into oblivion with Kellen at her side.

The faint mound of the sheet across Tessa's middle moved so slightly that Kellen wasn't sure if it even had. He lay quietly in the gray dawn light, propped on an elbow, watching intently. Again it came, a slight perceptible bounce. Tessa stirred sleepily and frowned, settling more comfortably against the pillow. Kellen held his breath, waiting, his disturbing blue gaze fixed on the same small spot. He reached out slowly, tentatively, and placed his hand on her stomach. Tessa smiled in contentment and slept on. There was a faint identifiable surge against his palm. It was a kick, quick and catlike—a deliberate measured pause, and then a second kick, stronger than the last. Tessa mumbled grumpily and turned on her side.

Kellen lifted his hand, smiling as countless fathers-to-be have smiled at the first faint movement of his child in its mother's womb. It was as new and wondrous to him as to all men before him. And all those who would come after him. A life link, his immortality assured in the continuity of life.

Yet not his baby to claim. Tessa seemed adamant on that point. Kellen frowned. How was it the two women destined to play such important roles in his life had pitchforked him into a dilemma so similar on the surface, yet so profoundly different. He didn't want Tessa to learn his painful secret. It would be a potent weapon in the hands of a woman determined to remain free of entanglements both legal and of the heart. And he couldn't trust her completely with the knowledge—not yet.

Kellen had never known a woman's real and unconditional love. He wanted to believe that Tessa had given hers into his keeping with her total surrender in his arms. But the sad part was that he couldn't be sure. That miracle had never happened to him before. There had been plenty of women to give him their bodies, some even their affection. But not their complete life-sustaining love. He could never allow himself the luxury of being vulnerable enough to accept such a gift. Now the one woman who could bring that long-dormant emotion to life carried his child. He ought to be the happiest man on earth. But he wasn't. Far from it.

All through the long night just past he'd loved Tessa passionately and well. Yet he felt as callow as a green youth. He sought to follow his own advice, put all their problems out of his head until sunrise; but he could not. Time and time again he found himself trying to tell Tessa what he felt. Why he was afraid to love. And always the words died unspoken as he caressed the

141

heavenly wonder of her breasts, feasted on the soft, sweet en-
chantment of her tender skin, her rounding belly pressed to
him, the small, fluttering kicks of his child communicating
through layers of muscle and sinew to pierce his very center.
Tessa wouldn't understand his reluctance to commit—his heart
—to love a woman again, to be that vulnerable. But he wouldn't
be cheated of the chance to know his child.

Kellen didn't want to believe—as his mind insisted on sus-
pecting—that Tessa had used him to create a baby for a dead
man. He refused to consider it seriously. He couldn't face it, if
the truth be told. But still he wanted to bind her to him. He
wanted her forever no matter why she'd chosen him. Perhaps
that was love and he was too jaded, too skeptical, too much a
fool, to recognize it? All Kellen knew with certainty was that he
didn't want to be alone.

He could be happy here in this valley with Tessa and his child
—his only child. She was too young to remember the scandal
that drove him from his birthright; the deceit that in the end
forced him to accept responsibility for a child not his own. It
made him fearful to risk his heart openly again. But he could
make Tessa love him if he only had the time. She was a stubborn woman. For whatever reasons, she'd hidden her pregnancy
from him. She would fight him all the way. He'd have to move
decisively and fast. She was his—that was as close as Kellen
could come to admitting that he loved. He would have them
both, mother and child. It would take all the strength of will he
possessed to overcome Tessa's stubborn refusal to be his. Kellen
didn't like the role he foresaw for himself in the days to come;
but he would pursue it with single-minded dedication. His
whole future depended on the outcome of his strategy.

When Tessa woke, Kellen was no longer beside her and she
sat up, suddenly chilled in the air-conditioned bedroom. Was
that what had brought her back from the hazy edges of sleep?
she wondered, vaguely distressed by formless imaginings. Or
was it a bad dream? Outside, the light was pearly dawn-gray, so
it must be very early still. Or had the rain clouds lingered along
the river and hid the morning sun? It didn't really matter. She
wasn't curious enough to get up and look outside or even turn
her head to stare at the bedside clock. Tessa was too satiated,

too contented with loving, to ponder the questions of time and weather. The only thing of importance was her lover's whereabouts and that small mystery was soon solved.

"Good morning, Tessa." Kellen appeared in the bedroom doorway and moved to tower over her. He was dressed and wide awake. Tessa glanced at the floor; only a damp circle on the carpet remained where they'd dropped their clothes.

"Your shirt is dry," Tessa said thickly, fighting off the dregs of sleep. "How did that happen?" He looked rakish and undeniably handsome in his clear gold, open-necked shirt with a day's growth of beard shadowing his strong jaw and chin. Tessa recalled its faint scratch on the skin of her breasts and the satiny smoothness of her waist and inner thighs. Her cheeks darkened and she was grateful for the poor light. Would her mind never cease to dwell on Kellen's abilities as a lover?

"Quite simply. I found your clothes drier downstairs. Thank goodness your kitchen isn't all antique." Tessa looked up quickly. His voice was harsh, businesslike. Where was the man who'd held her so tenderly through the long, stormy night. Who had whispered all the lovely things she wanted and needed to hear. Who compared her skin to the glory of the moon and stars, her eyes to a valley of aspens, her lips to the taste of cool springwater on a hot, sunny day? He certainly wasn't standing beside her at this moment. Tessa's laboring brain began to strengthen her neglected barricades with haphazard frantic haste. She didn't know what weakness to throw her artillery behind but she sensed a monumental battle in the offing.

"It's time to talk, Tessa," Kellen directed, sitting on the side of the bed, depressing the mattress along her thigh. "I have to get back to the house before anyone discovers I'm gone and Web comes after me with a shotgun."

"He'd never do that," Tessa defended, scooting up on the pillow. "You won't have any trouble getting in, we don't lock our doors around here." She felt more his equal sitting eye to eye. Tessa wished she were not still naked beneath the sheet she held to her breasts. It was Kellen the predator who sat beside her now, alert to any sign of weakness. Tessa raised her chin in defiance.

"I'll remember that." He didn't lighten the statement with his twisting smile, evidently sensing her small show of resistance. "I want you to come to the courthouse with me as soon as it's convenient." He met her puzzled green gaze and held it with a level blue stare.

"Whatever for?" Tessa murmured, her throat suddenly squeezed too tight to speak normally.

"To arrange for our wedding license," Kellen returned coldly. What had happened to the caring, loving man who'd taken her so tenderly, so totally last night? Had she only imagined him? This was the cold, blue-eyed stranger she dreaded. The adversary Tessa found it so hard to defend against.

"We're getting married," he repeated, as though for the benefit of an exceptionally dull-witted inferior.

We are going to get married. Not, will you marry me, Tessa. Or even, I want to marry you. Only, we are going to get married.

"No, we are not!" Tessa answered bravely, swallowing the coppery taste of terror in her mouth. An hour ago, five minutes ago, she would have wanted to hear those words more than any in the world. But not now. Not from this gimlet-eyed stranger. "No, we are not," she said again for emphasis, for courage. "There is no reason to be married only because I'm pregnant. I'll raise the baby alone as I've planned from the beginning."

"You'll marry me, because the child is mine," Kellen stated.

"No . . ." Tessa was too shocked to form reasonable arguments to diffuse his ultimatum. All her silly girlish dreams of a relationship with her baby's father crumbled to ashes around her. She'd been foolish to indulge in them at all.

"No?" Kellen mocked her throaty croak. "Are you trying to go back on your story of last night, my sweet conniving madonna? It won't work. You can disclaim it's my child now and for all eternity and I won't believe a word you say."

Tessa stared in mute horror. He wanted her baby. He meant to have him even if it included taking her into the bargain. "No, I'm not changing my story. I've admitted you are the biological father." Tessa blushed a pale rose as he stared her down, one dark brow arching toward his hairline. She faltered under his continued scrutiny, recalling her own voice, husky and aroused, pleading for his love, assuring him as his lips curved arrogantly against the budding dusky peak of her excited breasts—that anything and everything he gave her could never in her wildest

144

dreams be described as microscopic. Tessa winced, cleared her throat, and began again.

"If there is to be any further relationship between you and my child, it will be on my terms. Marriage is not included in the bargain."

"We have no bargain, Tessa," Kellen warned her ominously. "I want you answerable to me legally. Don't push me too far. You used me. Evidently with the express purpose of begetting a child. I don't like to be used."

"I didn't mean to hurt you. . . . You were never to know the gift you gave me. . . ." Tessa's eyes were huge pools of green-shaded misery. She bit her lips to keep them from trembling. The small pain was salutary. She had to keep her anger up front or tears would ruin her chances of making Kellen see reason. "Things just got out of hand. The physical act got out of hand. I intended—" She swallowed hard, mortified that she should have to explain her actions.

"To use that poor ass Gelbert as stud," Keller finished crudely.

"Yes." Her spine was stiff and straight. Tessa clutched the sheet with hands whose knuckles showed pale white in the morning light. "I wanted a baby very much. I'm going to be a good mother. But I needed a man and you scared him off." Tessa's spirits returned in a stinging rush of adrenaline that sent her pulses rocketing.

"You were ready to scream bloody murder when I showed up. I knew keeping an eye on you for Magda would only lead to trouble. I should never have trusted you that night but you looked so innocent—so loving. You do something to a man's brain. Short-circuit his common sense. . . ." Kellen made a gesture that seemed curiously as though he admitted defeat on some point Tessa couldn't grasp. "It hardly matters now. What's past is past. The child you carry is mine. I claim him." Tessa watched his strong lean hands curl into fists. "This baby will be a Sterling."

"A Litton," Tessa retorted hotly, rising up on her knees in her agitation. The sheet slipped to her waist and she didn't bother to cover her splendid nakedness. All her silly dreams of the night past eroded like a barren stretch of riverbank in a flood. She had hoped they might begin to build a future that would with patience and growing mutual trust overcome the hurdles they faced in this strange relationship and blossom in a love that could one day include marriage. Such foolish fancies, so easily shattered.

"Not a Mallory?" A muscle jumped in short jerks along Kellen's hard jaw.

"No . . . this child has nothing to do with Jacky." At least she could tell him something with total honesty. She had had to learn to live again, but Jacky was now part of the past. It salved a small part of her pain. "I wanted this baby for myself."

"I'm glad that at least is settled." He sounded oddly triumphant, back on the attack.

"My daughter will be a Litton. She'll be strong and resilient. I'll provide all the stability and continuity a child needs to grow and prosper. Alone."

"You seem to have overlooked something in your grand design, my sweet," Kellen went on, reaching out to run a hand over the heaving curve of her breasts, and lower, branding a line of fire over her rounding belly to the downy triangle between her legs. Tessa slapped at his roving hand, dragging the sheet back up to her chin. "The usual payment for the services of the stud is pick of the litter. Since you're roughly five months pregnant and not very big, I'd say it's a safe bet to guess there's only one bastard in your belly."

"Don't dare use that term," Tessa flared, tossing her gold-brown hair in an agitated negative shake of her head. "It's archaic . . . it's barbaric. . . ."

"It's a fact," Kellen grated. "I don't want my son—"

"My daughter," Tessa broke in on his words with a rude hiss.

"I don't want my child raised a bastard," Kellen continued grimly, ignoring her outburst. "I'll petition for custody if necessary. Have you declared unfit to raise a child on moral grounds."

"It won't hold up," she sniped more bravely than she felt. Her worst nightmares were coming true.

Kellen shrugged, an elegant lifting of his shoulders, the muscles rippling beneath the thin cotton shirt. "It may not. But I have another weapon. For the last dozen years I've had little else to do than make money. Lots of it. Add to that the prominence of a name that goes back to the Founding Fathers. I can provide a much better life for the child. Financially and socially."

Tessa's head whirled in a dizzying cyclone of kaleidoscopic images. Kellen didn't want his child raised a bastard. How ironic. She wanted to ask him what his reasoning for refusing to claim his other child had been. And as quickly as those words formed in her reeling intellect, there came the answer. Because the woman who carried that child tried to trap him—force him to give the child his name. He had acted according to type. She, Tessa, on the other hand, attempted to keep a child from him. Conversely, true to form, he wanted it. It was elementary psychology.

"You can't have my baby," she cried, in sudden fear that she'd pushed him too far. Often she sensed danger in Kellen; she didn't want it directed at her nurturing body. Tessa cradled her arms across her stomach protectively, bowing her head.

"Tessa." Kellen rose from the mattress, leaving her again at a disadvantage. A spasm of pain crossed his angled features and was quickly replaced by blank austerity. "Look at me," he ordered brusquely. Tessa craned her neck to look up at him rebelliously.

"I'll leave here, take my baby where you can't find me," she threatened recklessly.

"You won't leave Web or these vines. Give up, Tessa, bow to the inevitable. I won't make unreasonable demands on you."

She laughed hoarsely and took a ragged breath. "You *are* making unreasonable demands on me. You don't love me. How can you want to be married?"

Kellen ran his fingers through his thick black hair in frustration. It was too dim for Tessa to see the fine tremors coursing through his hand. When he spoke, the words were low and strained. "Would you believe me if I did tell you I loved you?"

"Love me!" Tessa's voice rose nearly to a shriek. Racking, screaming pain tore through her heart. "How could you expect me to believe that when you've threatened to take my baby?"

"That's why I didn't say it," Kellen answered quietly.

"I won't marry you," Tessa hissed through teeth that chattered despite her efforts to keep from betraying her fear. She rocked back and forth in mental agony. She refused to look at Kellen again.

"I can't offer you what you seem to want, but consider the alternative, Tessa. I'm not bluffing. I intend to have my child, with you or without you." He waited inexorably for her answer, a dark menace in the cool dawn.

"No!"

"Then I suggest you see your lawyer as soon as possible. I'll let you know when I've chosen mine."

CHAPTER TEN

For Tessa the next several days passed in a strange duality—divided equally into hours of torment and hours of ecstasy. During the day, when the sun was a bright, molten ball in the sky, she avoided Kellen with every ploy she could devise. It wasn't as formidable a task as she had feared. Mornings he spent in the vineyard or the winery; in the afternoons he disappeared in the direction of the city. Tessa's heart leaped into her mouth whenever she heard his rented car leave the drive, or the telephone ring. Was this the day he made good his threat to steal her baby? Worry ate away at her serenity, leaving her edgy and restless.

But at night she entered a parallel universe where everything was reversed. As the sun went down over the edge of the world, as the locust song gave way to monotonous chirrups of crickets and the tuneless piping of tree toads, her fluctuating moods collided head-on, hunger and longing winning out over unease. Kellen would come to her and she couldn't deny him.

Yet it was always in darkness. When even the moon chose to hide her light. Only then did it seem they could put aside the antagonisms that multiplied in the sun. In the cool quiet of her room Kellen gloried in her touch. And Tessa in his. They explored each other's bodies with amorous abandon, enjoying the taste, the scent, the contrast in texture, between his hair-roughened, angled contours and her silky softness and conforming curves. They didn't speak—their precarious truce holding—only exchanged whispered endearments, more sighs of pleasure, extensions of erotic caresses, than spoken sound.

Tessa lived for those brief moments when she could pretend to be loved and cherished by the tall, dark stranger who had so altered her life, and her outlook on the future. She wanted noth-

149

ing more in those hours than to fall asleep each night of the rest of her life in Kellen's arms.

Yet when she awoke, she was always alone. Her clamoring heart and conscience would begin to torment her again. They had no future together, she would remind herself. She was only storing up heartache and sorrow. Because Tessa knew, out in the world beyond the quiet neutral zone of her room, Kellen would have retreated once again behind a cold unbreachable barrier of iron will.

It was clear she faced emotional blackmail. Kellen was breaking down the crystal wall of her resolve with his sensual black-velvet assaults on her will, and the cold reason-confusing terror of his daylight threats of legal action. She couldn't win this lopsided war. All the odds were stacked in Kellen's favor. If Tessa agreed to marry him she would surely die of missing his love. He obviously couldn't—or wouldn't—offer her that part of him. And if she didn't agree would he take her child? Kellen wasn't a bluffing man.

Tessa didn't believe the intense physical appeal they felt for each other could survive the pressure of a forced marriage, or sustain a long-term relationship of itself alone. And if Kellen did concede to her desire to remain single, she would still be bound to him—perhaps for eternity—by that same overwhelming, devastating physical desire he aroused in her. But to be deprived of her child was the most terrifying scenario of all.

She could envision herself in a terrifying court battle, fighting for custody of her baby. His lawyer—the best that money could buy—would argue that she was an unfit parent on moral grounds. She'd seduced his client with the express intent of getting pregnant—of ripping off a baby—he would say, looking sternly in her direction. There were many women who became pregnant deliberately to force the father to accept financial responsibility for them and their child. He would insinuate she was one of them. That situation did happen frequently. But it had never been her intention. Yet how could she prove that? It was their word against hers.

Kellen's own questionable past might never enter the testimony. Far stranger, more unjust occurrences happened in courtrooms when clever lawyers argued points of law. Tessa was an unmarried woman, with centuries of bigoted prejudice weighing against her. Kellen was rich, socially prominent, highly successful. He could give his child everything.

Most people would look at it that way, find that her love for her baby wasn't enough to mitigate the handicap of her situation. Kellen was prepared to prove that he would provide the kind of advantages any child should have. Would that be enough? Could he take her baby away?

"Stan, do you have a moment for a small consultation?" Tessa questioned diffidently, bending to give a quick, hard hug to each of Laura's towheaded youngsters before they ran off to continue the game of interplanetary hide-and-seek her arrival had interrupted. Several times Tessa had pondered, with their parents, the peculiarities of heredity that produced for the couple a pair of blond children when Laura's fiery red locks and Stan's thinning brown pate held no golden tints. Her baby would have coal-dark hair and cerulean eyes like its father. Tessa summoned a smile for the children and waited for their father to speak.

"I always have time for you, Tessa. You're my favorite client. How did you come to find me here?" It was the day after her regular prenatal appointment. Laura had been too preoccupied with a waiting room full of patients for Tessa to confide her fears; Web was still too concerned with the Rieslings to burden him further. His health was too important to Tessa to risk it. She intended to rely on her own resources entirely, yet she needed to talk to someone. The infusion of courage Stan could provide would help her make her momentous decision.

"Your secretary said you were here with the children today." Tessa took the seat Stan motioned her to and waited as he reached out, gathering a squealing, giggling child under each arm. He deposited his son in the doorway leading to his playroom.

"You're right," he hollered, hoisting Megan into her playpen. "Laura's snowed under with this flu bug. It's rampant. The kids' nanny is suffering in solitude upstairs. I'm suffering in bedlam down here. Stay put while I talk to Aunt Tessa," he ordered in a practiced, no-nonsense father's voice. "Now what can I do for you, mother-to-be?" He sighed in mock exhaustion and dropped into his swivel chair behind a dusty, cluttered desk.

Stan was a wonderful father. Would Kellen be the same? Would she ever have the chance to know? Tessa pulled her random thoughts back to the subject at hand. "I don't have to name the father of this child on any document if I don't wish to do so. Isn't that correct?" Tessa made the question as casual as possible.

"No." He answered her as patiently as he might the children. They had been over this before when Tessa picked up her simple, explicit will and guardianship papers. "You don't have to name the father on the birth certificate. But I've already pointed out to you that the county officials won't be pleased. Bureaucrats like every *t* crossed, every *i* dotted. Are you having second thoughts? Do you still believe leaving the father's name blank is the best course to follow?"

"Yes." Tessa failed to meet his shrewd brown gaze. "I don't want the father to have any claim to the child."

"I see." Stan whistled through his teeth, balancing his swivel chair on two legs as he contemplated the acoustic tile on the ceiling. Tessa was sure he'd read a great deal of meaning into her words. Stan was a hard man to keep things from. And he was her friend. She felt a quick sting of shame at her evasions.

"What if the father finds out about the child—and recognizes him as such. Recent court cases have held that the biological father has equal rights with the mother in custody and visitation. Has that happened, Tessa?"

"No . . . no . . ." she fabricated. Tessa still wanted to solve the impasse privately, between Kellen and herself, if possible. It was essential to her image of herself as a successful, reasoning human being. A woman capable of raising a child alone. The prospect was decidedly less appealing than it had been a few short weeks before. "It wouldn't do any good to deny the man is the baby's father if that should happen?" She smiled brightly to show her unconcern. The muscles of her face were as taut as bowstrings. She was sure her smile was closer to a grimace.

"I'm afraid not anymore," Stan explained, tapping a pencil against his forehead, still balanced precariously on two legs. "Blood tests are now between ninety and ninety-nine percent effective in positively identifying the father of a child." He brought his chair back to the floor, emphasizing his next phrase. "Not only in disproving paternity. Add to that proof of cohabitation and intention to provide for the child and most courts will find in his favor."

"Give him sole custody?" Tessa's fingernails carved half moons into the leather armchair where she sat.

"Sole custody? Good heavens, no." Stan was a mild-spoken man. "Whatever gave you the idea we were speaking of sole custody?" He watched her with a level, unblinking stare. Stan was a good man to have in her corner if it came to a legal showdown with Kellen. Tessa took solace from the thought. "I assumed we were talking, hypothetically, of visiting rights and parental custody situations. Proving a mother is unfit to rear a child takes a lot more cause than the fact that the child was conceived and born out of wedlock. Although to be scrupulously honest all these circumstances we've just discussed would enter into a judge's decision if that situation should ever arise. But what it sounds like to me is a bona fide case of the single-mother heebie-jeebies."

"That must be it." Tessa laughed, relieved he didn't probe further. "You must admit I'm swimming against the current. I guess I'm entitled to a few misgivings and a slight bout of paranoia now and then."

"Hormones?" Stan inserted dryly, causing them both to laugh.

A few minutes later Tessa stepped out into the fading daylight, her pulse quickening as she counted down the hours until Kellen would come to her. Had she reacted too strongly to the situation as Stan suggested—although for the wrong reasons? There must be an equitable way out of this predicament. One that wouldn't leave her with a broken heart? That possibility was much harder to predict accurately. Yet there must be a solution. She had to trust in her own resources and stay the course.

Tessa looked up from the welter of newspaper, paint stripper, and steel wool that littered her deck. Kellen leaned negligently on the redwood railing, studying her kneeling form with narrowed blue eyes. He wore work clothes, snug-fitting faded jeans

153

and heavy shoes, a stained, buff-colored shirt that nonetheless bore the marks of an expert tailor. He'd come upon her so quietly Tessa hadn't known he was near.

"Have you been watching me long?" she asked, green eyes widening, her face flushed becomingly though the deck was shaded from the late-afternoon sun.

"Only a few moments. You were too absorbed in your restoration project to look up. I see you found my offering," he stated lightly, inclining his dark head toward the antique cradle she was preparing to refinish. Kellen's eyes were bottomless pools of reflecting blue that gave nothing away.

"Yes. But I thought my fairy godmother left it on the doorstep," she riposted with a rare soul-catching smile. "How did you know I wanted one for the baby?"

"A lucky guess?" His answering smile was quizzical.

This morning when she'd stepped outside and found the low hand-carved cradle on the deck, Tessa had resigned herself to having Kellen in the baby's life. It was a peace offering of sorts, she realized; it was also the straw that broke the back of her resistance. Kellen could have ordered an expensive replica and never missed the cost. Or chosen something so inappropriate that Tessa could have refused it outright. He did neither of those things. Instead he had taken the time and effort to find this beautiful example of the carver's art. He must care for the baby if not her.

"I'm afraid it's in pretty bad shape," Kellen went on, scowling down at the hooded cradle. "It looks worse in this light."

The wood was scarred and dented. In one spot, Tessa had discovered the indentations of small teeth. Several layers of pastel paint still adhered to the surface. But she had no problem looking past those defects to the pure lines and expert craftsmanship that lay beneath, confident that they could be restored to prominence. Kellen must have seen that potential, too.

"It's a lovely old piece," Tessa murmured, picturing mothers with their infants back through the years. She stripped off her rubber gloves, standing to rest the persistent ache in the small of her back. "Thank you very much for finding it for us." She patted her stomach, outlined under a faded plaid shirt of Web's. It was strained across her middle and she hoped the open zipper of her disreputable old jeans wasn't outlined also. This was her regular painting outfit, as the many-colored splatters testified. It would not be much longer, she realized ruefully. Tessa tugged at the shirttail self-consciously. "It's oak," she rambled on, slightly embarrassed at her display of emotion. Next thing would be tears if she wasn't careful. "It's perfect for the baby's room." Her voice was low and musical with a faint tremor as she bent forward to run a hand over the rolled edge of the cradle. The movement set it to rock gently.

"I thought you would want to refinish it yourself. But the proprietor of the antique shop will have it done professionally if it's too much trouble."

"Oh, no," Tessa answered impulsively. "I'm caught up in the lab and Web won't let me back in the vineyards as long as you're still spraying. I've needed some work to do with my hands. There is something so satisfying about reclaiming a fine old piece of wood. I enjoy it."

"As you've enjoyed restoring your home, remaking it into a fitting showcase for your talents and personality?" Kellen asked, coming up the steps to take her in his arms. Tessa didn't know how to react. It was the first time they'd touched in daylight since the storm. His hands on her skin challenged her and the reckless, soaring feeling stirred in her veins. What harm could it do to be held in his arms for a little while? She nodded acquiescence.

Tessa was more sure of herself as the days continued to add up, and Kellen did nothing further to bring her protective maternal instincts into play. Her mother's words returned to her—often at inappropriate times. She'd been right, as mothers so often are. Tessa did owe Kellen some claim to his child. It was too risky to refuse him all his rights; she was sure of that now. In her heart she didn't want to. With each passing day, Tessa yearned more and more to share with him the miracle of this new life they had created.

She knew her reasoning was inconsistent, based on feelings and not logic. But Stan's cautions had pointed out the folly, the possible grave consequences, of her earlier stubborn course. Today nothing was the same as it had been before Web's phone call to her in Indiana. If she had stayed with her family, never returned to see Kellen again and risk discovery of her pregnancy, she could have followed her master plan. But that was not the reality. Now she had to play by an entirely new set of rules. Kellen's rules.

Yet she couldn't marry without love. His love, complete and unencumbered. It was pride and the painful memories of losing love—of not being able to make love stay—that kept her from surrendering to him completely. For Tessa the problem now was to keep Kellen the father separated from Kellen her lover and the man she secretly loved.

It wasn't easy when he kept her in such a state of perpetual turmoil and unease—as his sudden appearance was doing now. For the last two long, hot nights he hadn't come to her, although Tessa lay awake until birdsong waiting for his step on the stairs. Yet he left the baby's cradle on her deck—as an offering. A gift of love for his child. She was convinced of that. What was the best course for all of them? Kellen was a puzzle to which she lacked a key. A puzzle to which she feared there was no solution.

He wanted her and yet he didn't. She wanted to love him, to allow him to be a father to her child, to be a family. Yet she was afraid to tell him so. Tessa dared not dwell on the intricacies of the situation for too long. Her head and her heart would explode from the strain. Other than her deeply hidden, self-deceptive fantasy of hearing Kellen say that he loved her and wanted to spend the rest of his life with her, she could only anticipate stolen days and bits and pieces of his life, those times when he was with his child. It was the most she could hope for. It was not a great deal to sustain her heart through the next fifty years.

"Come back, Tessa," Kellen whispered as her eyes focused on her surroundings once again. "You're a million miles away."

"I was." She smiled, nonplussed. Rapidly she cast back in her thoughts for the subject they'd been discussing. "This house needed rescuing just like the cradle," Tessa told him seriously, corraling her meandering fancy. She pushed at a recalcitrant strand of brown-gold hair with her hand. Her eyes were captured and held by the reflecting surfaces of his the moment she made contact.

"Rescuing humans—as well as inanimate objects—from destruction, giving them new hope and new purpose, fits your outlook on life, does it, Tessa?" Kellen's voice was low and dark, raising the gooseflesh on her arms. Tessa didn't attempt to fight its spell.

"I suppose you could say that. Helping people is the way I've lived my life. It's why I entered nursing. It's the way I'll raise my child."

"Your values and your roots. They mean a great deal to you."

"Of course. And Web, my family, and Vinifera. My loyalties go deep. Where is your home, Kellen? Not Sterling Hills, I know that's where you were raised." He frowned aside the personal question but Tessa plowed bravely on. She needed to know these things if he was to play a role in her baby's life. And she needed to know them for herself, for the image of him she was building in her mind and heart. The image of a man, always alone—encased in solitude.

"I have a place in New York. In Greenwich Village, as a matter of fact." Kellen grinned. "I don't spend much time there, actually. Magda always finds a room for me at San Luis when I need it. I'm a troubleshooter, Tessa. I go where I'm hired to go. But someday I'll be able to settle down."

He would settle down soon—with some beautiful woman, she mused. They would have everything. Everything but a child together—and they might want hers. Permanently.

Tessa couldn't bear to think of that. She must have some kind of arrangement with him now. One they could both live with. Not a sterile marriage, she couldn't endure that. But she could grant a nominal concession of visiting rights. Holidays, summer vacations, when the baby was old enough to leave her.

It made her soul ache to consider so far into the future. And always in the end Tessa saw herself alone. Waiting. That's not how she had dreamed it would be when she started her quest. But no one told her raising a child was a long series of partings. No one told her how great the longing to share this life-altering experience with the baby's father would be. It was something every woman must discover for herself. She hadn't considered that reality until today.

"Tessa, we have to talk. Make some kind of arrangement." Kellen broke into her wandering thoughts. "I can't stay much longer. I have to return to California to finish my business there. I want your answer soon. Today. It's too easy to forget everything else when I hold you like this. That's why I've stayed away—to give us both time to adjust—but it doesn't help. I still want you and I want my child. Both of you together —a package deal."

"I know you think you want us both, Kellen, but why?"

"This is why." His mouth came down on hers with strong, gentle force. His lips brushed over the moist, dewy sweetness of her, coaxing, teasing her to open to him. His hands settled lightly on either side of her throat, exerting a slight pressure until she could feel her pulse rushing against his palm. He smelled of rich black earth, hot sun, and sweat. Tessa's arms came around his waist with no hesitation, feathering light caresses along the tapering, flexing muscles of his back, straying lower to outline the tight leanness of his buttocks. How good his mouth tasted on hers, how welcome his exploring, probing tongue and the uninhibited ease with which she could return the invading kiss.

"I see your point." The contact left Tessa so dizzy she had to cling to Kellen for support. "We're intelligent people, aren't we?" she questioned in a husky, breathless voice. "We can carry on an important conversation about the baby's future without falling into my bed." She was shaky and weak in the knees. Tessa wasn't sure she believed her own words. "I serve an excellent cold salad supper. . . ." She trailed off, stunned by the intensity of need in his dark blue eyes.

"To hell with food," Kellen answered shortly. His breathing was as uneven and ragged as her own.

"I'm hungry," Tessa replied saucily, determined to keep her wits about her. If he took her to bed now they'd never settle anything. She would cave in to his demands, end up his hostage wife. She must remember she had become the means to his ends. "And I'm dirty." Her voice was shrill and Tessa swallowed to clear her throat. "So are you for that matter. Come back in an hour and I'll wine and dine you. I serve Vinifera wine. . . ."

Kellen looked down at her for a long, concentrated moment, his eyes still smoldering with subdued passion, his hands tracing small suggestive circles on the inner skin of her wrist. Tessa

158

shivered, half in anxiety, half in delight. He lifted his shoulders in the expressive gesture Tessa was beginning to know well. "Then by all means this is where we will . . . negotiate . . . our child's future."

CHAPTER ELEVEN

Tessa struck a kitchen match and touched the yellow flame to a pair of tapers on the walnut trestle table. The sharp smell of burning sulphur permeated her dining alcove and she shooed it toward the open window with a wave of her hand. The small brick house darkened early when the sun passed behind the pines, and the candles made a nice romantic touch.

Romantic. Tessa took a firm hold on her soaring fancy. Her hopes had been on a ride of highs and lows the last hour. In the kitchen Kellen dealt with a bottle of Vinifera red wine—Blue Eye—a hybrid that did very well in the valley. The usual wayward lock of dark hair rested on his forehead, dislodged while he wrestled with the stubborn cork. Tessa reached up on tiptoe to smooth it away.

Kellen smiled down at her. The sexually arousing, heart-twisting smile that turned her bones to water. Allowing him back into the house and therefore back into her life—the reality that existed between sunrise and sunset—had been a mistake, Tessa decided, her spirits dropping like a mercury thermometer on a cold day. The gift of the cradle had lulled her misgivings temporarily, but nothing had actually changed. They were still adversaries.

The refrigerator door slammed shut on her reverie, punctuating Tessa's unease. Kellen placed the bottle of wine on the counter and reached out to take the cold, clear glass bowl of salad from her hands. Tessa stared at her handiwork critically. It was bright with fresh tomatoes, peas, and baby carrots against a dark background of endive and garden lettuce. Kellen never glanced at it as he deposited it beside the wine. "The Blue Eye needs to breathe. We can eat later. I want to talk to you now."

"I thought you said you were hungry." Tessa tried a smile but it deserted before it reached her lips. Her unruly heart beat a syncopated cadence against her ribs.

"I said I was hungry for you. But this subject is more important still." Kellen took her hand and pulled her close, trapping Tessa between the lean corded length of his body and the sharp edge of the countertop. Her nerves stretched tighter with each surge of blood through her veins while her body responded to the primitive appeal of Kellen's embrace. "There's something I have to tell you. . . ."

"I intend to give you visitation rights." Tessa rushed into speech, adamant that the conversation stay on track. "Is that what you want to hear?" She paused to clear her dry throat, wishing she had a glass of wine from the bottle behind her. She needed something to do with her hands so they wouldn't be drawn irresistibly to the collar of his shirt. "I was wrong to deny you any right to the child once you found out I was pregnant. It's not your fault my plan went awry." She gave up the struggle to keep from touching him. Tessa rested her hands against the carved planes of his chest, her cheeks tinted a deeper pink. "I wanted to blame you for making me share my baby. That's selfish and childish. Babies are a miracle of sharing all in themselves. I won't accept any financial support from you. But I can offer you access to your child. I'm sorry I tried to keep you apart." She looked down at the buttons of his camel-colored knit shirt. Its warm golden tones complemented his skin and contrasted vividly with his inky-black hair. The tiny irrelevant details distracted Tessa. It hadn't been an easy speech for her and not at all what her renegade heart wanted her to say.

"Visitation rights aren't enough, Tessa. I told you that the first night I stayed with you." Kellen was on the hunt again, sensing her weakening in his predator's way. "I realize you want to be independent. That your longing for this child is deep and your motives for becoming pregnant were sound. But I intend to marry you and make the child legitimate," Kellen said clearly, without a hint of softer emotion to take the edge off his words.

"My baby will be legitimate," Tessa retorted, goaded past discretion. She twisted in his arms, but Kellen only tightened his hold, quelling her small rebellion effortlessly. "I'm his legitimate mother," she sniped, her words darts of anger in the quiet room.

"Don't split hairs, Tessa," Kellen answered shortly. "You know as well as I do a child born out of wedlock is a bastard."

"Stop drowning me in semantics," Tessa cried, flinching away. The pleated folds of her fuchsia float dress swirled around her long, golden legs in a graceful curve as Kellen released her. "Stop throwing all these legal technicalities in my face." Her hands made agitated gestures in the air. "I wanted to create a beautiful, loving baby, to give him a happy life and all the love I have stored in my heart. All the rest of the world is concerned about is whether or not I'm married to his father." She laughed shakily and brushed past Kellen's arm to blow out the candles. Her appetite was ruined, her hopes of an amicable settlement dissolving like smoke from the snuffed tapers. Her heart ached from solitude. She was very much alone in this dangerous venture.

"Tessa." Kellen came up behind her and enfolded her in a warm, spice-scented embrace. "I'm not trying to criticize your reasons for starting this pregnancy. I've told you that. But I intend to claim the right to hold you like this. You and our baby together. I'm his father. I want to be proud of what I've given you. Even if it was unintentional on my part." Kellen chuckled low and deep, his breath hot and exciting in her ear. Tessa shivered as he turned her to face him. She found him almost irresistible in this mood. She avoided looking into his eyes but stared instead at the full, sensual curve of his mouth. "I want to lay my hand on your belly and feel the baby move inside you. My baby, our baby." He traced the outline of her figure with his palm. His hands on her body were gentle, sensitive, and inquisitive.

"You must understand, Kellen . . ." Tessa began, making one last attempt to keep to the chosen path. She shut her mind to the traitorous pleasure of his words—and his touch. They were meaningless taken out of context. But exactly what she needed to hear. He knew that. Tessa dared not succumb to her weakness for him, her burgeoning desire to keep him and their baby safe and happy for the rest of her life.

"Do you love me, Kellen? Love me enough to be faithful to

the vows you insist we exchange? To spend the rest of our lives together?" The tense silence that followed her unexpected words stretched out between them. She didn't know where she'd found the courage to speak them aloud. Her ears hummed with the whirring, clicking mechanical heartbeats of her kitchen.

When Kellen finally spoke, his words were low and she strained to hear. "I don't think I know what love is, Tessa. I feel committed to you and our baby."

"I know you do," Tessa sighed. The words settled over her like a shroud. "I've known that since you gave me the cradle. But it's not enough," she whispered sadly, tracing the curve of his lean cheek and the downturned curve of his mouth while his hands settled possessively on the crest of her hipbones.

"Not enough? You're a strange woman, Tessa. Most women demand a commitment."

"And they're fools," she murmured. "Commitment is precisely what love is not. Don't you understand?"

Kellen shook his sable head in puzzlement. "Tell me, lovely Tessa, so I'll know the difference between love and commitment."

"It's so simple. One word. Obligation." Tessa stared recklessly into his mesmerizing cobalt gaze. She could almost believe she saw sadness equal to her own. But that would only be a reflection of her emotion. "People make commitments because they've sustained an obligation. A sense of obligation isn't love. I had real love once. I couldn't make it stay. It wasn't my fault, although I blamed myself for Jacky's death for a long time. Now I won't settle for less than that kind of love again. Even if it means spending the rest of my life alone."

"So you decided to have a baby—on your own—to share your love."

"That's part of the reason. Time is running out. I wasn't in love. . . . I mean there was no man. . . ." Tessa stopped, squared her shoulders, and went on. "I love children. I've wanted babies all my life."

"We will have a child soon, Tessa. That's a good beginning to a relationship isn't it?" Kellen coaxed, capturing her stubborn chin between his thumb and forefinger, arching her neck to meet his shaded blue gaze.

"Kellen, you're making this so difficult for me." Tessa's voice broke and she bit her lower lip to keep it from trembling. It could have been the best beginning in some other relationship—but not this one.

"I'll have to show you then what we still can't communicate with words." Kellen folded her close to him, feathering her cheeks, her brows, the tip of her nose, with light tingling caresses.

Tessa's restrained, sharply curbed passion blossomed upward in a heated, swelling rush. He knew her weakness. She wanted him so badly, needed his strength to go on. Loved him so hopelessly. Hopeless—his last words proved that. They were worlds apart in understanding. It would create great difficulties sooner or later, and the baby would be caught between. She couldn't risk that. You couldn't overcome such a fundamental gap with kisses and caresses alone. Still, when he was with her, holding her, touching her, Tessa could almost believe it might be enough.

"Tessa, do you love me?"

The question came from out of the blue like a bolt of summer lightning. Tessa's mind reeled as the earth shifted on its axis. What could she say? Yes, I could love you. I do love you. What if she should take the dare? Grab onto the intangible ounce of courage she needed and launch herself into the void? Would she soar free or fall to her doom? Doom. Doomsday. Those three words—I love you—had the explosive power of a doomsday weapon in Kellen's hands. It would give him eternal, total control over her happiness, over the baby's future. Tessa was afraid. Much too frightened to show that vulnerability. Saying those words wouldn't enable her to fly, but they might clip her wings forever.

"I'll be a good husband, a good father, Tessa. You could teach me how to love." Tessa cupped his face in her hand, searching the solemn features for something to reassure her. Some sign to tell her she should do what he asked. Kellen lowered his head to nuzzle her neck enticingly.

Tessa's mind stretched upward to grasp the shining ring of courage. "Kellen . . ." The shrilling of the phone's bell stilled her tongue, cutting into her rush of thoughts.

"Don't answer it," Kellen mumbled against her throat. "I

want you to tell me how you feel. Now." Tessa couldn't ignore the mechanical summons. She'd never been able to allow a phone to continue ringing in her life. And it might be Web.

She stretched one golden arm across the barrier of Kellen's back and lifted the receiver from the hook. "Hello?" Her voice was low and bemused. Her thoughts still ranged far from the place she stood.

"Tessa? This is Stan Hunt. I think we need to have a long talk." He sounded serious, grave almost. Tessa could feel her spine stiffen and a quickening of her pulse.

"Stan, what's the matter?" Kellen's tongue followed the shell curve of her ear. He sensed how close she had been to surrendering that last dangerous knowledge into his keeping. But for Tessa the spell was broken. It had been replaced by unease. Something was very wrong.

"I had a visit just now from Silas McCormick. He wants to meet with us and . . . his client . . . tonight. At Vinifera."

"Silas McCormick?" The famous, controversial attorney's name was a byword in Ohio legal circles. "And his client?"

Kellen. Kellen was his client, of course. Alerted by the words and tone of her voice, he dropped his hands from her shoulders and attempted to take the phone from her convulsive grasp. Tessa shrugged him off without thinking, suddenly icy cold with fear.

"The one and only Silas McCormick," Stan grated in her ear. "What the hell's going on, Tessa?" She stared out the sliding glass doors with eyes blinded to the beauty of the scented, colorful garden as Stan continued speaking. "Counselor McCormick was very casual, very off-the-record. But he's also very interested in you. Everything about you from your credit rating down to your favorite restaurant. Was our little hypothetical question-and-answer session the other day, less than hypothetical?" Stan sounded impatient now, and Tessa cringed. She was no good at subterfuge. This whole disastrous state of affairs existed because she was such a poor liar.

"I'm sorry, Stan. I should have told you everything from the beginning," she apologized. Tessa couldn't bear to look at Kellen. Couldn't bear to have him so near. She stepped away. She had been within a life's breath of telling him she loved him. And he had betrayed her.

"Be careful, Tessa. I don't trust McCormick. I'd better get over to Vinifera as soon as possible and get all the facts. You can bet if his client is the father he wants more than visitation rights or he wouldn't have retained McCormick. Level with me, Tessa. Does the biological father know about the baby?"

"Yes." At least this conversation required simple answers. Tessa didn't know how much longer she could keep from bursting into frightened tears. Kellen watched her closely. When she'd backed away from him he no longer attempted to take her stiff-backed figure in his arms.

"Did you know the man was planning something like this?" Stan asked, exasperated.

"I was afraid it might happen," she confessed wretchedly. "I thought I could handle it myself." Tessa knew Kellen could see the misery deepening her emerald eyes to smoky pine. She turned her back to him, winding the phone cord around her fingers in distraction. "How soon can you get here, Stan?"

"As quickly as I can drive it. We'd better have our strategy planned before McCormick and his client pull in the drive."

"I'll explain everything. But up at the big house. Not here." Tessa replaced the phone in its cradle without saying good-bye.

"Tessa, you're going to have to let me explain . . ." Kellen began, pulling her hands away from her temples where she'd lifted them to massage the painful tension building in her head.

"Your lawyer has contacted mine as you probably gathered from the conversation," Tessa replied coldly, fending off his embrace with shaking hands. "What did you intend? To have them find us in bed together? Did you want me compromised so badly I'd gladly marry you or anything else to keep my baby? Is there a photographer hidden in my dressing room? You didn't even tell me you'd planned a meeting for tonight so I could have Stan with me. Why?"

"I hoped it wouldn't be necessary, that's why not. Nothing gets accomplished with two lawyers in the same room. That damned prima donna McCormick must have decided to run the show himself. There are papers I want you to sign, Tessa. I swear that's all. Your attorney didn't need to be notified at this point in the proceedings."

"Proceedings? Papers for me to sign? What are you talking about?" Tessa slipped through the sliding doors, almost suffocated by the warm closeness of the redolent kitchen. Panic welled up in her, cutting off her oxygen supply. She took several deep, sustaining breaths, leaning heavily on the redwood railing for support. She tried to order her thoughts but the wrenching pain of betrayal that squeezed her heart made it hard to think at all. It was the beginning—the opening shots fired in the battle over her child she feared more than death itself.

"I want this settled before I leave for California again. I meant every word I said." Kellen sounded angry and defensive in his turn as he followed her out of doors. He didn't try to touch her quivering body. Tessa's stubborn intractability had eroded his usual controlled reserve. "These papers have nothing to do with custody rights . . . they're for my own peace of mind."

"You liar!" Tessa rounded on him like a gold and peach fury. Her cheeks flushed a deep, dusky rose and her eyes shot emerald fire from beneath tear-spangled lashes. "You want all of him. You want my baby."

"Tessa. Don't say anything we'll both regret later. Stay calm. I will explain . . ."

"No, you won't," she hissed, backing away, poised for flight at the top of the steps. "I was willing to offer you everything you wanted. The right to see your child whenever you wished. Vacations . . . holidays. I would even have been your mistress, because God help us both, I can't seem to keep my hands off of you."

"I don't want you as my mistress," Kellen grated, closing the small distance between them. Tessa darted down the steps, throwing her words over her shoulder as she retreated in the direction of the big house and Web's comforting presence.

"No. You want me tied to you legally. Dependent on you for everything I have."

"I want you and our child to have the dignity of my name. What's so wrong with that? You're not the kind of woman to go through life as any man's mistress." Kellen nearly shouted the words. Tessa had never heard him raise his voice in quite that manner before. She faltered, slowing her steps enough to allow him to catch her hand. Kellen swung her to face him. Tessa continued to back away until her skirt snagged on the thorns of a rose bush. "Stand still." She halted, as he plucked at the captured skirt of her dress, freeing her. "You will be my wife." Again those one-syllable commands she found so hard to disobey. "You can stay here. Live at Vinifera. Never see me alone again, if that's what you wish. But there will be no more schemes like this one. Get that straight right now. If you want more babies they will be mine."

Tessa jerked her hand from his grasp, stung by the unconscious arrogance of his words. "I don't want you to touch me again," she croaked. It was another lie, as transparent as all the rest.

"Don't speak too rashly. I don't think one child is enough for you. Your instinct to mother goes too deep. This will be a marriage in name only—if you prefer. But it will be forever. I won't divorce you. And if you make a fool of me with another man I'll take the child."

"Don't insult me any further, Kellen Sterling. I'm not afraid of you." He'd awakened her maternal defenses. He had gone too far. Tessa suddenly felt strong enough to take on the world. She could bury the pain of her splintering heart under this adrenaline surge of courage that would help to keep her baby safe. She put the sudden image of Kellen, squatting beside the cradle, his big hands tracing wonderingly over the carved wood, out of her mind. More of his babies, the words echoed past restraining barriers. How dear they would be to her. But he didn't care. Not really. Not enough. "Why are you so determined to have this child? Is it revenge because I used you in California? I told you I was sorry. More sorry than you'll ever know. Your pride won't suffer from sharing me with other men. There will be no others. I'll never get you out of my system enough to make room for another relationship. That should be the perfect revenge for you, to teach a woman the kind of passion that she could never bear to share with another man. Why do you want to claim this child when you ran away from the responsibilities of the child you already have?"

Tears threatened her pain-bright eyes once again, smudging the outlines of the twilight garden. Tessa wanted to sink down on the gravel path and cry her eyes out. That's what she needed as the adrenaline surge faded, leaving her tired and drained. A good cleansing bout of tears. But tears were a sign of weakness in this male world and she couldn't indulge the urge. Tessa stood straight and tall, her face cold and proud in the fading sunset light. Kellen didn't say a word. He was an image carved of black oak; just as he had been that evening in Web's study. As Tessa watched, a fine tremor passed through him, as though he were in pain.

"How long have you known that?"

"Since the beginning. Why do you think I allowed you to make love to me?" Tessa said recklessly, needing to hurt him as his words hurt her. "I was aware you'd already fathered a child. That was my main consideration that night. Your potency," she explained venomously. It was amazing how quickly the tendency to cry disappeared when you were desperate to keep the lifeblood of your shattered heart from soaking into the ground at your feet.

"Tessa!" Kellen's voice was a snarl. "Don't push me too far. I've never hit a woman in my life but you are dangerously close to being the first, pregnant with my child or not. Who told you about this other child?"

"The seamstress at San Luis," Tessa confessed, cowed by the dark danger in his face. His hands were like lead weights on her shoulders. Tessa had come to the end of the graveled path. His grip tightened painfully. Any thought of breaking free died. She felt cheap and tawdry admitting her hidden knowledge of the scandal.

"Tell me what you learned." Kellen shook her once, hard, so that her head snapped back. Tessa glared at him defiantly. They were so close to the trellised silver lace vine near the lab that showers of tiny white petals drifted down over Tessa's head and shoulders like angel's tears. They clung to her eyelashes and the dark, curling hair on the back of Kellen's hands and wrists.

"She told me you are the father of your sister-in-law's child," Tessa hissed, truly angry now. "That your brother caught you together. Was it in your bed?"

"Keep going." His voice was inky menace. Tessa began to shake despite her anger. Kellen did look ready to beat her. But what emotion lurked deeper beneath the cold mask of rage? Tessa kept receiving short-circuiting vibrations from his tight-coiled body. Was it regret? Sadness? Her own responses were too overloaded to sort through the neural information rationally. "Your brother turned the poor girl out, she said. You denied responsibility and she was forced to file a paternity suit to get you to recognize her position. After that I . . . I don't know exactly what did happen." Tessa stumbled to a halt, her thick tongue tripping over the words. She didn't know what had happened next in Kellen's life. Her information was sketchy at best. Her thoughts seldom took her past the poor pregnant girl's feelings of anxiety and panic—of empathy for her predicament.

"After that I found myself the father of a son that isn't mine. And isn't my brother's," Kellen ground out between clenched teeth. "It's time you learned the truth, Tessa. All of it, for what good it will do either of us now."

"I can't understand what you mean," Tessa said, after a long, deep breath gave her lungs enough force to form the words. "Please tell me. Explain yourself. I'm so confused."

"The child you're carrying is the only child I've ever fathered."

"I don't understand. . . . The seamstress said it was in all the papers . . . your sister-in-law . . ."

"Is an amoral bitch," Kellen said, biting off each word as though they made a bad taste in his mouth. "She used me. She's used my brother for nearly fifteen years. I've been exiled from my home, estranged from my family for close to half my life, because of that woman."

"Her child isn't yours?" Tessa whispered. For the first time she had no trouble deciphering the emotions in his blue eyes. There was anger, so deep and profound it frightened her by its intensity. And pain—fundamental and long-lived. Tessa reached out to gather him close, her anger forgotten in a rush of love and compassion. She couldn't have stopped the comforting instinctive gesture even if her life depended on it. At the most primitive level of her existence it did.

"Don't pity me, Tessa. I can't accept that." His body was rigid beneath her caressing hands.

"You're not the kind of man any woman pities, Kellen Sterling," Tessa answered with complete conviction. From the beginning she'd known that a strong emotion existed between them—for days it had seesawed between love and hate. Love had won out. She would have to accept her fate from this point forward.

He took a long jagged breath, stepping into her embrace, twining his fingers through her soft brown hair, talking in a low, tightly controlled voice that held far more sadness than tears. Kellen stared through her, past her, to a place Tessa couldn't follow.

"I met Helena when I was nineteen. At Davis." The sentences were short and clipped—a litany of regrets. "Everyone there remembered my brother Derek. Most knew of my father. I let the attention go to my head, I suppose. Helena was several years older. She seduced me, and I was more than willing. She was the prettiest girl I'd ever seen, huge silver-blue eyes, freckles scattered over her nose, so tiny I was afraid to hold her too tightly for fear she'd break. I fell head over heels in love." Tessa stood quiescent, hardly daring to breathe for fear she would break the spell of his reminiscences. For years Kellen had kept his pain to himself. She didn't want to stop the fragile flow of words and jeopardize this chance of understanding what made him the way he was.

"I was so proud she'd chosen me to love. I took her home to meet my family at Christmas break my junior year. She flirted with my brother, charmed my mother, flattered my father. I never saw what was coming. She was always asking questions about Sterling Hills. The way it was run, the way it was financed, how it would be divided between Derek and me eventually. That should have been my first clue. But it wasn't. I was so besotted I just assumed she simply loved it as much as we did."

Although Tessa could guess what was coming next, she knew the telling of it was more important than any sympathy she could offer. Lancing a festering abscess was necessary before any healing could take place. She could only make the surgery as painless as possible.

"Sterling Hills belongs to my father and my brother," Kellen tried to explain. "It did then. It still does. When she discovered that, Helena began to back off from our affair. My brother is ten years older than I. He was already a skilled vintner when I was in high school. You just don't turn over an operation like Sterling Hills to a green kid. Helena grasped that fact almost immediately." Tessa nodded. She could do little else, held so tightly in his arms. "I had at least a year of college left, military service staring me in the face after that. Then a long apprenticeship.

171

Helena couldn't accept that. She didn't want to marry a penni-less boy. She wanted a man."

"You'd asked her to marry you?" Tessa looked up into his face, the carved lines harsh in the fading light. His smile was stark and bitter. "Countless times. She always said no. But so charmingly. Not that time. We fought. I went back to school. Helena didn't. She married my brother six weeks later. I was best man at their wedding."

Tessa's heart ached for the proud hurt boy inside the man in her arms. How difficult this confession was for him, she could only imagine. Around them evening sounds came alive. The air was hot and heavy and Tessa's back ached from her living bur-den and the strength of Kellen's arms around her. She didn't complain, tightening her own hold, relishing the contour of strong muscles under her hands.

"I stayed away from Sterling after that, except for one short trip home. After graduation I came back—just before I got drafted. Helena was so changed. Pale and drawn, not laughing or carefree. I thought perhaps it was worry over my brother's health. He'd been in a serious auto accident earlier in the spring that year."

"That was when you'd come home?" Tessa could see the direction his story was heading and her stomach churned with anger and disgust. She already hated Helena: an unscrupulous, ambitious woman, far different from the poor innocent girl Tessa had wrongly sympathized with for so many months.

"I was far off the mark about why she looked so ill. It was worry all right, but not for my brother's health. It was for herself. Helena was pregnant. She must have been bored stiff before the honeymoon was over. My family eats, sleeps, and lives for Sterling Hills. Helena thought she would be joining the jet set, not a family of hardworking vintners. She must have taken a lover while my brother was still convalescing."

"She told you that?" Tessa was appalled by the callous scheming of the woman who had shaped Kellen's distrust of all her sex.

"Of course not. But I had plenty of time to figure it all out for myself later, belly down in a stinking rice paddy."

"Go on, Kellen. Tell me the rest," Tessa cajoled as she might a reluctant child. He needed to put the anger into words and

172

purge it from his mind and heart as she'd done with her grief for Jacky.

"She wanted me to take her away. Said my brother didn't love her anymore, didn't want the baby. That she'd made a terrible mistake. She begged me to tell him the child was mine so he would set her free. It helped my bruised ego to believe she might still love me. But before she could twist me completely around her finger, Derek did find us together—just as your informant said."

Tessa flushed and failed to meet his shadowed, questioning look. She picked at one or two of the snowball petals that adhered to his shirt collar. "Were you making love to her?" She didn't know why she even asked. Helena was no longer a threat to her peace of mind.

"No! She was my brother's wife." Anger flared briefly in his cobalt eyes then died away. "Are you jealous, Tessa?" His mouth softened, relaxing the harsh lines, almost as if he sensed a turning point in her thoughts and feelings.

"I think I am," Tessa admitted softly. "Go on. I want to know the rest. I need to know."

Kellen nodded shortly and shifted his gaze to stare back into the past once again. The words came no more easily than they had before. "Helena told him the baby was mine. That we'd made love several times while he was in the hospital. She was so sure of me, and very convincing. She's even better at it now, but then she's had a lot more practice. My brother went crazy. I think he would have killed us both if he had had the strength. I couldn't fight him. I couldn't reason with him—so I left. Hell, Tessa, I was young. I looked guilty as hell. I didn't know what else to do. Derek wouldn't see Helena again. That's where her little plan backfired. When neither of us would accept responsibility for the child, she panicked, and filed a paternity suit. That's about the time the papers got hold of the story and played it to the hilt."

"Did you try to explain to your brother and your father?" Tessa could barely get the words past the lump in her throat. She was ashamed of herself. How wrongly she'd judged him. She'd based all her bias, all her reasons for doubting him, on lies.

"Just before I left for Nam, Derek had a relapse. Helena

173

came back to nurse him. Pregnant and sad eyed and very contrite. Derek fell for it hook, line, and sinker. She must have been frightened enough to behave herself for quite a while after the baby was born. She still takes every precaution to keep her affairs secret. I see to it she keeps in line. She married the wrong brother for the circles she wants to travel in. But she learned her lesson well. Being Mrs. Derek Sterling, of Sterling Hills, means more to her now than anything else. Far more than her son. She won't jeopardize her life-style."

"And your brother?"

"You won't let it go, will you, Tessa?"

"Not until you've brought it all out in the open." Her voice was soft but firm; inwardly she cried for the younger disillusioned Kellen.

"He wanted to know if it was my child. He said he could forgive us both if that was the case. He thought Helena always did love me more."

"Oh, Kellen." The quiet cry was filled with his pain.

"What could I say?" He gave a short, mirthless laugh that was a groan. "Helena watched the whole scene and never batted an eye. I admitted responsibility for the child. I couldn't break his heart by telling him it must be someone else's baby. It was my fault Helena ever came into our lives in the first place. I knew Derek would be a good father. He worships the boy. I signed over my rights in Sterling Hills to my brother to be put in trust for my son." Kellen's voice faltered on the last words. "Three years later Derek adopted the boy. I didn't change the arrangement. When I was home last month I got to know him. He's a good kid, Tessa. He'll be a good vintner some day. Telling the truth now would only make things worse. I don't even hate Helena as much as I used to."

"Does your brother know the truth?"

"I think he suspects. We never spoke of it. All the legal proceedings were conducted through our lawyers. He still loves Helena, she'll always be between Derek and me, not the boy. I've seen love make people do crazy things. That's why I've steered clear of any entanglements from then on. No involvements, no commitments—until now."

Tessa couldn't meet his gaze. Didn't see the longing and hope fade slowly away to be replaced by the deep angry bitterness she'd encountered so often before. Her thoughts turned far inward, chastizing herself for her lack of compassion, for all her vain self-serving judgments of Kellen's character. She'd never asked him to tell her these things; just gone blindly on believing the worst because it made her own chosen path easier, safer to follow.

"Maybe I do remember how it felt to be in love," Kellen said in the low, even tone Tessa intuitively shrank from. "I won't force you to marry me. Or even to see the child if that's what you want. For me loving was all pain; I can't take that again. All I ask is that you come to the house and sign those papers. It's a trust fund." He tipped her head back, forcing her to engage the steely blue eyes. "I fly a hundred thousand miles a year. I have no idea what arrangements you're making for his future. I want to make sure our baby's taken care of if anything should happen to either of us. Surely you can grant me that peace?"

"No, Kellen." She wanted to tell him not to speak of dying as though it were a release, not to equate loving with pain, but the words didn't come quickly enough.

One strong hand crashed into the palm of the other with a crack like a pistol shot. Tessa stepped back instinctively. "You win, Tessa. I won't ask you even that concession. I'm going to the lab and pack up my final reports for Web. When McCormick gets to the house I'll tell him to leave the papers. You can look them over with your lawyer when he arrives. Or burn them. It doesn't make any difference to me." He set her aside, causing another shower of sweet-scented white petals to cover them both. "I do love you, Tessa," he grated. "I just wanted to hear you say it first."

Tessa was alone, too stunned by his words to move from the spot where she stood. That was all he'd wanted, to hear her say first she loved him. They were both victims, afraid to admit to loving. Tessa because she had had it all and lost it. Kellen because he'd given his heart unwisely and had been betrayed so cruelly. They'd lived inside their separate strongholds for too long, each refusing to be the first to surrender. It was time to tell him she'd loved him almost from the first moment of meeting. Let him know how deeply she wanted to share the baby with him. That she was sure now as her mother had always been sure that a baby needed two parents. She was terribly afraid she'd delayed too long already.

Where had he gone? Tessa sorted back through the jumbled mass of recollections. Their conversation had been so emotionally charged, so enervating, she had trouble recalling his destination.

The lab, of course. Kellen was a professional. He wouldn't leave Vinifera without completing his work for Web.

Tessa flew down the walk as if she had wings. The door of the lab banged shut behind her. Only one light, above the work table, illuminated the cool stone-walled room. Close by, a beaker topped with a coiled glass tube bubbled gently over a Bunsen burner. Web was checking something, Tessa cataloged absently, he'd probably be back shortly to monitor his experiment. Tessa stood silently at the bottom of the stairs while Kellen shoved papers haphazardly into a leather briefcase. His back was turned to her, ramrod straight, unyielding.

"Kellen." She sounded too timid, too hesitant. She needed to be positive, so sure of herself he couldn't doubt her words or her sincerity ever again. What would be best? A baby needs two parents to love and cherish him? No, that didn't say enough. I want to spend the rest of my life with you? Better, but still not best. Tessa shook her head, her hair swinging around her cheeks like gold-brown streaks of light. Quit beating around the bush. It only takes one simple three-word declarative sentence. "Kellen." He spun around, his face bleak and shadowed in the dim light. Hard fists slammed down on the tabletop in frustration, his unnatural control snapped at last in a fury of pain and hurt.

"Damn it, Tessa! What do you want from me now?"

"Kellen, no!" Her startled outcry came too late. Whatever his frustrated words would have been, they were lost in the crash and splinter of breaking glass as the unstable shelving teetered and buckled under the battering vibrations of fists on marble.

Tessa's hands flew up to shield her face as a rolling metal beaker dislodged the Bunsen burner from its stand. Volatile, flammable chemicals erupted in a burning rain as they came in contact with the open flame. The force of one small explosion pushed Tessa into the wall with stunning force, leaving her dizzy and disoriented for several life-threatening seconds. The fumes were a greater danger than the flames; they filled the room, making breathing arduous. Her eyes stung and tears ran down her face.

"Kellen, where are you?" Tessa gasped, what had begun as a scream barely making it past her constricted vocal cords in a strangled whisper. "Kellen!" Only the crackle of flames answered.

Miraculously his voice came out of the spreading inferno, an oasis of calm strength in the maelstrom. "Get out, Tessa. Now!" He was backed into a corner made by the table and the wall—almost directly across the room from her. They were separated by a growing ring of fire.

For the first time Tessa had no trouble at all disobeying a command. "No. Not till you can come with me." The heat was intense. She coughed as each breath drew more acrid smoke into her straining lungs.

"I'll be out in a minute. As soon as I get my breath. This damn smoke." He shook his head as though to clear it. "Here, take this." The briefcase came sailing over the building wall of flame. He couldn't get out. Now or never. The hairs on the back of Tessa's neck stood up in terror. Kellen was trapped.

She clawed her way to her feet, blind hands seeking the fire extinguisher on the wall by the door. She had to get it down. She was too close to finding love again to be cheated by death a second time. With a wrenching jerk she freed the cylinder from its clamps. How did they work? Her mind screamed in silent frantic waves of fear. How many fire drills had she sat through in her life? The wire guard twisted off in her hands as she aimed it blindly into the smoke and heat. Kellen's figure was completely obscured by the dense smoke. The fire didn't appear to give off light in the darkened room. The flames seemed to have a life of their own, feeding off the feeble glow of the overhead light, sucking it into their orange-and-yellow hearts to feed off its energy and augment their own. Tessa squeezed the trigger and a heavy, smothering cloud of foam arced out into the room with the hiss of a thousand snakes. Flames sizzled and died under the suffocating blanket of chemical snow. Endless moments later Kellen dove through the small path to relative safety and grabbed the extinguisher from Tessa's singed hands.

"Get out of here before everything else on that shelf blows."

"I'm not going without you. . . ." Tessa gasped clinging to him for dear life. She had no intention of leaving without him.

"Stop trying to have the last word all the time. Get out for the baby's sake if not your own. Get Web. Call the fire department. But get out!" His voice was hoarse and raspy. The smoke was much worse. He couldn't survive alone for more than a few seconds.

"No. Come with me."

"Get the briefcase and get out. All the papers, all our research." Kellen coughed. "Go. I want my son born alive and healthy." His tone held no softness; he meant every word he said.

Tessa turned, bent to grasp the briefcase, and stumbled to the stairs. Kellen's last words had cut through to a deeply rooted maternal instinct. "I love you, Kellen Sterling," Tessa said fiercely. It was only a croak. She cleared her throat to try again, afraid he hadn't heard her at all.

"I know." Kellen smiled, his face darkened grotesquely by smoke and flames. "I know you do. Now do as I tell you, for God's sake." His words were lost in the dizzying nauseating whirl inside her head. Tessa crawled up the last few steps and opened the door to slip through. Not wide, no strong drafts to feed the flames.

Outside she tried to stand and failed. Voices and light confused her reeling senses. She hadn't been able to summon help. Why were they here?

Web's voice came out of the miasma, his big strong hands reached out to steady her. Laura's face bent over her. Laura? Stan's voice hollered roughly down the steps and Kellen's answered him faint but strong. The meeting. She'd forgotten, but their presence was the answer to a thousand silent, fervent prayers. Web took the briefcase from her protesting hands. "Kellen's inside," Tessa whispered, using the last of her reserves. "Help him. Don't let him die, Web, please."

CHAPTER TWELVE

With an impatient fist Tessa pummeled the feather pillows on her bed, adjusting them more comfortably behind her back, dissipating a small amount of nervous energy in the process. Satisfied, she leaned back and smoothed her flower-sprigged, mauve-colored nightgown over her expanding middle.

It was her wedding night.

In the adjoining bathroom the concentrated rain of the shower spray ceased, and mentally Tessa followed Kellen through the interesting—soon to be familiar—male rituals of brush and blow drier and splashing cologne. Fireflies flickered past her line of sight, their tiny blinking beacons nearly as bright as the running lights of barges on the river. Beyond her window, open to the unseasonably dry and cool August night, faint sounds of revelry floated on a summer zephyr.

For Web, who'd given her away and contended he'd known what was coming the moment he first saw them together in the morning room—"I've always been good at counting on my fingers and your traveling salesman story had a lot of holes in it, Tessa honey," he'd teased, taking her hand and giving her a quick peck on the cheek before the short ceremony—for Stan and Laura who'd acted as witness; for her brothers, their wives, and her mother, the small, happy wedding party continued.

Only Tessa had been banished to her room as early as the children. Even Kellen lingered, taking a few more minutes to speak with Frank and Web. Tessa was close to pouting.

In the five days since the fire she'd seen very little of her brand-new husband. Tessa fingered the wide gold band on the fourth finger of her left hand, letting her mind skip back over the press of that night's terrifying events. It was true Kellen never left her side for a moment after he emerged, smoke-blackened, coughing, and gasping, but safe and unharmed from the burning lab. Tessa's recollections of the next few hours were hazy at best, but it was Laura who'd taken over command of the confusion, directing everyone with calm efficiency.

"I'll bless you always for coming with Stan that night," Tessa had told her, accepting their wishes for future happiness after the brief ceremony. Both women were near to sentimental tears.

"Hormones," Laura sniffed, brushing off her thanks as she fumbled for a tissue in her bag. "I know you'll be happy for the rest of your lives. Who wouldn't be with a man like that!" the plump M.D. sighed, only half teasing. Tessa blushed as deeply as any new bride. "I think I'll talk to Stan about that new addition to the house," Laura went on with a sly smile in her gray eyes. "I have a feeling your obstetrical fees will keep me solvent for the next few years."

Laura could be flippant now, the danger was past, but Tessa knew how close she'd come to losing it all. A portable oxygen cylinder from Laura's car had relieved the tortured pain of her smoke-filled lungs. The fire was out; the ambulance summoned so quickly that almost before she knew it Tessa found herself in a hospital bed, hooked up to a bewildering array of monitors, sedated, and effectively silenced by additional supplemental oxygen. That unsatisfactory and uncomfortable state of affairs lasted two long days and nights.

Since her return from the hospital she'd faced the equally frustrating boredom of her room while everyone pitched in to restore the lab facilities to working order before vintage. Her family's arrival helped reduce the tedium of enforced solitude, but her mother's pointed "I told you so" looks and aggravating agreement with every word of caution Kellen uttered made Tessa want to scream. And she would have if it hadn't been so comical to see her strong-minded mother manipulated with such skill by her tall, dark husband-to-be. Margaret Litton swore she'd fallen in love with Kellen at first sight; just as her daughter had done, she added coyly.

On the thought Kellen appeared in the doorway of the bathroom catapulting Tessa back to the here and now with a rush of purely sexual desire. He was clad in nothing but light gray pajama bottoms that hugged his slender hips and enhanced, rather than obscured, the rugged virility of his body where they clung to his still-damp skin. Tessa squirmed against the pillows. It had been a long, long week since they had made love. She ached to belong to him once again. Hard work, her convalescence, and a gaggle of nieces and nephews underfoot had kept them apart as effectively as any chaperon could wish.

Tessa was heartily tired of being treated like a very pregnant, very fragile china doll. She was a woman, passionately and eternally in love with the man she'd married. When Kellen insisted on the formality of a wedding immediately, Tessa gave a good imitation of her mother's recent behavior, obeying his command with gratifying meekness, offering not a murmur of protest. Why bother? She wanted Kellen bound to her, legally and totally, for the rest of their lives.

Yet there were still obstacles she knew must be overcome. He had retreated some distance from her since the fire, when during the emotionally trying dangerous hours of that long night he'd kept her sane with random memories of his boyhood and dreams for their future together. After they knew she wouldn't lose the baby, he'd pulled back into his shell of reserve, his shield against too much caring, too much pain. Kellen, so strong on the outside, so giving—so truly vulnerable within. Tessa was saddened by the lingering evidence of his years of solitary pain. Tonight she intended to complete the healing process the fire had interrupted. But matters weren't proceeding quite as she had wished.

"I thought you'd be asleep," Kellen said casually, adjusting the window before sliding in beside her, close but not touching. He smelled of soap and clean skin. Tessa scooted near as he reached over to flick out the bedside lamp. "Laura says you need plenty of rest."

Tessa stared sightlessly into the image-spangled darkness near to tears. Kellen rolled over, pulled himself up beside her, and placed a light kiss on her nose. "Good night, Tessa, love."

It was the last low, hesitant word, spoken in the husky, deep burgundy voice, setting her mind afire, that opened the floodgates of self-pity. Tears overflowed, rolling down her face. After a few moments she felt Kellen's fingers on her cheeks. The bedside light sprang back to life. "Tessa darling, don't cry. What's the matter? Are you ill?"

"I'm fine." She sniffed peevishly. "It's our wedding night,"

Tessa wailed, as if that explained everything. She buried her head in the hollow of his throat; her arms circled his neck, holding him tight.

"Laura wants you to take it easy. We don't want any delayed aftereffects from the smoke and fumes you inhaled." His voice sounded strained. Kellen reached down and patted her stomach proprietarily as if she might have forgotten it was there.

Tessa sobbed louder, wetting his chest with her tears. "You are so damn smug because the baby is a boy, just as you said it would be. I shouldn't have let Laura go ahead with the amniocentesis. You only married me for the baby, after all."

"I married you because I can't live without you," Kellen said curtly. "And admit it. You went through with Laura's tests because we both wanted to be sure our baby is healthy and well, which thank God he is," Kellen coaxed, gathering her closer into the comforting circle of his arms. Tessa would have sold her soul for much less than his embrace.

"You're right," she sighed, stretching like a kitten before a fire. "Laura could have talked me into anything that night. I've never been so frightened in my life. Not being able to breathe, not knowing if the baby's oxygen supply was impeded also. I was terrified." Tessa shuddered at the nightmare memories. "Thank you for not leaving me alone, for telling me everything I so needed to hear, for keeping my hope alive."

"Shhh. Let's talk of something else. Get your mind off the fire, so we can get some rest. I have to leave for California early tomorrow. I can't put it off any longer."

It was the second worst choice of subject from Tessa's point of view, only slightly less upsetting than the fire. She sniffed dejectedly. "I don't want you to go, Kellen. I don't know how I can adjust to a nomad's life," Tessa confessed sadly. Leaving Web and Vinifera was a sad ache in her heart. "California tomorrow, New York next week, Europe the month after that. . . ."

"I wouldn't ask that of you, Tessa love. Your roots are too deep."

"I don't want to be here without you either," she said with complete lack of concern for the rules of logic. "I'll hate having you gone so often."

"I won't be gone more than a few days."

182

"You won't?" Tessa sat up, running her fingers along the angle of his jaw, feeling his lips curve into the sensuous inflammatory smile she adored. He kissed her fingers where they rested on his mouth. Tessa's tears dried miraculously, replaced by a shining light of passion. "Are you giving up consulting?"

"As of next week. I have a new job," Kellen boasted proudly. "Web's asked me to stay on. I'd like to. Vinifera's a pioneering effort, Tessa. One I want to be part of with you. We can travel as much as you wish—or as little. I'm more than ready to settle down. But I'd like to keep my hand in," Kellen admitted with a grin. "Consulting in the wine industry is pretty lucrative and—being the great businesswoman you are—I'm sure you'll agree new capital is always appreciated."

"Amen," Tessa caroled in return. "And as I told you once before, the winters here are long and cold. Can we do your consulting somewhere warm and sunny?"

"I think that can be arranged."

"Oh, Kellen. That's the answer to my dreams. The best of both our worlds." Tessa flung herself against him, but Kellen held her back.

"Careful, you'll hurt yourself."

So they were back to square one. "No, I won't hurt myself but I'm within an inch of smacking some sense into your thick head, Kellen Sterling," Tessa blazed, but the anger in her green eyes was playful.

"What do you mean by that threat, Mrs. Sterling," Kellen retorted. One eyebrow lifted quizzically as he entered into the spirit of her game, puzzled but anxious there be no more tears.

"I'll spell it out for you in words of one syllable so you will understand. This is my wedding night."

"Our wedding night," he interrupted maddeningly.

"Kellen!"

"Yes, dear." He settled back on his pillows, one arm behind his head, the other resting intimately between her parted legs. Only the thin material of her gown kept his touch from scorching her skin. Kellen watched her so intently that Tessa nearly stumbled over her next words, losing the thread of her teasing thoughts under his continued, arousing scrutiny.

"I was married, practically at a moment's notice—in my matron of honor's hand-me-down maternity dress."

"You were a lovely, albeit pleasingly plump, bride." His hand had stolen higher to capture an opulent rounded breast in a kneading caress.

Tessa gave him a sharp glance that melted into an audible sigh. She plunged on, leaning into his touch, ticking off her grievances with ivory-tipped fingers against his naked chest. "I was banished from my own reception like a small, sleepy child. Now you crawl into our marriage bed, kiss me on the nose like a maiden aunt, tell me to get some rest, you'll be back from California in a week—as if nothing is at all unusual about the situation."

"Your doctor told me . . ."

"My doctor, bless her, is very tipsy on Sterling Hills champagne. She won't remember a word she said by tomorrow morning." Tessa pressed against him with wanton seductive intent, her hands feathering light, bold caresses over his waist, tracing the long, corded line of his thigh, moving upward to rest possessively on the source of his power. His response was immediate and electrifying. Tessa felt the jolt through her entire body. "Kellen, I'm pregnant, not terminally ill. I love you. I ache for you. Please, let me show you how much I need you."

Tessa pushed the sheet away from his body, tugging at the drawstring of his pajamas, pushing the soft fabric down over his narrow hips as he lifted himself to facilitate her task. Tessa's breath came in short, panting jerks as she viewed the fluid, muscular lines of his body. He was so beautiful, so very dear to her. Kellen reached up with a long, lightly muscled arm to plunge them into darkness. Tessa stayed his hand, carrying it to her lips, pressing her mouth against his palm, kissing each individual fingertip, lingeringly, evocatively. "Don't turn out the light. I want to see you with me. I want to tell you all the things I've kept in my heart these past days; as you told me your secrets the night of the fire. I don't want to hide in the darkness tonight."

Her nightgown joined his pajamas on the floor. Kellen was as anxious to be joined as she. Her widening figure never entered either of their thoughts. Tessa was a beautiful, fertile goddess. She was a woman loved and in love. She molded her body to his, fitting herself into all the hollows and angles like a missing piece in a jigsaw puzzle. Her hands roamed over him with delicious abandon, caressing every inch of his lean hardness, memorizing the contours and textures as she spoke in a low, sweet whisper of sound.

Tessa told him how Jacky had died, how she'd blamed herself for so long. That she had put her love for him where it belonged, in her memory and into the past. Her melodious voice spoke of her love for Web's kindness in those dark days, her envy of her brother's happy family life, her desire to give her love to a child of her own. All the reasoning that had gone into her decision to have a baby.

"I thought I could make it alone, Kellen, but I was wrong. I hoped I could pick a man who meant nothing to me, at random, and I was wrong. I think I loved you the moment I saw you through the boutique window that day. Surely when you appeared out of the night and sent Larry Gelbert packing. Only I couldn't admit it. It threw all my carefully laid plans into confusion."

"You threw all my carefully planned future into confusion," Kellen chuckled against her ear, his hands making such inroads on her concentration that Tessa found it difficult to continue speaking. She was silent, drinking in the intoxicating power of Kellen's voice. "I loved you, Tessa, and I didn't even recognize the emotion. I only knew I had to have you back."

He pulled her closer, half covering her with the heated warmth of his body. Tessa snuggled into the sheets like a kitten with a fuzzy blanket. "I didn't want anything to do with relationships, or families, all the things loving demands of you—and Helena cheated me of. But once I'd possessed you I knew I was never going to be free. From there it was only a few short steps to considering a long-term relationship. When I found you carrying my baby it was the perfect excuse to insist on marriage. Our child would bind you to me for eternity."

"I wanted to tell you my feelings when Stan's phone call interrupted us," Tessa mumbled, her words airy and far away where she flew free among the stars. Kellen's hands had found the tender buds of her nipples; his erotic circling caress drove her wild with wanting.

"I should have jerked the damn thing out of the wall. Don't talk of that anymore," Kellen moaned, shifting his weight, pulling her under him. His mouth covered hers for a brief moment before he retreated to place a flurry of small, demanding kisses on her eyelids, her cheekbones, the cleft of her chin. Tessa's hands moved across the mat of hair on his chest to trail along the sleek contours of his buttocks, increasing the contact of their lower bodies. His lips moved down to circle a dusky peak, drawing it into his mouth for a long, soothing bite that stole her breath.

"I need to tell you these things, Kellen," she pleaded. "You make it so difficult to hold on to my thoughts."

He became still, ardor held firmly in check. "We are lucky that way, my love, our bodies speak for us." His hands swept her tumbled hair back from her cheeks as his eyes held her captive and her breath returned to her lungs.

"It's important to share our feelings. When the baby first moved, I knew I wanted you with me—to share our miracle. Some women can accomplish—can be successful—at what I tried. I admire their courage. But I'm not one of them. My baby needs two parents. I knew that with my heart, I fought it with my head. I need to share my life and my love—with you."

"We have shared. I've known since the moment you took me in your arms under that blasted weeping bush that you loved me. Even though you still believed I had fathered a child I wouldn't claim you loved me. I was too stupid to realize it immediately, but when you followed me to the lab I was almost sure. The fire only interrupted this conversation, not the miracle that revelation produced."

"Kellen!" The baby kicked, hard, between them as though annoyed by his father's weight. "That hurt," Tessa pouted, coming to earth with a rush. Kellen chuckled indulgently, turning on his back, pulling her atop him in a single, sustained movement.

"I think we will have to make some adjustment in our sleeping arrangements—for the duration." He grinned wickedly up at Tessa's startled face as he parted her legs with his own and positioned her most intimately. "It could be a very enjoyable experiment." Tessa opened to his tender dominance, anxious to be one with her lover, inflamed by the simple rhythm of joining, of drawing in and absorbing the power of his long, sleek strokes. Kellen moved slowly, provocatively, increasing the tension in Tessa's lower body until she wanted to cry out with

186

mingled pleasure and pain. She hadn't forgotten the sorrow and longing of their pasts, the problems with Kellen's family still to be resolved; but together, as they were now, they would build a future for their children and themselves at Vinifera.

"I didn't believe in love at first sight," Tessa mumbled, her words wispy as she sucked air on a delighted moan, her body moving in perfect unison with his. Already tiny, foreshadowing ripples of delight coursed through her, making speech difficult. She soared far higher than ever before.

"I didn't believe in love at all," Kellen rasped, his voice reedy with concentrated passion. "Until I found you, my precious, willful madonna." They didn't speak again. With pleasured sighs they communicated the special wonder of shared dreams, each carrying the other to new worlds, the fiery heat of their ecstasy forging a bond that would last into eternity.

Life could be very good when you loved and were loved in return. Tessa believed—and Kellen shared the precious knowledge in his heart. Their relationship would grow and mature with the fullness of years. Their love would become more complex and valuable as time passed—as precious and long-lasting as the most prized of vintage wine.

LOOK FOR NEXT MONTH'S
CANDLELIGHT ECSTASY ROMANCES®:

CANDLELIGHT
Ecstasy Supreme

$2.50 each

Candlelight
Ecstasy Romances™

$1.95 each